His Majesty's Sailor *and the Girl in the* Blue Coat

MICHAEL D GILSTON

◆ FriesenPress

One Printers Way
Altona, MB R0G 0B0
Canada

www.friesenpress.com

Copyright © 2024 by Michael D Gilston
First Edition — 2024

Book Contributors

Editing Victoria Straw - London, England
Cover Design David Prendergast - Dublin, Ireland
Cover Art Chris Gilston- Ottawa, Canada
Research Robert Gilston - Llanfynydd, Wales

All rights reserved.

No part of this publication may be reproduced in any form, or by any means, electronic or mechanical, including photocopying, recording, or any information browsing, storage, or retrieval system, without permission in writing from FriesenPress.

ISBN
978-1-03-918797-9 (Hardcover)
978-1-03-918796-2 (Paperback)
978-1-03-918798-6 (eBook)

1. FICTION, HISTORICAL, WORLD WAR II

Distributed to the trade by The Ingram Book Company

Dedicated to Dad, Kenny

I love and miss you.

Table of Contents

1 *Special Thanks*

3 *Prolog*

5 Chapter 1: Holy Loch

15 Chapter 2: Daily Rum Ration

23 Chapter 3: Off to Church

27 Chapter 4: A Wedding in West Derby

33 Chapter 5: Lime Street Station

39 Chapter 6: Travel en Route

47 Chapter 7: Off to Work

51 Chapter 8: Gironde Estuary

55 Chapter 9: Letters from Home

61 Chapter 10: Finishing the Mission

71 Chapter 11: The World Atlas

75 Chapter 12: Fire Watch

79 Chapter 13: Albany Road

89 Chapter 14: Christmas in Liverpool

97 Chapter 15: Back to Plymouth

105 Chapter 16: Christmas in Crewe

109 Chapter 17: Back to It

121 Chapter 18: Working out the Bugs

127 Chapter 19: Trouble and Change

137 Chapter 20: Crewe Memorial Cottage Hospital

141 Chapter 21: U-Boats in the Norwegian Sea

147 Chapter 22: Getting Better

155 Chapter 23: Time to Go Home

163 Chapter 24: Back on Her Feet

171 Chapter 25: *Tuna* at War

179 Chapter 26: Buckingham Palace

199 *Epilog*

200 *Appendix A: Dominic King*

207 *Appendix B: London Gazette*

208 *Appendix C: Operation Frankton Team Members*

230 *Apendix D: N94 HM Submarine Tuna War Patrols*

Special Thanks

The story of Dominic King would not have been able to be written without the research conducted by Robert Gilston, my paternal first cousin who is our family historian with a naval background. Robert spent many hours sifting through records at the London National Archives, Kew. Dominic's Service Records and HMS Tuna's log entries were researched. They provided great detail about when and where he was deployed.

The website Uboat.net was invaluable with its information on the Tuna and Totem's placements during the war.

A copy of the London Gazette dated Friday, 29th October 1943 and published Tuesday, 2nd November 1943, identifies the officers and crew whose actions aboard H.M. Submarine Tuna resulted in a Distinguished Bars and Medals being awarded. For the sailors Dominic associated with on other watches, I used surnames from across the British Isles.

Finally, Evelyn Sylvia Gilston (nee Jackson), my mother, provided the colourful history of what her life was like before and during the war. She shared my grandmother's stories of Dominic and of her experiences in Liverpool, Crewe, and London as a child during World War II.

Lost to History

While this story was being researched and written, there were many questions that have been left unanswered, the truth lost to history. For instance, while the Marines were being transported by HMS *Tuna* to a location ten miles off the Gironde Estuary, would they maybe have been offered a cup of grog along with the crew of the *Tuna*?

Prolog

In the fall of 1942, Britain had been at war with Germany for over three years with no end in sight. Cities like Liverpool and London received very heavy bombings both day and night. Towns around these cities were collateral damage, receiving daylight air-raid bombings due to their locations in valleys and low-lying areas.

The Luftwaffe launched air attacks on Britain from Norway and France, with various single and twin-engine bombers concentrating on large industrial centres of Manchester and Coventry. Britain defended itself with Spitfires, Mosquitoes, and Hurricanes, fighting for air superiority with the Battle of Britain.

The Royal Navy fought in the seas of the North Atlantic, protecting convoy routes from North America, and throughout the Mediterranean Sea—the people stationed there would see the fall of northern Africa and the allied invasion of Italy.

There are countless stories of people who lived through the war at home, in the air, and at sea. This is the story of two individuals who were touched by the conflict in very different ways.

Dominic King was the oldest son of John and Ellen King and their seven children, who joined the Royal Navy at an early age. He served on submarines during the war, getting awarded by King George VI for his bravery under pressure while in battle. His niece Evelyn Jackson, a ten-year-old girl with her family, was relocated to Crewe to try and escape the heavy bombing of Liverpool.

Both lived through the war that would shape their lives forever.

Michael D Gilston

HMS *Tuna*, Pennant N94

Ordered on 8 December 1937 and built by Scotts Shipbuilding & Engineering in Greenock, Scotland, *Tuna* was originally one of four boats ordered. *Tuna* was joined by sister ships *Triad* and *Truant*, built by Vickers Armstrong in Barrow-in-Furness. *Tuna* weighed in at 1095 tonnes surfaced and 1575 tonnes submerged, with an overall length of 275 feet.

She was Laid Down on 13 June 1938, launched on 10 May 1940, commissioned on 1 August 1940 as HMS *Tuna*, and was a Triton T-Class submarine with two 2,500 H.P. diesel-electric motors.

Tuna had a total complement of 63 officers and sailors.

With ongoing engine problems, *Tuna* was kept to local waters: in the North Atlantic off the Scandinavian coast and in the Bay of Biscay off the coast of France.

Tuna was instrumental in the Operation Frankton raid on the German cargo ships in Bordeaux, which saw participants go on to be called the "Cockleshell Heroes."

Skippered between 4 July 1940 and 1 September 1945 by twelve different lieutenants and Lieutenant Commanders at the helm of 21 war patrols. *Tuna* was credited with destroying three U-boats under the command of Lieutenant Desmond Martin, who was awarded the Distinguished Service Order with two bars.

In service: 1 August 1940 - 24 June 1946

Chapter 1: Holy Loch

30 November, 1942
Glasgow Docks

Two troop trucks stopped at the garrison gates.

A corporal approached the first driver's door, saying, "How can I help you?"

The driver handed him papers that were emblazoned with *High-Level Clearance*; no further communication was required. The corporal stepped back and motioned to the second sentry to raise the white barrier. The trucks proceeded through, passing the sandbag sentry posts with their anti-aircraft guns and armed sailors.

They drove to Pier 2, where a Royal Navy transport boat was moored alongside the dock. It was manned by three seamen in white jumpers. The passenger in the lead truck cab announced into the back of the truck they had arrived.

"Time to offload," he yelled.

Out of the back of the truck, twelve Royal Marines climbed down onto the wharf. They started offloading their rucksacks, duffle bags of equipment, and six flattened canoes from the second truck. Each canoe would be required to carry 150 pounds of equipment.

Major Herbert "Blondie" Hasler instructed the Marines to load their gear onto the transport boat. There were few words said amongst the men. Everyone knew what was required. Their kits and canoes were placed on the boat. Each marine took a seat on the vessel when they were done and settled into the next part of their mission.

All the men were part of the Royal Marine Boom Patrol Detachment, trained with explosives and for setting limpet mines, along with small ordinance weapons and the handling of the Mark 2 canoes.

When the offloading of their equipment onto the troop transport by the Marines was complete, the three sailors stowed the last of the food supplies being ferried back to their submarine. There was the pilot (or "helmsman") and two crewmen helped man the transport boat. Crewman Dominic "Bommy" King was standing on the dock. He unhooked the mooring rope and stepped back onto the boat. The ropes were coiled as the boat revved and pulled away.

The Marines and sailors travelled down the River Clyde towards the south side of Holy Loch, their destination Ardnadam village. Travel time across the 28 miles should be two hours and twenty minutes. The wind was from the northwest, and the sea spray was in their faces. The boat travelled along the south shore, passing farms and cottages along the way.

The Marines were sitting together in pairs, some checking their equipment, others shutting their eyes.

Dominic ventured over to one sitting by himself.

"Good day. How are you?" he asked.

"Fine, thanks. How much longer until we get to Ardnadam?" Norm Colley asked.

The boat was passing Greenock on the left shore. "About forty-five minutes across the Firth of Clyde, and we'll be there," Dominic replied. He had made the Ardnadam to Port Glasgow run a couple of times when their submarine, HMS *Tuna*, was moored in Holy Loch.

Norm asked, "How long have you been serving on your sub?"

"Since March of last year," he replied. Dom thought about how much had transpired in the past year and a half, and he elaborated a bit. "This is my sixth submarine. I was on the *Regent* in Singapore, the *Perseus* and the *Tetrarch* in the Mediterranean, and the *Parthian* and the *Turbulent* at Gosport, with patrol areas in the Atlantic. Where are you Marines from?"

"We've been training at Lumps Fort, Southsea, Portsmouth," Norm replied.

Dom counted six folded canoes. Each was equipped to carry two Marines.

"There seems to be one extra of you?" he said.

"That would be me, unless there is a major cock-up and one of the twelve cannot go. I am the spare wheel—along for the ride, so to speak," Norm replied. "I have practised with them, but more than likely, I will not be deployed on the mission."

Dominic could see the disappointment in his eyes.

As the troop boat passed the middle of the Firth of Clyde, HMS *White Bear*, an Armed Yacht, was anchored in the waters.

The skiff now approached Ardnadam, where the submarine maintenance ship HMS *Forth* was docked, with her black and white dazzle camouflage. There was a submarine moored alongside in the small harbour. The troop boat came alongside the submarine, where mooring lines were cast up to waiting sailors who tied them off.

The Marines stood up and prepared to disembark with their equipment. They formed a chain to offload onto the deck for'ard of the fin. Finally, the six canoes were passed across and stacked flat on the submarine's deck.

Lieutenant David Brown instructed two Marines. "Follow the crewman down the for'ard hatch."

Marines Ellery and Fisher climbed down the ladder onto the torpedo room.

"You can place your canoes on the port or left side torpedo racks," the crewman said.

The canoes were passed down one at a time and placed on the torpedo rack. When all six canoes were loaded, a rope was lashed to them so they would not move while in transit. The rucksacks, duffle bags, and oars were passed down and stored along the submarine's outer hull.

Meanwhile, the quartermaster and head cook, an Irishman, John "Cookie" Cooke, was recording the food provisions against the manifest. Bommy had helped unload the food rations onto the deck. He had been an assistant cook since joining the *Tuna*: Bommy had learned long ago that the cooks were always sure to eat.

Not that the Royal Navy did not feed them well. Submariners were fed the best of all the armed services. When stationed in Alexandria and Malta, Dominic would wander the food markets while the *Perseus* and the *Tetrarch* were in port, picking up spices not found in England at the time—Cumin and Cardamom. While in Singapore, he'd buy paprika and a blended spice called curry. The spices and herbs had long since run out, and Dom wondered if he would ever have a chance to replenish them. Would he be sent back to the Mediterranean or Far East? In the meantime, he still enjoyed helping cook when his watch would allow.

Cookie had to record where the two and a half tonnes of food were being stored inside the submarine. All the food had to be secured throughout the boat, so it would not come loose during an enemy attack. The food also had to be evenly distributed to trim the boat both fore and aft, as well as side to side. Fresh meat was placed in the small refrigerator located in the galley. Bread and potatoes were stored in the for'ard torpedo room and canned goods in the electric motor room. There would be plenty of food for the anticipated fourteen-day war patrol, even with the thirteen extra guests.

The afternoon sun was setting behind the hills to the west when the last of the food provisions were stowed. Finally, two-hundred tonnes of diesel fuel was pumped in two tanks under the control room in the submarine's centre. *Tuna* was now ready for her mission and 16th war patrol.

Lieutenant Commander Richard Raikes called his senior officers and Major Hassler to the control room map table. A map of eastern France, the Bay of Biscay, and Bordeaux were laid out on the table.

Major Hassler started talking about the Royal Marine Boom Patrol Detachment and the 34 men under his and Captain John Stewart's command.

"The detachment is based at Southsea, Portsmouth, with training in Commando Tactics at Lumps Fort and in the Portsmouth Harbour," he said. "In nineteen-forty, I suggested small boat attacks manned by divers, but Combined Operations HQ deemed the project impractical. In light of the human torpedoes that struck battleships Queen Elizabeth and Valiant in March nineteen-forty-one with explosive motor boats in Alexandria harbour, COHQ became very interested very quickly, and here we are."

The mission timelines were laid out for the submarine officers. Lieutenant Commander Raikes had already been briefed on the major parts of the mission: he informed his officers that they would be joining up with HMS *White Bear*, an Armed Yacht currently moored in Firth of Clyde.

His Majesty's Sailor *and the* Girl *in the* Blue Coat

"HMS *White Bear* will provide *Tuna* with an escort down through the Irish Sea. Travelling to the Bay of Biscay and the Bordeaux Gironde estuary is anticipated to take seven days. After your mission is underway, the submarine will return to Devonport, where the *Tuna* will get a refit. Are there any questions?"

All the officers shook their heads and the tactical meeting ended.

The mooring lines to HMS *Forth* were released, and the diesel engines fired up. The rumble of the engines could be felt on the deck, with big puffs of black smoke belching out of the exhaust. The submarine was ready to depart. The man and torpedo hatches were closed and secured. The submarine headed eastward towards where HMS *White Bear* awaited her arrival.

At 2000 hours, the watch was changed: Dominic was off duty now until 0400. He would have a bite to eat and get some shut-eye. Cookie had made a light meal of preserved meats and reconstituted potatoes. That should tide everyone over until midnight, when he would start cooking dinner while they were on the surface.

Dom headed to the bunk that he shared with two other crewmen. There was no hot bunking tonight, since no one had slept in it for the day. A couple of Marines were sleeping in the general area, and the rest had been scattered throughout the boat.

As he lay there, Dominic was thinking of home. He'd been able to post two quick letters to his wife, Gertie, and to his mum, letting them know he would have shore leave in two weeks. He had not been home in over two years and looked forward to seeing his family again. He grabbed his letters from home from his duffel bag, hanging at the end of the bunk—he had a bundle inside that he had read multiple times. There were a couple from his mum and Gertie, and from his older sister Dorothy, who his wife was living with in Crewe. He read them for the umpteenth time and fell asleep thinking of home and the women he loved.

At 2030 hours, Tuna met up with HMS *White Bear* and headed on, bearing 175 degrees. Lieutenant Commander Richard Raikes instructed the submarine to dive to 40 feet. This was to check the trim of the boat and ensure that the weight in the submarine was evenly distributed. The submarine surfaced again and continued using diesel engines while charging its batteries.

Dominic awoke to his bunk being kicked. "Time to get your ass in gear," Crewman Cooney said.

It was 0330 hours, and the Tuna was on diesel mode. That meant she was on the surface, charging its batteries. Since they were on the surface, he could have a smoke. "You have thirty minutes 'til you're back on the helm."

Dominic needed the head or a bucket to take a pee, and he needed to go badly. His bunk was located beside the seaman's mess, right behind the torpedo storage compartment.

Walking past the petty officers' mess, he saw Charles "Spinner" Watkins nursing a cup of coffee. Before he entered the control room, he passed the engine room artificer mess and the captain's wardroom. When walking through to the galley, he had to make it quick.

William "Sparks" Richard Huthwaite, the signal operator, received naval commands at 0400 hours from Rugby, central command. The dispatches, when received, were then given to the skipper or the officer of the watch.

"Good morning, Cookie. I could smell your porridge cooking," Bommy said.

Cookie replied, "Should stick to your ribs."

Bommy grabbed a bowl, some biscuits, and a couple spoonfuls of sugar for the porridge. Dominic drank the essence coffee hot and black, not with condensed milk. As he walked back to the seamen's mess, he noticed Norm Colley, the 13th Marine. They nodded to each other.

Acting Temporary Leading Seaman John "Willie" Wilband, a Welshman, was sitting in the mess.

"*Bora da*, Bommy. Did you have a good night?"

"I did. Thanks for asking. Nothing like the diesel engines to lull you asleep," Dominic said.

Dominic had the rudder as the ship's helmsman, and Willie manned the for'ard and rear hydroplanes. There would be a third coxwain if at action stations, manned by a Petty Officer. As the skipper or officer of the watch's command, the coxswain was the boat's helmsman. They were

His Majesty's Sailor *and the Girl in the* Blue Coat

a well-oiled machine on the red watch, now on duty for the next eight to twelve hours depending on circumstances. The boat's depth and tilt gauges were displayed for easy reference.

"It will be a very crowded place for the next six days while we are en route with them. They seem like nice enough chaps," Willie said.

"I met the thirteenth, Norm Colley. He will not go unless someone goes tits up, and like you said, nice enough chaps."

The diving-klaxon sounded twice.

"*Tuna* is going under water, Mister Wilband. See you at the wheel," Bommy said. He was glad now that he had relieved himself, as his watch was about to begin.

Sixty-three crew members, including the skipper, made up the three watches. There was always somebody manning the equipment or sleeping in a bunk. The goal was to have the red and white watches sleeping during the blue watch overnight. A new day watch began at 0400, with the dispatch from Rugby and the boat needing to surface in order to receive a message.

Time to switch with Davey Jones—"DJ"—and Glen Walker, who were at the end of their blue watch.

"Red watch is now on duty, gentlemen. Time for you to go get some breakfast," Bommy said as he approached the wheel. "Here he is," he continued, as the coxswain took his station. Willie to the rescue." Both were ready to take the helm on the port side of the control room. They sat down, hands on the wheel, and their watch began.

Tuna was being tracked by other ships using their hydrophone detection. They were listening for the *Tuna*'s propellers.

The First Lieutenant Travers who was in command of the boat. As Number One and officer of the watch gave the command to dive to 60 feet. Acting Chief Petty Officer Alfred James "Jimmy" Mallett gave the order to change from diesel engines to battery power now that the boat batteries had been charged to 98 percent. Victor Lammin, the Electric Room Artificer, fourth class, manned the diesel motor controls in the control room.

11

With the noisy diesel generators switched off, the vibration that they caused ceased. Now on battery power, the *Tuna* was silent and shudder-free.

Number One gave the order, "Bearing 175 degrees and 8 knots."

An engine order telegraph was sent from the control room to the engine room. CPO Mallet confirmed that the order was sent and received. Bommy turned the rudder as Willie handled the forward hydroplanes. With the ballast tanks flooded, the submarine submerged.

Their escort ship, HMS *White Bear*, left the Tuna to join a naval exercise in the Inchmarnock waters south of the Isle of Aran.

Life on Board the HMS Tuna

> When the submarine departed port for their war patrol, the crew and captain were prepared for any and all emergencies that may arise. The seamen were always at the ready, having changed into the clothes and boots that they would wear for the duration of their mission. Seaman would don their woollen white jumpers when weather and sea conditions warranted it being worn; other than that, they stayed in the same clothes for the duration of their patrol.
>
> Potable water was pumped aboard while at port, and used primarily for cooking and for the crew's daily hydration in the forms of tea and coffee.
>
> With temperatures in excess of 100 degrees in the engine room, the submarine can become quite stifling and airless. Between the diesel fuel exhaust, smoking, and a lack of continual ventilation, carbon dioxide levels can become dangerously high.
>
> Smoking aboard a submarine was limited to when the boat was on the surface and running the diesel engines. Smoking was not allowed while standing on the bridge: a lit cigarette could be seen for miles at night.
>
> Now Bommy, in the early years when he was assigned to HMS *Devonshire*, had swabbed and swilled out his share of toilets. As an Able Seaman on the *Tuna*, however, he left the mucking and cleaning out of the head to the junior ratings. If the facilities got

plugged up—from the use of 63 officers and crew, along with the Marines—those junior ratings would have to clean it out.

The heads were equipped with a macerator that ground up the solid waste before pumping it into the sanitary holding tank. If the macerator got plugged, an air pump cleared the head and emptied the contents into the septic tank. The line out could sometimes get plugged, however, and then there was a possibility of the person trying to clear the jam of "getting your own back"—hit with spray back—if the toilet valve was not fully closed. Not a pleasant experience, and would certainly ruin somebody's day.

HMS Tuna

Chapter 2: Daily Rum Ration

1 December, 1942
Inchmarnock Waters

The submarine headed south-southwest with the blue crew ending their watch, and in stepped Bommy into his position. They had to stand at the helm wheels for endless hours not long ago. The powers at the Admiralty, in their wisdom, allowed for both positions, rudder and forward stabilizer, to sit on a wooden chair cobbled together at the naval yard in Plymouth. This allowed the helmsmen to sit down on a hard plank of wood. It was easier than standing to man the controls.

Right in front of him was Tuna's nanometer, that showed the submarine's depth to the keel, and the clock. It was hard not to focus on how slow time went, when he stared at the clock's hands as the minutes ticked away. When Bommy had been on HMS *Dolphin*, in Gosport, Portsmouth, from May to September 1938—just after he got married—he'd been training to be a submarine seaman. He'd met Dave Williams, a new submarine recruit like himself, and learned to stare at the gauges and controls in front of the helmsmen. Bommy learned to count in his head to keep his concentration on the helm's position. All submarines had a clock in the control room; the trick was not to watch it.

Bommy didn't mind the red watch. It started in the early morning, but it finished—more importantly—with a tot of rum at noon.

As the minutes ticked by, Bommy started to drift, losing his concentration, and a cold chill came over him. *One, two, three...* he counted in his head to one hundred, then he counted backwards to one. The exercise was both a distraction and helped him keep alert. The counting helped. It passed about three minutes, counting to one hundred and back.

The crew was in good spirits, with the Marines as their guests. The atmosphere, in general, was good, with laughter coming from the seamen's mess as the Marines were mucking in well.

The ache in his belly started every day at 0830. He could feel his heart rate increase and his breathing faster and shallower. "Three hours to go," Bommy muttered to himself.

He was holding it together. The counting helped him focus on only the nanometer—not the feeling in his gut or the chills on his spine—as he clutched the wheel.

A *pang* was how it felt. The ache in the belly, and the wanting—needing—his daily tot! It helped settle the nerves, and he was waiting on his today.

As time was always right in front of the helmsmen, it was hard not to watch the seconds tick by.

Minute by minute…

At 1100 hours, the submarine was travelling on a heading of 200 degrees at a depth of 100 feet.

ERA Victor Lammin was at his station in the control room, and the clock on the wall clicked to twelve o'clock. He said with his voice on high, "Up spirits."

This was followed throughout the boat by a chorus of, "Stand fast, the Holy Ghost."

Since the boat was not at action stations, there was no reason to postpone the daily ration of grog. Grog, being a daily ration of two parts water to one part rum offered to all of age Ratings. Petty officers too were entitled to a tot of rum.

The line for the grog started at the petty officers' mess. ACPO Alfred "Jimmy" Mallett was joined by Spinner Watkins, and they dispensed out of the daily ration of rum. Though everyone was entitled, not everyone wanted it: Jimmy Mallett practised temperance and did not partake in the shot of rum. All those not having a tot were recorded in the log as with a *T*, and received three pence extra a day. There were not many that practised

His Majesty's Sailor *and the Girl in the* Blue Coat

temperance on the boat, but there were a few—Willie Wilband had a T recorded for his daily tot too. The Welshman was a Methodist and completely abstained from liquor.

As soon as Dominic had finished his watch, he joined the line for his tot. As the line drew closer to the petty officers' mess, he noticed a couple of glasses of grog already poured. One of those would be his.

Dominic stepped up to Spinner Watkins and asked for a tumbler of grog with a smile on his face. A full glass was handed to him. He raised it and said, "To the Queen."

He then downed the concoction.

There was a warming down his throat and into his belly. "Ah." He nodded to the petty officer as he placed the glass on the table. "Thank you," he said, with a rasp in his voice, then walked forward to his mess.

His bunk was open. Should he have some shut-eye or have some lunch? Offerings of canned Spam and Corn Beef made more appetizing with tomato ketchup and chutney.

Dominic decided to hit the hay and get some sleep. Cookie had asked for help with the evening dinner. He jumped into the bunk and pulled the canvas drapes closed. He laid back and closed his eyes. He was asleep in no time.

Dominic awoke after a quick nap on his cot. His head was a little fuzzy after the tot of rum, but with a cup of coffee he would be right as rain. Dominic swung his legs over the side and stood up quickly, finding his sea legs. He walked across to the seamen's mess where Willie was sitting, nursing a cup of tea. He looked like he was about to fall asleep sitting at the table.

Dominic said, "Why don't you go for a quick kip? The bunk is nice and warm."

"I'll be all right. I'm getting my second wind now," Willie replied.

Dominic went to the galley, got a cup of black coffee, and had walked back to the mess when Gerald "Boomer" Watson, the torpedo armament artificer, came and sat at the table. He held a small stack of envelopes containing letters from home in his hands. Boomer's mail had caught up with him while the sub was in Holy Loch. He sat down and arranged the letters in the order of the postmarks on the envelope. Boomer's wife was quite the prolific letter writer, and from the stack, she appeared to have been quite busy: he easily had between fifteen and twenty letters to read.

Now, Boomer liked to share the stories his wife had written to him, and would tell them to anyone who may be around the mess table. Boomer started to recall one of the letters from his wife.

"The house cat has gone missing," Boomer told Dominic. "It was let out, and it never came back. My wife thinks the cat has been nicked because it was black." In Liverpool, families of sailors would keep black cats for good luck—but unfortunately, they were often pinched.

Dominic thought back to the cat his family had when he was a young lad. It was not as much a pet, but a prolific mouse catcher. Whiskers had been adopted by the family: he was already an old tom when he first accepted food left outside the back door for him. He was not invited into the house, but was always near while the family lived on Albany Road. His brothers and eldest sister, Mary Ellen 'Eileen', had been friendly to the cat, but his older sister Dolly hated the moggy and would shoo it away whenever it came around.

Boomer had opened another letter. "My wife found a neighbour a couple of streets over whose cat had kittens, and one was a black female with white socks. She is going to call it Luna."

Dominic took a sip of his coffee. The caffeine had kicked in, and his head felt much better now. He sat there listening to Boomer tell stories about the goings on at home. Like all servicemen, Dominic relished getting letters from home—but unlike Boomer, he liked to read his letters in private. He received mail from his mum, and his sister Dolly, usually a bunch at a time when the Navy delivered them to the base while the submarine happened to be in port. He had not received a letter from home in a while, which made the ones he had received all that more precious.

Just then, there was a glint of light from the chains on a peg on the wall between the petty officer's and the seaman's mess. The Navy did not allow sailors to wear any jewellery or chains while serving at sea. They were taken off and placed on the peg until the sailor was on leave. There were six chains with medallions hanging on the peg. First, there was his, a silver chain with a small crucifix. His mother had bought the chain and cross just before he left home for the Navy. He had told his mum that he was not allowed to wear it while at sea, but she did not care.

"You wear it when you can, and the good Lord will help keep you safe," she'd said to him.

Dominic smiled to himself. He wouldn't forget to put it back on when he went on leave at the end of this war patrol.

After finishing his coffee, Dominic walked aft and into the galley where Cookie Cooke was starting to prepare the evening's supper. Dominic asked, "What's for dinner tonight? I'm here to help."

Cookie replied, "We'll be havin' brisket of beef, potatoes, and vegetables. Would you like to start peeling?"

"Okay," Dominic said as he grabbed the paring knife and a bucket and started peeling potatoes.

Now, where Boomer was full of stories, Cookie preferred the quiet. He did not talk too much and kept his concentration on the matter at hand. Dominic did a quick calculation on the number of crew and Marines. Then, he decided to start to peel about the hundred pounds of potatoes they would be having for that night's tea.

A hum came from the engine room, and a slight hot breeze with the exiting air from the generator and equipment fans. Dominic got to work peeling, and his thoughts drifted to going home. He missed his wife and family, but they should be getting together for the Christmas dinner he hoped to have with his mum and sisters. His next eldest sister Dolly should be there, with her daughter Evelyn—who Bommy called "Kate." A smile came to his face. He thought she looked like Katherine Houghton, who had been in his class at school when he was at Christ the Redeemer in Liverpool. The two shared the same mischievous smile.

The peeled potatoes were slowly accumulating in the metal pans of water. The work was therapeutic in settling his thoughts. Dominic had learned the expression while at St. Vincent, Gosport, Portsmouth, where he started his naval career. Kingsley Holt was a cadet with Dominic, who was in the mess kitchen peeling potatoes with him. He said once that peeling potatoes was very therapeutic, and that all you had to worry about was not cutting yourself.

"What's therapeutic?" Dominic had asked.

Kingsley had replied, *"It's Greek for 'just do it.'"*

Dominic never complained about peeling potatoes since learning that it was "therapeutic."

After the fourth pan of white peeled—and now cut—potatoes, Cookie said, "That'll just about do it." Cookie had already prepared the carrots and onion in another pan.

They heard the order to surface come from the control room. The generators would soon be started up. Then, finally, the hatches opened, and the brisket cooking could begin on the brazier.

Once on the surface, the white watch would be going topside. He could take the rubbish bins and peelings up and dump them, while Cookie would carry on cooking the evening meal. Dominic lifted the bins and walked over to the rear hatch that had just opened.

ACPO "Jimmy" Mallett was on the watch.

"Permission to go topside, Sir, to get rid of the rubbish?"

The watch officer replied, "Permission granted."

Bommy walked back to his bunk to grab his jumper. There, Willie was in a deep sleep. He took his jumper off the peg at the side of the stacked cots. He grabbed a cigarette from its package, stuck it between his lips, and crossed to the seamen's mess, where several sailors were sitting lit up. ERA fourth class Wilfred Jarvis, who was seated, offered Bommy a light off his. Bommy thanked him and walked aft to the rear hatch.

He walked back to the rear man hatch ladder, standing there having a smoke was Acting Temporary Leading Stoker Thomas Abraham. Who nodded to Bommy and said "taken the rubbish out? I'm looking forward for our tea tonight." "Wer hav'n a brisket, potatoes and veggies tonight." Said Dominic. "Cheers mate, I'm famished tonight" replied Thomas as he finished his smoke and returned to his duties.

Finishing his smoke, he tied one end of the rope to the bin handles and climbed the rungs topside while holding the other end of the rope. As he straddled the hatch and started hoisted up the bins, he realized

His Majesty's Sailor *and the Girl in the* Blue Coat

soon enough that the bins were heavy enough, let alone two at once made pulling them up challenging.

"Fool," he muttered to himself as he continued to pull. He should have pulled them up one at a time, but he wanted a little longer deck time.

He finally lifted the pair of bins onto the deck and untied the rope from around the handles, then fastened it to the hatch latch. Dom picked up the bins and walked aft to the rear of the submarine, where SSC Rodney Leahy was on watch at the stern of the boat. They nodded to each other as Dominic walked to the end of the flat deck. Just above the rear of the boat, he dumped the contents onto the deck. The rubbish would be swept away when the sub went under. He walked back to Stoker Leahy was standing.

"Nice evening tonight," Bommy said to Rodney.

Rodney replied, "A lovely evening indeed."

Bommy relaxed for a moment and breathed in lung full of fresh air, he turned to the stoker saying, "Have it good for the rest of your watch."

He walked to the rear hatch, untied the rope, and reattached it to the bin handles again. This time, they were a lot lighter as he lowered them down the hatch opening. Once he and the bins were at the bottom, Bommy coiled up the rope and stowed it for next time.

Back in the galley, Cookie had the meat and vegetables cooking. It smelled wonderful. He walked back to his cot to hang up his jumper. Willie was starting to stir on his cot. "Tea's not for another couple of hours," Bommy said to Willie, who was slowly getting up.

"*Rwy'n effro*, I'm up." Willie yawned. "I was having a wonderful dream about home and the wife."

Bommy walked back to the galley, asking Cookie if he would have time for shut-eye while the supper was on the broil.

Cookie said, "Be about an hour and a half." Cookie would catch some sleep after tea was served, usually around 0200 hours.

Bommy walked up to his mess, and his cot was open. Willie was sitting in the mess. He jumped into the hot bunk—"hot", because the mattress still warm and damp from Willie.

Dominic thought back to when he turned twenty years old, serving aboard HMS *Devonshire*, a heavy cruiser assigned to the Mediterranean fleet. Dominic had tasted rum before his first grog, and he preferred his rum straight-up. Back on the *Devonshire*, the honour went to a senior boatswain mate who would proclaim, "Up Sprits." In the eight years that he has been entitled to his daily tot, he has never once initiated the call, "Up Spirits" at eleven o'clock Since joining the *Tuna*, he left it to the junior ratings, the twenty years old who would now take up the daily call. He would always join in the chorus reply of. "Stand Fast the Holy Ghost."

With the gentle hum of the generators, he was soon fast asleep.

Chapter 3: Off to Church

5 December, 1942
Crewe

Evelyn asked her mum if she could use the alarm clock. She did not want to sleep in and miss ten o'clock Mass at St. Mary's Church tomorrow morning. Her dad was on midnights, and mum wouldn't need the clock. She wound it up, set the time for 0830, and placed it on her night table before kneeling beside her bed.

Eve quietly said her nightly prayers. "…name of the Father, the Son, and the Holy Spirit, Amen." She then made the sign of the cross again and climbed into bed.

Evelyn had her atlas open in bed, scanning the countries on the map and dreaming of far-off places. She had a game with her dad: He would give her three cities to find, whether it was a capital, a province or state, or the country. She loved geography at school. It was her favourite subject.

Eve was starting to feel tired. She did the timing in her head again. Her school friend Maureen Yates came by at nine-thirty, and it was a fifteen-minute walk to the Church. Her alarm was set for plenty of time to get ready.

It was about ten minutes before Eve was fast asleep.

The following morning, the alarm went off at eight-thirty. Eve hit the button on the alarm and jumped out of bed. She liked to go to Mass at St. Mary's, because the priest, Father Mulcahy—who was Irish—was uplifting. He wasn't too stuffy like Father Breen, who was more fire and brimstone. She got dressed and went downstairs, where her mum was in the kitchen. Eve's aunt Gertie was in West Derby at the McCardles' house for a short visit. Gertie would sometime walk with Eve and Maureen to the church. That morning, the girls would be going alone.

Evelyn said, "Morning, Ma'am," as she walked into the kitchen. Her mum was in her housecoat, sitting at the table having a cup of tea.

"Good morning. How did you sleep?" her mum asked.

"Well, thank you," Eve replied.

"Are you going to have some breakfast before you go to church?" her mum asked.

Eve looked at the clock. She could not eat before having Communion.

"I'll have cereal when I get home," she said and sat down at the table.

Normally if her dad, Jack, was awake on a Sunday morning, they would have been having bacon and eggs for breakfast after church—when the food rations would allow—but he'd gotten home earlier this morning and was asleep.

Maureen will be here shortly, Evelyn thought, as she ran up the stairs to get ready.

A short time later, there was a knock on the door. "That will be Maureen," Evelyn announced from the top of the stairs.

Her mum walked out of the kitchen and opened the front door.

"Good morning Mrs. Jackson. Is Evelyn ready?" Ten-year-old Maureen asked.

"She'll be right down. Do you want to come in to wait?" Eve's mother, Dolly, asked.

"Thank you," Maureen said as she stepped inside.

"Hey Maureen, I'll be right down," Evelyn called from the top of the stairs.

Eve just had to put on her coat and was ready to go. She opened her wardrobe in her bedroom and pulled out her blue coat. Eve loved her sky-blue coat. She had gotten it from her parents on her last birthday.

Eve ran down the stairs. "Let's go. We don't want to be late." She called to her mum in the kitchen, "See you after Mass." Eve and Maureen went out of the door and then walked at a good pace. They did not want to be late for mass.

When they arrived at the church, the parishioners were filing into the front door, and they noticed Father Mulcahy welcoming everyone into the sanctuary. The girls genuflected before walking into the pews and sitting down. They both knelt and said a quick prayer.

There were a couple of children from her school sitting around the church. Up at the front, walking in to the right of the altar in the ambulatory, were the nuns from school, including their teacher—Sister Mary Margaret—and the imposing figure of Mother Superior. The nuns walked in a straight line, coming out from the Rectory, and each knelt before taking their seat in the front pew.

The service started shortly after the nuns took their seats. As the service began, Eve and Maureen followed along with the Mass. When it came time for Communion, they stood up and walked up to the altar. After Evelyn received the Host, she turned to the right and walked right by the nuns. Sister Mary Margaret smiled at the two girls as they passed. Mother Superior had a very stern look on her face. It was like she was unable to smile. They walked back to their pew and knelt, saying their prayers as the priest was finishing the service.

When Mass had finished, the girls walked to the back of the church, made the sign of the cross with the holy water from the font, and left. They walked home in relative quiet, thinking about Father Mulcahy's homily: about keeping the spirit of Christmas all the days of the year, especially with the war in its third year. When they arrived at Eve's home, Maureen said she would see her tomorrow for school. Eve would stop at her house and walk together to school.

As Eve walked in the front door, she was reminded that her dad was still sleeping. She made a lot of noise that morning when she was leaving. She would be quieter now. Her mum asked from the kitchen, "How was Mass?"

Eve said it was fine and walked up the stairs. She had schoolwork that needed to be completed for tomorrow. She best not waste time. Eve spent the better part of the day in her room doing mathematics and reading her school books.

When her dad woke up later that afternoon, she had finished her homework, and he was looking to spend a little time with her before he left for work.

25

Chapter 4: A Wedding in West Derby

30 April, 1938
Liverpool

Six-year-old Evelyn was woken by her mother. "Rise and shine, sunshine. We have a wedding to go to," her mum said as she opened the curtains. "And we can't be late."

Evelyn sat up, stretched, and said, "I have never been to a wedding before."

"Well, your Uncle Dominic is marrying Gertie McArdel at St. Paul's in West Derby this afternoon, and we cannot be late," her mum said. "I have pressed your yellow dress, and your dad has polished your Mary Janes, so get washed and dressed."

"I'll get ready," Eve said.

After she was dressed, she went downstairs. Her dad was having his breakfast with a cup of tea.

"Hello, my love, did you have a good night?" her dad asked.

"Yes, I did, until Ma'am woke me up," Eve replied.

"Well, we have a big day today. We need to take a couple of trams to get to West Derby, so we have to leave soon," her dad said.

Dolly came downstairs all dressed and walked into the kitchen.

Evelyn asked her mum, "Will Sonny be there too?"

"Yes, he will, but I do not think David will be there," her mum said. Sonny and Dave were Aunt Rose's children. Eve loved to play with Sonny when they got together. However, Dave was only three years old and maybe too young to attend.

"We are leaving within the hour," Dolly announced.

"Well, I am all ready to leave," Eve declared.

"Go get your world atlas, Evelyn. See if you can find Athens on one of the maps while we are waiting. I'll give you a hint: it is the capital of a country," her dad suggested.

Eve ran up the stairs to her bedroom to retrieve her Rand McNally Atlas. She'd received it for her last birthday, and she had been learning where the different cities and counties were around the world. She grabbed her book, returned to the settee in the living room, and opened the book.

"Athens, where to start looking?" she said to herself. "Let's try Europe."

This gave Dolly and Jack time to finish getting ready.

Dolly and Jack had finished getting ready, and they were putting on their shoes when Eve declared, "I found it. It's the capital of Greece."

"Good job Evelyn," her dad said. "Now, let's get to the tram stop. We don't want to be late."

Eve was proud of herself for finding Athens. She enjoyed looking at the atlas with her dad and learning about the different places around the world.

Jack held the house keys as he ushered Eve and Dolly out the front door. He closed and locked it as they walked down the path to the street. They walked down Timpron Street to Earle Road, turning right to Tunnel Road to catch the tram at Widney Close.

They did not have to wait long for the tram. Her parents paid their fare and went up the stairs to the top of the double-decker, where her parents could have a cigarette as Eve watched out the front window where they were going. They passed through Edge Hill and up to Kensington, where they got off. They walked over to Sheil Road, where they caught their connection. The tram travelled north to Rocky Lane, where they disembarked and walked to the next stop. There, they did not have to wait long. The tram that would take them to West Derby arrived after a few minutes.

They boarded the tram, decided to stay on the lower level, and found two sets of seats together where they could sit. The tram travelled up Rocky Lane and along West Derby Road. They arrived at Queens Drive and exited the tram. Jack took the map that he had drawn, of the streets to

His Majesty's Sailor *and the Girl in the* Blue Coat

walk to Saint Paul's Church, out of his pocket. "It should be just up the road," Jack said.

They crossed the street to Mill Lane and walked up the street. It changed to Barnfield Drive. They were nearly there. They crossed over to Town Row and walked up to Spring Grove. They could see the church up on the right when they turned the corner.

Jack looked at his watch—and they had made it on time.

People were milling about the front archways as they walked up to the church. Eve noticed her Nana King first. And there, playing on the steps was her cousin Sonny. A big smile came to Eve's face when she saw her cousin.

She ran up to Sonny. He was a year younger than Eve, but just as tall. "Hi-ya, how ya doin'?" Sonny asked Eve.

"I'm all right," Evelyn replied.

Just then, there was an announcement from someone at the church door. "Would everyone please come in and take a seat? The wedding would be starting shortly," the registrar announced.

Eve ran to her mum and asked, "Could I sit with Sonny?"

"As long as you both be good," her mum said.

"We will be good," Eve replied as they all walked into the church.

Eve walked into the church. There were her aunts and nana sitting in the pews on the right. Sonny and Eve sat behind her parents.

Eve looked up to the front of the church to see her Uncle Dominic standing in a light grey suit standing beside her Uncle Charley. Sonny had told her his dad was Uncle Dominic's Best Man. Her mum called Uncle Dominic "Bommy," but she had heard her nana King call him Dominic. So, she just assumed he had two names.

An organ started playing, and the wedding was about to begin. A young lady in a dark blue dress with a light blue collar was walking down the aisle with an older man. Evelyn had only met Gertie a couple of times, but she was very nice and kind when they did meet.

The priest was standing at the front of the church, and a couple of altar boys were helping with the mass. Gertie and the older man reached the front of the church. Gertie and Dominic smiled before they turned to face the priest who started the ceremony.

Eve could not hear all the priest was saying, but she did hear Gertie and Dominic say, "I do."

The Mass proceeded on to the Sacrament of Holy Communion. Evelyn watched as her aunts walked up to the altar and took the Host. She was looking forward to making her first Communion next year.

They had reached the end of the wedding ceremony when the organ started playing again. Gertie and Dominic walked to a small table and signed some papers. The priest asked everyone to stand as the couple walked down the aisle, right past where Eve was sitting. Dominic looked down at Eve as he walked by, and waved at her, and then everyone filed out of their seats and walked to the back of the church.

Outside the church, the families gathered. People were lining up to hug Gertie and shake Dominic's hand. Finally, it was Eve's turn as she was standing with her mum and dad. Her mum gave Uncle Dominic a big hug and a kiss on the cheek, and her dad shook his hand. Dominic looked down and said, "My goodness, Kate, you're growing up so fast. You'll be as tall as your mum before you know it." Eve wasn't sure why Uncle Dominic called her Kate, but that was all right. It seemed like everyone had another name that they were called by. Eve gave both a big hug to her Uncle Dominic and her Aunt Gertie.

The man who walked Aunt Gertie down the aisle was giving directions to her dad on where their house was on Darly Drive. The twelve or so in the wedding party started walking towards the McArdles' house.

They arrived at the house. A small garden was behind the hedge as they walked up the path to the front door. The house was full when Eve walked in with her mum and dad, full of people mingling and chatting with each other. Evelyn decided to stay close to Sonny.

Eve overheard her Uncle Dominic telling her dad that he was last serving aboard HMS *Escapade*, a Destroyer. He was on five days' leave before he started submarine training in Gosport, Portsmouth, early next week. Dominic and Gertie were to be married in June, but his transfer came in for the HMS *Dolphin*, and the wedding was moved forward.

Everyone was asked to sit around the large dining room table. There were not enough chairs, so Evelyn and Sonny crawled under the table to escape. As food was passed around and everyone served themselves. Dolly handed down two small plates to Eve and Sonny. As the serving plates were passed around, her mum passed them down some food. The two kids both sat cross-legged on the floor, eating bits and bites that were being offered to them. They could not see what was happening, but there was a toast to the bride and groom, wishing them the best and a long life together.

Finally, they brought out the desserts and sweets. Everyone around the table felt sorry for Evelyn and Sonny, having to sit under the table—each started passing pieces of cake and biscuits down to them, until they were both stuffed with all the treats they had been offered.

It was getting to be later in the afternoon, and Eve overheard her dad say to her mum that it was time they started to head back home. So Eve said goodbye to her Nana King and Aunt Eily, who were about to leave too.

They walked down Darley Road to Eaton Road, turning right to get over to Mill Lane. Their trip home to Toxteth took about as long as it did to get to West Derby.

When they arrived home, they were all tired from the walking and the excitement of the wedding. Jack felt like a nap on the settee. Eve was still buzzing from all the sugar she had eaten. Eve asked her dad, "What is another city I can look for?"

Jack thought for a second, "Well, we started with A. How about Adelaide?"

Eve asked, "Any hints?" Her dad replied, "It is on a coast."

With that, she grabbed her atlas and went up the stairs to her bedroom, and the house was quiet for the rest of the afternoon.

Chapter 5: Lime Street Station

2 September 1939
Liverpool

Seven-year-old Evelyn was sitting in her bed playing with her doll Lilly, at 0800 hours, when she heard the radio turn on in the living room.

Downstairs, Dolly and Jack had tuned in to BBC News. The radio announcer came on with ominous news.

> *"At 0445 hours yesterday, Friday, September 1st, German Forces invaded Poland without a declaration of war. Immediately British and French demanded a German withdrawal from Poland, and the British army has been mobilised."*

Dolly looked at Jack and asked, "What does this mean?"

"It does not sound good," Jack replied.

The radio announcer continued.

> *"Evacuations of young children from London and Liverpool and other vulnerable areas have begun. Over the next couple of days, children will be evacuated to north Wales and Scotland."*

Dolly asked Jack, "What are we to do? Should we be evacuating Evelyn too?"

"I do not want to see Evelyn shipped off, but the government would not be sending off children if there was not a good reason for it," Jack said.

Dolly said, "Let's get our breakfast, and we'll see if there is any more news. I'll go get Evelyn. We got some bacon from the market yesterday; we could have a nice meal before we decide."

With that, Dolly walked upstairs and into Eve's bedroom.

Eve was sitting on her bed when her mum walked in.

"Good morning. Did you have a good night?" her mum asked.

"Yes, I did," Evelyn replied.

"Your dad has put on some bacon. Go get yourself washed and changed. Your green dress is cleaned in your wardrobe. Put that on and come downstairs," her mum said.

Jack had sliced off the bacon and started cooking it in the frying pan. It was one of his favourite activities to cook breakfast on the weekends.

By the time Evelyn came downstairs dressed, her dad was about to put on her egg and toast.

"One egg, fried?"

"Yes, please," Evelyn replied, with a big smile on her face.

Jack placed the rashers of bacon and sunny side egg and toast onto a plate and placed them on the table where Eve was sitting. Eve picked up her knife and fork.

"Thanks, Dad." She started in on her breakfast.

When Eve had finished, her mum asked her to come into the living room.

Her mum asked her to sit on the settee, and she sat beside her and spoke.

"Sweetheart, you will have to take a trip by train, but we will not be able to come with you."

"Why not?" Eve asked.

"Because it is only children who will be taking the trip. Adults will not be going," her mum said.

"Where will I be going?" Eve asked.

"It sounds like Conwy in North Wales," her mum replied.

"How long will I be gone? Will you come and visit me?" Evelyn asked.

Dolly was unable to answer her. She started to get choked up and was about to begin to cry. Dolly cleared her throat. "It may be a while before we can come to visit. But it is best that you go while you can. Your dad and I will take you to the train station, so get your knitted sweater and gas mask. We must be leaving soon," instructed her mum.

34

Evelyn asked, "Can I bring Lilly with me, too?"

Her mum smiled. "Sure, you can. She will keep you company while you are away."

Eve was happy that she could take her doll, and went upstairs.

Jack had been listening from the kitchen and said, "I think we are making the right decision."

"I hope so," Dolly said as she wiped the tears from her eyes.

Evelyn came down the stairs with Lilly, her sweater on, and her gas mask over her shoulder. Eve had become very proficient at putting on her gas mask. Since getting it back in the spring, she had been practising at school and could now put it on without any help.

Dolly and Jack were now ready, too. They all left the house, Jack locking the door behind them.

Eve and her parents walked down to Upper Parliament Street and over to Grove Street. They waited for the tram to take them north, past the University of Liverpool and the Liverpool Royal Infirmary and up Russell Street. Lime Street station, with the arch covering the tracks, was on the left.

As they walked up to the train station, there was a crush of people. Many young children were being accompanied by their parents to the station. There was a sign instructing parents about where the evacuated children were to be taken. There standing in line, Eve looked around. She had not been on a train before and was looking forward to taking it. The line reached a table where ladies were helping the evacuees.

"Hello," one of the ladies said. "What's your name?"

"My name is Evelyn Jackson," Eve said.

"That is a very nice dolly. What's her name?" the lady asked.

"Her name is Lilly," Eve replied.

The lady took a preprinted placard board and wrote Eve's name. "What is your address?" the lady asked.

Jack spoke up, "Nine Timpron Street."

The lady wrote on the board. She then took a piece of string, attached it to the board, and placed it over Eve's head.

"All the children are to queue over there. It's best that you say your goodbyes before she gets into line," the lady said.

Dolly and Jack looked at each other. They had to let Eve go now. Dolly started to cry again. She did not want to cry in front of Eve and get her upset. They stepped out of the line and started walking to where the children were being lined up to go into the station.

"We have to say goodbye now, my love," Jack said to Eve. "Remember your manners, and we will write to you as soon as you have been settled."

He bent over, picked her up, and gave Eve a big hug. "You take care."

"I will," Eve said.

Dolly was still holding back her tears when she bent over to give Eve a hug.

"We love you dearly. We miss you already. You be good a girl," her mum said.

They walked up to the line where the children were waiting. Both gave Eve a final hug and kiss.

Eve watched her parents. They turned to wave as they walked away.

There was the toot of a train whistle from within the station. Eve turned to see if she could see the train.

There was a young girl standing in the line. She, too, had a board around her neck. All the children in line had boards around their necks. A railway guard opened a gate at the front of the line, and all the children filed into the station. There was a line of children that had already formed on the platform. Eve and her group were told to stand and wait for further instructions.

As Jack and Dolly walked out of the station, Dolly could no longer hold back her tears and started sobbing. Jack held her as her sobs slowly subsided. He took out his handkerchief and offered it to Dolly, which she used to dry her eyes and blow her nose.

They both walked out towards the street in silence.

Eve was still waiting patiently in line. Every so often, it would move, as the queue wound its way into the station and onto the platform. She could see children at the front of the line getting into train carriages.

Jack and Dolly had got as far as Lord Nelson Drive when Dolly stopped in her tracks. She shook her head. "No." She turned to Jack. "I cannot let her go. We have to go back."

Jack did not know what to say. He knew that there was no letting go once Dolly got something into her head. "We have to go get her," Dolly said—and with that, she turned on her heel and started heading back to the train station.

They walked past where Evelyn had been dropped off. What if Eve had already been placed on a train. There was a line up inside the station and onto the platform.

Dolly started to run now, as she passed children that had been lining up along the platform. Was she looking in the right queue? She continued along the line. All the children were starting to look like Eve. She kept walking, checking the children as she went by.

Evelyn started talking to a boy who was standing in line with her. His name was Kenny, and he was from Knotty Ash Liverpool with his younger brother John. The queue kept moving towards a red and black carriage.

Jack was keeping pace with Dolly and scanning the queue, just in case. Dolly could see a carriage in the distance with children climbing the stairs, and the queue was on the move. Dolly started to run. Was she already on the train? *No, keep looking.*

Although Eve was standing in the queue with her back turned, Dolly saw the sweater, green dress, and shoulder-length auburn hair. She grabbed her by the shoulder and turned her around: It was Evelyn.

Dolly was so pleased she threw her arms around her daughter as Jack came up behind, panting, and put his arms around them both. Dolly said, "We all go together."

Eve was happy to see her parents, and that they were all staying together. She was unsure why she'd almost been sent away, but she was grateful to be with her parents again. They all returned to the original table where the same lady was serving another child. When she finished, Dolly approached her and said, "We have decided to stay together."

She took off the placard, handed it back to the lady, said thank you, and walked away.

They started walking home, but Dolly decided to walk across Albany Road to see her mum, Evelyn's Nana King. It was a twenty-minute walk or just a mile in distance. By the time they arrived, they were tired from all the walking and this morning's excitement.

Dolly knocked on the door and walked in. Her sister Rose stood in the hall with her sons—six-year-old Sonny and two-year-old Dave—running around. Evelyn saw her cousins, and she was off to play with them.

"You decided not to send Sonny?" Dolly asked.

"Nah," Rose replied. "Dave is too young, and I didn't want to separate them, and with Charlie away in the Royal Navy, I'd be lost without them."

Dolly informed her sister and mum of the morning's going on with Evelyn's evacuation. "I just couldn't let her get on the train."

They both completely understood.

By the time Jack, Dolly, and Evelyn walked down Brownlow Hill, they were all tired. Just a bit further to Timpson. When they arrived home late afternoon, they were knackered. After a light supper at six, they each had an early night and slept well.

Chapter 6: Travel en Route

03 December 1942
Off the east coast of Land's End

The boat travelled south, on a heading of 170 degrees at a steady 11 knots, only surfacing at night to charge the batteries with the diesel engines. The Marines had intermingled with the crew, bunking beside the seamen's mess. Some were playing card games, others playing chess at the petty officers' mess table, and a couple Marines were sitting with others writing letters to their loved ones. They would ask one of the petty officers to mail the letters for them when they arrived back at port. There was a quiet calm within the submarine, considering the tight quarters.

The nice thing about helping the cook was you got to sample the fayre being cooked. Beef and chicken would be a part of the daily dinner served at midnight (while the fresh meat lasted.) The meat was grilled in the small electric oven, and the aroma and smoke soon filled the boat. Topside hatches were opened when the sub charged, letting in the fresh air.

Topside, on the bridge, Lieutenant Travers was the officer of the watch. The blue duty watch watched the skies for any aircraft with their binoculars. Though they were still in friendly waters, they would soon be in hostile territory and in harm's way.

The galley was behind the control room with the wireless compartment, and ahead of the 2,500 BHP diesel motors and the Engine Room Artificers, ERA, Tiffys' territory. The ERAs were a collection of boilermakers, shipwrights and enginesmiths. They were, every one of them, addressed by Tiff or Tiffy. They maintained the diesel motors and charged the 336 battery cells.

The stokers shared the area with the ERAs, responsible for the diesel fuel when the submarine was charging the batteries. Acting Temporary Lead Stoker Thomas Alexander Abraham was on duty.

Signalman William Richard Huthwaite was on duty in the wireless compartment. A dispatch had just been received and was given to Lt. Travers. He read the dispatch and gave the communique to ACPO Mallett to record the transmission into *Tuna*'s log.

Just then, the skipper, Lt. Richard Prendergast Raikes, emerged from the Captain's cabin. APO Mallett handed the latest dispatch from Rugby. "Increased German air coverage off the east coast of France, it's like they're expecting us. What is our position, Mister Blake?"

"Approximately five miles east of the Isles of Scilly, heading 170 degrees and 11 knots," Sub-Lt. Ronald Blake Navigating Officer replied.

Raikes and Blake headed to the map table, rummaging through and pulling out the English Channel and the east coast of France. Lt. Travers and ACPO Mallett joined them at the table.

"We will be in the English Channel with aerial surveillance by Focke Wolf 190s out of Brest. We are going to be right on the doorstep tomorrow night. Have the white watch rested up. We will need extra eyes topside while running on diesel."

"Aye, Sir," Lieutenant Travers confirmed.

Dominic was preparing to start grilling 75 chicken legs, one for each crew and marine. Cookie had joined him in the galley to prepare the evening meal. Fourth Class ERA Wilfred Jarvis had been enlisted to help in the galley too. He was handed a potato peeler and 40 pounds of potatoes. He grabbed the slop bucket and started peeling into the bucket, putting the finished peeled potatoes into a metal basin that had water on the hob. The potatoes were quartered and placed into a large pot to boil.

The galley, situated on the starboard side, had metal counters with rail guards so the cooking trays would not topple over while on the surface in rough seas. There were a couple of wash basins for the crew to wash and prepare food. Food was stored throughout the boat, with the fresh meats were consumed first. The crew would be eating lamb, beef and chicken for the first couple of days, and then frozen, canned and dried foods as the war patrol continued.

The sea was not too rough while travelling on the surface. The winds were favourable, with a light wind coming from the northwest with the blue watch topside.

Stoker John Wilkinson was on the bridge with the binoculars. "Aircraft spotted port side. Looks like a Messerschmitt 410, as it has two engines." Lt. Nicholas Traverse took note of the aircraft for the boat's log.

08 December 1942

At 1600 hours, the sub was off the east coast of France near La Pallice, France, in the Bay of Biscay. The port city had a German airbase and a U-boat base. The routes in and out of ports were heavily mined.

Lt. Raikes called *Tuna*'s lieutenants to the map table in the control room.

"As we pass off the coast of La Pallice, the Germans are known to have laid mines out along the shipping lanes on the Rochebonne and Aquitaine shelves. The area has a depth of 25 to 50 fathoms. It is unknown if they have deployed moored contact or magnetic mines. We will have to surface as soon as it's dark and charge the batteries. It will take us eighteen hours to get to the disembarkation area off the coast of the Gironde Estuary. We are going to have to travel carefully through this area."

After his own briefing, Lt. Travers called the petty officers together. ACPO Alfred James Mallett, Stoker PO Charles Spencer Watkins, and PO Second Class George Crawford joined him in the petty officers' mess.

"Gentleman, we will be passing through a hazardous area over the next twenty-four hours. With a sea mine barrage laid throughout this area, our passing will be particularly dangerous. We will be travelling at reduced speed, and all available seamen and stokers will be on alert for mines. We will position two seamen at the bow and in the crew areas, listening for any contact with a mine mooring cable as we travel through the area. At the first sign or sound of contact, the boat will come to a complete stop. Red watch will start immediately in position. They will be relieved by white watch as blue is currently on duty. Any questions?"

The petty officers all nodded; PO Crawford confirmed, "Good to go."

When the confab ended, PO Crawford walked forward to the seaman's mess. Crew members King and Wilband were sitting quietly, sipping cups of tea.

"Gentlemen, are you feeling rested?"

Bommy piped up, "What do you have for us, Sir?"

Petty Officer Crawford laid out the plan. Bommy and Willie would start their watches at the submarine's bow, in the for'ard torpedo compartment. Seamen James Wray and Sidney Griffith had been lying on the bunk and had overheard the petty officer talking with King and Wilband. They got off their bunks and wandered over to the seamen's mess. Crawford said that Wray and Griffith would relay any sound report that King and Wilband heard to the control room.

"We are certain that the mines have been laid off the east coast. We just have to punch on through this area," added Crawford. "To your positions, men."

Bommy knew that the fore torpedo compartment would be cool. He walked across to his bunk and grabbed his and Willie's jumper. He handed the jumper to Willie.

"*Diolch,*" Willie replied.

"It will be cool up front. No need to shiver me timbers while waiting," Bommy said.

They opened the man hatch into the torpedo storage compartment. The for'ard Davis Escape Trunk was on their left. Six stacked canoes were stored on top of the port-side torpedo racks. Torpedo Artificer Gerald "Boomer" Boynton was checking on them.

"Boomer, were movin' on in with you, mate," Willie joked. "We'll be up front for some time to come."

Willie took the port side, and Bommy took the starboard, standing between the six for'ard torpedo tubes and the pressure hull. The metal surfaces were cold to the touch.

Bommy quipped, "It could be worse."

Willie replied, "Not by much, mate."

It was eerily quiet in the front of the boat. With the electric motors engaged, and so far removed from the remaining crew, there was no sound in the compartment as both Willie and Bommy settled in for the duration of their watch.

After about 30 minutes, PO Crawford came for'ard to check on Bommy and Willie. The submarine was travelling at a heading of 160 degrees, at a speed of four knots. "Gentlemen, how are you faring?" he enquired.

"Right as rain, Sir," Bommy replied.

"Good to hear. We are not sure how long we will be passing through this German shipping lane, so any contact with a mooring line, yell," Crawford stated emphatically.

"Aye, Sir," Willie and Bommy said simultaneously.

PO Crawford walked back to the control room.

"There you have it, Bommy. We'll be the first to know if we strike a mine," Willie joked. "Keep your ears peeled." Bommy laughed with him.

Listening for the scraping on the outer hull, the two men stood at the ready.

"Thanks for remembering the jumpers. We would have been two blocks of ice if we had to stand here without them. Are you looking forward to getting home, Dom?" Willie asked.

"Don't be saying things like that. You'll be jinxing us," Dominic replied.

"Ah, that's the Irish in you. We Welsh look on the bright side. With any luck, this will all be behind us soon enough."

Just then, a scratching noise filled the compartment. Bommy's heart jumped at the sound. "It must be a mine mooring cable." The sound came from all around them.

"It's on your side," Willie yelled.

Bommy cupped his hands around his mouth and yelled as loud as he could. "Mine cable, green side starboard."

Jimmy Wray had been standing in the hatch at the gangway in the mess area. He turned to yell towards the control room. "Mine, green-side starboard."

Lt. Raikes was in the control room when he heard the dispatch from the front of the boat. He said to commanded, "All stop."

ERA Second Class David Reid switched off the power to the propellers. "Power is off, Sir."

The mooring lines crept backwards, scratching along the side of the submarine.

"We're not stopping," Willie said, exhaling hard.

"There is a lot of boat for it to run down," Bommy said as he held his breath.

He could hear his heart beating in his ears.

The mine mooring line hit the starboard hydroplane, and there was the sound like a rasp as the cable moved across the leading edge of the plane. Dominic, still holding his breath, thought to himself, *was the submarine caught on the mine?*

As it raked the edge, the cable slapped back against the outer hull of the torpedo compartment, and both Dominic and Willie jumped at the sound. They slowly walked into the torpedo compartment. The scratching noise continued down the side of the sub.

The cable ran up to the for'ard auxiliary machine space, where the submarine's side started to bulge out.

They walked into the gangway of the mess. The rasping sound was now coming from behind the bunks.

"It sounds like we are slowing down," Willie said, sounding hopeful.

The submarine was coming to a stop.

Lieutenants Travers and Brown were standing with Lt. Raikes in the control room.

"With no for'ard momentum, the boat's buoyancy will be lost, and we will sink," Lt. Raikes stated. "Gentlemen, I am looking for options."

Lt. Brown stated the obvious, "We cannot rise, or we will strike the mine. It must be a contact mine. If it was an influence mine, it would have already been triggered by it catching the mooring cable. But if we continue forward, there is a chance that the mooring cable will snag the rear hydroplane."

Finally, Lt. Travers said, "If we go hard to starboard with the rudder and pulse the screws, we may be able to nudge ourselves off the cable."

Lt. Raikes thought for a second, then said, "Make it so. Hard to starboard with the rudder, and we'll tap the motors gently with five seconds of rotation with the starboard screws only."

Seaman Walker was at the helm. He turned the wheel clockwise until it stopped. There was a thirty-degree angle to the rudder.

ERA David Reid was at the electrical panel. He turned the motor on to the right screw for five seconds, then off again.

Lt. Raikes said, "Again."

Bommy and Willie were still standing in the gangway of the mess area. The sound of the rasping noise started again.

ERA Reid tapped the screws again.

The sound was not as loud, but it was still making noise as it moved further back towards the for'ard ballast tanks.

Lt. Raikes called out, "Again."

Reid tapped the screws.

Bommy and Willie, standing in the control room, heard the sound lessening. There was not as much pressure from the cable on the side of the hull.

"Again," Lt. Raikes ordered.

Reid tapped the screws again, and all of a sudden, the scratching noise was gone.

"Keep hard to starboard. Tap the screws again," Raikes ordered.

Reid tapped the screws.

"Okay, now straighten out the rudder," the skipper instructed.

Seaman Walker, at the helm, turned the rudder back to straight.

There was no more scraping. They were free of the mine mooring cable. Bommy took a deep breath, looked at Willie, and nodded.

Lt. Raikes said, "We're clear. Well done. We don't know if we are still in a mine barrage or were, we were lucky enough to snag a loner? Continue with the watch for the next hour to make sure we are clear."

PO Crawford walked back into the mess area.

"Seaman Wray and Griffith, you are up front. King and Wilband, since you didn't shit your pants, you're both to now be the relays. Good work, guys."

Wray gathered up his and Sid the Kid's jumpers from their bunks. "We're going to need these," he said.

For the next hour, the submarine travelled on a bearing of 170 degrees at five knots, and it did not encounter any more mines.

Chapter 7: Off to Work

8 December, 1942
Crewe

There had been no air raids yesterday. There was heavy cloud cover, so there were no German bombers. The Cheshire area of England has been quiet these past couple of days. Everyone had guarded optimism that the British Spitfires and Mosquitoes were stopping them on the east coast, where German bombers would traverse the North Sea heading for the rail yards in Crewe and the docks in Liverpool.

The Jackson family was waking to a new day on that grey morning.

Evelyn was still asleep when her dad, Jack, woke up with his alarm clock. Her mother, Dorothy, stirred as she rolled over and fell back to sleep. There was the familiar sound of her snoring as Jack swung his legs to the side of the bed. It was 0445, and he had less than an hour to get ready for work. He was scheduled to start his shift at the Rolls Royce Plant in Crewe at 0700 hours. He stretched and rubbed his eyes before putting his glasses on.

"Another day in the mines," he muttered.

Starting early in the morning and finishing after dark, there was no chance of seeing the sun.

Jack walked downstairs and got a bowl of Weetabix and milk while he boiled the kettle on the stove for a cup of tea. When he listened to today's weather last evening, the weatherman reported *"Forty-five degrees today, but the chance of rain in the Cheshire area."*

Jack sat quietly finishing his breakfast and his cup of tea.

By the time he finished his tea, it was time to get ready to leave. He opened the larder to grab the lunch Dolly had made for him the previous evening: There was a brown paper bag with a sandwich and a couple of biscuits. He grabbed his lunch box, opened it, and placed the brown bag inside. Dolly had reused the brown bag and wax paper he had brought home in yesterday's lunch. Jack prepared his milk caddy for his tea at work. The small oval tin had one side for sugar and the other side for condensed milk, and he placed it in his lunch box and latched the lid.

As Jack put on his coat, Dolly walked down the stairs and asked, "Did you get your lunch from the larder?"

"Yes, thank you," Jack replied.

Dolly reached up to straighten the collar of his coat. "Can't have you going out like an unmade bed, now, can we?"

"No, I suppose not. Ta-ra, my dear."

He kissed her on the cheek, put his cap on and walked out of the front door. He turned back to wave to Dolly as he walked towards Victoria Avenue, where he would catch the tram to the plant.

Dolly closed the door and went into the kitchen. she filled the kettle with water and placed it on the hob. Evelyn would be up soon for school, so she had time to have a cuppa' and start her day quietly.

Eve woke up to the sound of her mum and Aunt Gertie talking in the kitchen. She couldn't sleep in today—she had to get to school. Evelyn put on her dressing gown and went downstairs. "Good morning," Eve said.

"Good morning, Ev," Gertie said with a smile. "Did you have a good night?"

"Yes, thank you," Evelyn said.

"Would you like a boiled egg?" her mum asked. "I have one ready if you would like it?"

"Yes, please, and toast, too," Evelyn said as she sat at the table.

Dolly placed a slice of bread under the grill and watched while it toasted one side at a time. Then, she used a spoon to take a boiled egg out of the saucepan and placed it into an egg cup as she flipped the piece of toast.

There was a slight smell and a whisp of smoke coming from the grill. The toast was done. Dolly placed the toast on a side plate and served it to Evelyn, who said thank you.

When Evelyn finished her breakfast, she asked if she could leave the table.

"You may," Dolly said. "Go and get yourself ready for school."

Up the stairs she ran. Eve quickly got washed and dressed, putting on her blue blouse and gymslip. After Evelyn got ready, she picked up her school books and went downstairs. She kissed her mum and Aunt Gertie goodbye, put on her coat and shoes, and ran out the door.

She walked up the street towards her school friend Maureen Yates, who was in her class at St. Mary's Catholic School. Maureen lived on Langley Drive, which was on Evelyn's way to school, and the two walked together.

Evelyn was in a good mood that morning, and she started to skip up the pavement to Maureen's house. She walked up to the door and knocked. Eve could hear footsteps coming to the door, and then it opened; Maureen was ready. She yelled goodbye to her mum and walked out the door, shutting it behind her.

While they walked towards the school, Maureen asked if Evelyn had finished her homework.

"I do not understand ratios and geometry," Maureen said. Their teacher, Sister Mary Margaret, had just introduced the two subjects to the class yesterday, and Maureen was struggling with them.

Evelyn didn't want to boast, but she understood what their teacher said about geometry and angles. There were 360 degrees in a compass, and geometry was about angles and measuring distance, shape and size. Evelyn also like geography, learning about the different countries around the world. She would ask her dad for help with geography questions—things like the difference between longitude and latitude, and why the prime meridian was in London.

As they walked towards the school, other children arrived, the younger pupils being dropped off by their mothers. Evelyn saw a small group of pupils from her class waiting for the school bell. When the bell rang, each pupil was expected to wait outside the door and enter the school by walking into it in two lines. Once inside, they then walked down the hall to their classroom.

When the pupils were lining up, Mother Superior was standing beside the main doors. Her black veil and white wimple set off her high cheeks and dark eyes. She was a stern-looking woman. Since starting at the school, Eve had been on her best behaviour—she followed the rules.

It was different from when she went to school at Sacred Heart in Liverpool. There were air raids almost daily, and running to the school or air-raid shelters for cover. Evelyn remembered how, living in Liverpool over a year ago, she had won a real Christmas tree in a school raffle. One evening, the candles and ornaments on the tree had been shaking as the bombs were exploding all around their house.

Chapter 8: Gironde Estuary

09 December 1942
10 miles off the coast of France

Major Hasler and Lieutenant Mackinnon called the Marines together at 1600 hours.

"We are nearing the disembarking area off the Gironde Estuary. Teams will put on each other's face paint. Lieutenant Mackinnon has green and black tubes to hand out to you. When we arrive at the disembarkation location, A Division will go topside, and B Division will pass the equipment and canoes through the man hatches and the torpedo hatch. When the equipment is unloaded, have your torches at the ready. Depending on the wind, we will deploy on the lee side to launch the canoes."

At 1700 hours, *Tuna* was travelling at eight knots, heading of 175 degrees at a depth of 80 feet. Lt. Raikes gave the order to go to periscope depth, 35 feet in depth to the keel, and the for'ard-looking periscope was raised. Looking south by southeast, the waves were between three-to-four-foot swells with the north-westerly wind. "Poor weather topside. Take her up," ordered Lt. Raikes.

The submarine crested the surface. The boat was trimmed down, not at full buoyancy to reduce the boats silhouette and aid in the launching of the canoes "We are not here long enough to run the diesel. What are our battery levels?" the captain requested.

"Tiffy" ERA Fourth Class Victor Lammin confirmed, "The for'ard banks are at 35 Ah, and the aft are at 33 Ah, Sir."

The skipper calculated that there were six hours of battery life. He didn't want to run the batteries below 10 Amp-hours as it could damage the battery plate electrodes.

Major Hassler and Lieutenant John Mackinnon were standing in the control room, waiting for Lieutenant Raikes's order to offload.

Corporal Albert Laver and Marine William Mills were on their feet. There were about 900 pounds of equipment stowed in the steering gear compartment; once the rear hatch was opened, the equipment would be loaded topside. Bommy waited to hear that the sub had surfaced, so he could climb the ladder and open the hatch. The wind lashed his face, and he was glad of his jumper on. There was a cold spray with the wind. He was followed up the ladder by Willie, and the two climbed onto the freeboard.

Marines Ellery and Fischer passed the rucksacks and oars up the ladder to Corporal Albert Laver and Marine William Mills, who had gone topside. They could see the Marines climbing out at the front of the boat, carrying the canoes behind the conning tower.

Laver and Mills climbed the ladder when all the equipment had been unloaded, then started walking to the bow to help carry the for'ard-stowed equipment to the rear.

Corporal George Sheard and Marine David Moffatt were starting to unfold their canoe, *Conger*. Bommy and Willie walked to the fore hatch as Sergeant Samuel Wallace and Marine Robert Ewart were passing up canoe *Coalfish*.

Bommy grabbed hold of the front of the canoe and started to pull up out of the hatch. A gust of wind hit the two holes, and the canoe popped open.

"Whoa," Bommy said as he steadied himself. He did not want to get pushed off and into the water. The canoe was clear of the hatch as he started to walk to the rear freeboard, with Willie carrying the back end.

Marines Ellery and Fisher came to the fore hatch to unload their canoe, *Cachalot*. It was being passed up when the wind gusted again, this time lifting and twisting the canoe. Marine Ellery lost his grip, and the canoe quickly flew to the side, hitting the hatch. Bommy heard a rip as the locking clip punctured the side of the canoe's canvas.

"Bloody hell," Ellery yelled. Major Hasler heard the cursing, and came to see what the commotion was about.

His Majesty's Sailor *and the Girl in the* Blue Coat

The canoe was lifted out of the hatch. Major Hasler asked for a torch, and he shone the light onto the side of the canoe. There was an eighteen-inch rip on the right side of the canoe, down below the waterline. "We can't repair this," Major Hasler said. "It's too damaged. Cachalot is scrubbed from the mission. Ellery, Fisher, secure your equipment."

Lt. Mackinnon asked, "Should we pitch it over the side?"

Major Hasler stopped for a second to think. "No, we'll ask the skipper if we can load it back onto the sub. It will go back to Southsea if it can." The sub was due back in four days at Plymouth. Ellery and Fisher would take it back, along with Marine Colley.

Lt. Travers came over to investigate. "Can we help you, Major?" he asked.

"Yes, Lieutenant, could you ask the skipper if we can take this damaged canoe and two additional Marines, Ellery and Fisher, back to Portsmouth?"

The remaining five canoes were each unfolded, and the 750 pounds of rucksacks lashed to the tops of the canoes.

Division A canoes *Catfish*, *Crayfish* and *Conger* were all launched on the starboard side of the submarine, their main rope still held by the sailors of the blue watch as Division B's canoes were loaded. The Marines were already sitting in the canoes with their oars.

Lt. Travers walked to the edge of the submarine.

"Major Hasler, the skipper says he will take the Marines and canoe back, and wishes you Godspeed."

"Thank you for the hospitality, Lieutenant. We must now leave," Hasler said.

The five lines were tossed back to the front canoe as they paddled off to the right, towards the shore—where lights could be seen. It was about ten miles to the coast.

Lt. Travers gave the orders: "Close all the hatches."

Bommy and Willie returned to the stern man hatch, closing and securing it behind them. They walked through the motor room into the galley, where Cookie sat on a wooden bin.

"Bommy, are you helping me with tonight's dinner? We have the last of the lamb and beans."

"If I could have a quick kip until we resurface to charge the batteries, I'll help with tonight's dinner."

"Aye, have a good snooze then," replied Cookie.

Bommy smiled and headed to his bunk. He was spent. Even a couple of hours is better than nothing. He was happy to help with cooking the night's dinner, but right now, he needed to close his eyes.

As he walked back to the seaman's mess, he passed Marines Ellery and Fisher, who were sheepishly washing the paint off their faces with Norm Colley standing with them.

No words were exchanged, but Bommy saw the disappointment in their faces.

Chapter 9: Letters from Home

9 December, 1942
Crewe

Dolly sat at the kitchen table with a pen in her hand. They had purchased paper and envelopes from Ryman House Stationary in town for all the letters that Gertie and Dolly wrote to Dolly's brothers in the service.

As Dolly sat there looking at the blank paper, she was not sure who to write first. She had written to her four brothers since the start of the war. Filled each letter with the comings and goings on of their homes, not saying anything about the war effort; information like that would not pass the censors at the post office.

With Dominic coming home soon on leave, she decided to start a letter to John, who had been a prisoner of war for the past three years. He had written a couple of letters since he was taken prisoner in France. His latest letters had come from Stalag 39, highly redacted, with black markers blocking out chunks of his text.

Dolly wrote to her brother about their moving to Crewe, but not the reason why knowing that it would be censored—she did not want to get into trouble with the military or the civil postal censors. She kept the information to their family, telling him of his sisters, his niece Evelyn, and Rose's sons, Sonny—ten now—and Dave, three.

As Dolly was finishing the letter to John, Evelyn walked in the door, ready for lunch. "I'm home," Evelyn called.

When she got in, she could not remember if her dad was on days or nights—was he sleeping or at work? Better to not raise her voice, since he might be sleeping. Eve walked into the kitchen, and her mum stood up from the table.

"How was your morning at school?" Dolly asked.

"We were learning more about ratios and geometry, and Sister Mary Margaret asked if I would do problem-solving on the board, and I got it right," Evelyn said proudly.

"Good for you."

Dolly had heard of ratios and geometry, but had no idea what they were about. "Come sit down, I have a tomato and cheese sandwich for lunch."

"Yes, please," Eve said.

The early afternoon was spent talking about John being a prisoner of war, and time got away from them both: when Evelyn looked at the clock, she had less than fifteen minutes to get to school. She kissed her mum goodbye and ran out the door.

Evelyn ran down Valley Road towards the school. She would not be stopping at Maureen's on Langley Road, as Maureen would not have waited for Evelyn. She continued to Dane Bank Avenue, where she turned left. She crossed the road, and the school was in sight.

The schoolchildren were playing and running in the school playground. She was happy that she was not late. Evelyn stepped onto the school driveway when the air-raid siren started.

Every child in the playground stopped and stood still. No one moved. Evelyn heard the wailing siren and started running towards the school door. Standing on the steps was Mother Superior; she looked down at Evelyn, who was out of breath from running from home.

"Child, we do not run. We walk when the sirens sound. We can't have children running around. When we hear a siren, there must be decorum and sedateness, or children will get hurt." By this time, the children had all started to walk to the door and line up. "When you get to class, tell Sister Mary Margaret you must come to the office."

With that, Mother Superior stood back from the doors as the children filed in.

Evelyn did not know what she had done wrong. When she was at Sacred Heart in Liverpool, everyone ran when the air-raid sirens wailed their warning. She walked to her classroom, where her teacher stood beside her desk, and she walked up to her.

"I have to go to the office. Mother Superior told me to tell you that I had to go."

The nun looked puzzled. What could Evelyn have done that required her to see Mother Superior? Evelyn was very obedient and respectful, and Sister Mary Margaret could not imagine what she would have done. As the pupils in her class filed in and sat down, Evelyn walked out into the hall and towards the main office.

The school halls were empty as Evelyn walked down to the main office. She did not know what to expect as she stepped inside the office. The main secretary looked up and asked, "Can I help you?"

Evelyn's head was down, and she said, "Mother Superior wants to see me."

The nun said, "Come with me." She stood up and walked down the short hall to a door on the right.

There, standing erect with a whipping cane in her hand, was Mother Superior. "Come in," she said to Evelyn. Mother Superior told Evelyn again about the school rules and how they cannot be broken without consequences. She said, "Hold out your hands."

At that moment, Evelyn realised she was going to get the cane. She had never been punished at school before, either when living in Liverpool or Crewe. She gingerly put her hands out.

"Palm up and stick them out farther," Mother Superior sternly said.

Evelyn turned her hand over and started to outstretch her arms as the Mother Superior raised the cane and lashed both her hands. There was an immediate burning sensation on her palms. Eve wanted to pull her hands back, but she knew that would only enrage Mother Superior even more.

The nun raised her hand again, and then the cane came down on Evelyn's hands. This time the pain was even more intense, and she was not sure if she could take another blow. Just then, the third lash came down upon her hands.

Evelyn looked down at her palms. There were three bright red lines across her palms and fingers. They were now stinging badly. She wanted to cry but did not want to cry in front of the nun.

Mother Superior put the cane down and told her to return to her classroom.

Evelyn walked out of the main office and started back to her classroom. She tucked her hands under her arms to try to ease the pain. When she reached the door to the classroom, she wiped the tears from her eyes on her sleeves and opened the door.

All the pupils looked up as she walked into the classroom. Not a word was said. Evelyn walked to her desk and took a seat. She did not look up. Instead, she stared down with her head hanging low.

Sister Mary Margaret was covering geography, a subject Evelyn really enjoyed, but her heart was not in it. She could not concentrate as her hands were still stinging from the caning. She looked down at the welts that had started to rise to ridges.

By the time school ended that afternoon, Evelyn had kept herself composed. When she met Maureen in the school yard to start walking home, Eve asked if she could walk alone.

Maureen wanted to ask what had happened and why she got the caning, but she understood that Eve wanted to be alone. So, she crossed the street, leaving Eve to walk home alone.

When she reached her house, Evelyn walked up to the door, quietly opened it, and went inside. She just wanted to go up to her room and close the door—but just then, her mum walked out of the kitchen into the hall. Dolly knew at once something was wrong. Seeing her mother, Evelyn could not hold the tears back any longer. She started crying.

"What's wrong? What happened?" her mum asked.

Through the sobs, Evelyn told her mum how the air-raid siren started when she got to school, and she ran to the school for the bomb shelter as she had in Liverpool, but this time she got the cane. With that, she started to cry even harder.

All Dolly could do was console her little girl. "Who did this to you?" she asked.

"Mother Superior," Evelyn replied.

Dolly was furious. She could not believe her daughter would be caned for running to the bomb shelter. "Come on, we're returning to that school and seeing the headmistress."

Evelyn did not want to return to school, but her mother was determined to get to the bottom of this. She put on her shoes, grabbed her clutch purse, and walked out the door with Evelyn at her side.

There was no talking on the way back to school. Dolly walked with determination in her stride, and it was all Evelyn could do to keep up with her.

They walked through the school's front doors and down the hall to the main offices. The same nun who had taken Evelyn to the Mother Superior's room looked up as they walked into the office.

"Can I help you?" the nun asked cordially.

"I want to see Mother Superior at once," Dolly demanded.

"I will see if she can see you now," the Nun replied.

"She'd better see me, or I am not leaving until she does," Dolly said, in a loud booming voice that everyone could hear. Just then, Mother Superior walked out of her office towards where Dolly and Evelyn stood.

"Yes, you wanted to see me. Can I help you?" Mother Superior asked.

Now, Dolly was not much more than five feet tall, and Evelyn nearly saw eye to eye with her. Mother Superior looked to tower over both of them as Dolly walked up to her.

"Did you cane my daughter because she ran when there was an air-raid siren?" Dolly bellowed.

"We have rules here at St. Mary's, and if they are not followed, there are consequences," Mother Superior said.

"Rules? You pretentious, highfaluting bitch. You're a pompous over-starched penguin," Dolly started in on her. For the next three minutes, Dolly took a strip off Mother Superior. She was not given a chance to say a word. Finally, Dolly finished, "If you ever lay a hand on my daughter again for no good reason, I'll be back here to break that cane over your backside." And with that, Dolly grabbed Evelyn's arm and walked out the door.

They were halfway home before Dolly said a word to Evelyn. She had turned red with anger in the school office, and the natural colour was returning to her cheeks when she spoke up. "Listen," Dolly said. "I'll tell your Dad about what happened today. So, you won't have to worry about that."

Evelyn was so pleased with that. She did not like disappointing her dad, and this would certainly upset him. She looked down at her hands. The welts had started to shrink, and they didn't sting anymore; however, there were still thick red lines, and the lash marks were still tender.

Dolly and Evelyn walked the rest of the way home in silence.

Chapter 10: Finishing the Mission

9 December 1942
Gironde Estuary

At 2200 hours, HMS *Tuna* had been travelling on a heading of 270 degrees, at ten knots for the past two hours. This was to clear any further sea mines that may have been set in the Gironde Estuary, before turning north at 330 degrees.

Lt. Travers was officer of the watch in the control room. The batteries had just over 13 Ah of charge left and were getting dangerously low. The boat would have to surface to charge the batteries. He gave the order to go to periscope depth at 35 feet, the main ballast tanks were blown, and the front and rear hydroplane were tilted to fifteen degrees up angle. Tiffy Henry Higgins raised the for'ard-looking periscope when they had reached the depth. Lt. Travers scanned around. There were no lights or any sign of ships in the area. He gave the order to surface.

Stoker Rodney Leahy was in the motor room waiting for the order to switch to diesel. Stoker PO Spinner Watkins was in the hatchway between the galley and the 2,500 HP diesel motors. Lt. Travers gave the orders to switch on both diesel generators. Leahy hit the switch to turn them on, and the two diesel motors rumbled to life.

Topside hatches were opened with Seamen Wray and Griffith on White Watch going up first. Then, Lt. Travers climbed the ladder in the control room up the conning tower to the bridge.

The weather was still poor, with high winds and pelting rain. However, the poor weather would provide good cover for the submarine while they surfaced.

Dominic had a quick nap in his bunk when he was woken by Cookie asking for help to cook the evening meal.

"Dom, if you're not on watch, could you give us a hand with dinner?"

He stretched and rubbed his eyes, "Yes, I'll be right there."

He might still get a little more shut-eye before he started his watch at 0400. In the meantime, he would help Cookie with the lamb and beans.

As Dominic walked back to the galley, he passed Marines Ellery, Fisher, and Colley, who were sitting in the engine room artificers' mess while the Tiffys were busy charging the batteries. The three Marines were sitting quietly. Marine Norman Colley saw Bommy approaching and flashed him a wry smile.

"Hey, Norm," Dominic said as he closed in on the ERA mess.

Colley replied, "Hello, Dominic. Are you helping with dinner again tonight?"

"Yes, no rest for the wicked. How are you guys holding up?"

"We're well, settling back in for the return to Plymouth. Is there any guess on how long it will take us to get back to port?"

"If there are no further delays with sea mines, we should be returning in a couple of days. So that would make it around Sunday the 13th," Dominic replied.

Marine Ellery said, "That is the day that we would have been in Bordeaux and undertaking our mission."

Dominic could tell they were deeply affected by not being able to proceed with their mission. There was nothing he could say that would change how they were feeling. He gave a nod of acknowledgement to the trio as he walked into the control room on the way to the galley, where Cookie was waiting for him to help.

In the galley, Cookie was preparing the evening dinner. All the fresh meat had been eaten on the journey south. The food stores were down to frozen and dried foods to prepare. Cookie was defrosting lamb chops and soaking red beans for tonight's meal.

Dominic grabbed a cup of coffee. This would help clear the cobwebs as he drew water and placed it on the boil.

The dinner was prepared for twelve midnight, and the batteries had been half-charged while travelling on the surface.

The crew had settled into the return to Plymouth. The mood on the boat was jovial, with laughing and merriment being heard throughout the vessel. A number of the crew would be going home on leave, as Dominic would.

As he laid back on his cot, he thought of home and seeing Gertie again. God, did he miss her. He said his prayers and fell off to sleep.

The boat was off the northwest coast of France and would change to a heading of 20 degrees once they had reached the English Channel. There was a high risk of being spotted there in the Channel by German air patrols coming out of Brest when they had to surface next and U-boat bases in Lorient and St.Nazaire. They were too close to finishing their war patrol for something to happen now—there was guarded optimism that they would soon be safe back in Plymouth.

12 December 1942

The submarine had made good time travelling across the English Channel. There were no sightings of German aircraft on air patrols over the last couple of days. The boat was heading directly to Plymouth. They should arrive early tomorrow morning.

At 2230 hours, Marines Ellery and Fisher asked Dominic if they could go topside for some fresh air now the submarine surfaced to charge the batteries. "Could we go up top one last time before we get back to port?" Eric Fisher asked. "We are starting to climb the walls in here. Could you ask the skipper?"

"I'll ask Lieutenant Travers, who is the officer of the watch. I'll be right back." Dominic walked back from the mess area into the control room. PO George Crawford was in the control room. Dominic asked him if he could ask Lt. Travers about the Marines going topside—he didn't have an issue, and Dominic climbed the ladder to the bridge.

Lt. Travers was standing at the front of the bridge. Seamen Wray was standing in the for'ard 4-inch gun turret, and Griffith was in the rear anti-aircraft tower.

"Sir?"

Dominic stood on the bridge, and Lt. Travers turned around. "Yes, King?" he replied.

"The Marines have asked if they could come up topside for some air. I think that they are going a little stir-crazy and need a bit of a break. What should I tell them, Sir?"

A thin smile came to Lt. Travers' face. He said, "Yes, that will be fine, they can come up for a couple of minutes. You will have to stay with them while they are on deck."

"Aye, Sir. Thank you. I will let them know."

With that, Dominic climbed back down the ladder. He walked back to the mess area, where the three Marines stood as Dominic walked up to them. "The Lieutenant said it would be okay for you three to go topside. We'll go out from the for'ard man hatch."

The Marines picked up their coats as Dominic grabbed his jumper off his bunk. Willie was fast asleep as Dominic walked by.

"Somebody's getting some shut-eye," he muttered.

They walked for'ard into the torpedo storage compartment. The hatch was open and a draught of cool air spilled down through the hole.

Marines Ellery and Fisher took out their cigarettes, and they offered one to Dominic.

"Thank you," he said.

Ellery lit a match and lit Fisher's and Dominic's cigarette. He blew out the match and lit a second match to light his own and Colley's. Dominic smiled. He knew it was bad luck to light three cigarettes off a match. When they finished their smokes. Dominic said, "Remember, the freeboard can be as slippery as snot, so watch your footing. We don't want to have to pull you out of the briny," he reminded them as they went up the ladder.

The foursome stood together in silence, the waxing moon reflecting on the calm sea as stars glimmered in the cloudless sky.

When they started to feel the chill, they climbed back down the ladder. They thanked Bommy for being able to go topside. The Marines then walked back towards ERAs' mess—still empty, since the ERAs were still busy with charging the batteries. Dom was sure that letting them go topside would help their morale, if only for a couple more hours.

When Dominic returned to his bunk, Willie was sitting up with his legs over the side. "My turn before we're back on the helm," Dominic said, taking off his jumper.

He still had a couple of hours before his 0400 hours start. Dominic sat on his bunk, swung his legs over, and laid back. He felt the vibration of the diesel motors through his body, and he was asleep in no time.

Willie woke Dominic at 0345, when the boat was submerged on battery power. "Rise and shine, sunshine," the Welshman coaxed. "We're nearly at Plymouth."

A smile came over Dominic's face. If all went well, he could start his leave once the boat arrived back in port.

He knew that he would have to help unload the unused food. As the boat would receive a sonar unit while he was on leave, all the food and rations would have to be offloaded so they did not spoil while the *Tuna* sat unused. Plus, any food left unattended would become a cockroach fest. They lived in the shadows and under the duckboards—sometimes two inches long, vile, nasty-looking creatures.

Cookie had the master list that he started with, showing the food and where it was stored throughout the boat. Fortunately, there were only boxes of dried provisions left: all the fresh and frozen meat had been eaten, along with some of the canned stuff, and most of the other food had also been consumed.

Dominic and Willie were on the red watch for the final leg of the war patrol. The skipper and Lt. Brown were in the control room as Lt. Raikes gave the order to raise periscope. Tiffy Victor Lammin threw the switch and raised the periscope. Lt. Raikes scanned the area; there were no ships in the vicinity and no planes overhead. They were within sight of the coast.

"Take her up Lieutenant Brown."

Brown gave the order to surface. They were still a couple of nautical miles off the coast of Plymouth and they should arrive by sunrise. Dominic asked Lt. Brown if he could help Cookie start the collection of stored food.

"Go ahead, now that we are surfaced," he replied.

Dominic went back to the galley, and Cookie was checking his list. "There is food in the rafters of the for'ard torpedo compartment and some in the rear stokers' mess. We'll gather all the food and place it into the rear stokers' mess, then all we have to do is carry it out the rear hatch."

"Sounds like a plan," Dominic said. For the next hour, they gathered all the remaining food and stockpiled it at the back of the boat.

When they had finished, they both climbed up the rear hatch, and there off to the left was Plymouth.

"Whitsand Bay: we made it," Cookie said.

With that, a smile came over Dominic's face, and he said, "We're home."

The submarine travelled across the Tamar Estuary and then up the River Tamar. There on the starboard side was the Devonport Submarine Base.

"Prepare for harbor stations." Ordered Lt. Brown

As Dominic was on the red watch, he helped with securing the submarine to the dock. Naval seamen on the dock threw lines to attach and secure the sub to the jetty. A gangplank was rolled out and over onto the rear freeboard.

It took a couple of hours to clean out the submarine of all the remaining food and provisions. Auxiliary lines were attached to the boat to supply power and to discharge and empty the septic and bilge tanks.

The Marines had unloaded their equipment and damaged canoe through the torpedo loading hatch. There they waited for a truck to take them to their compound. Dominic came over to them to say goodbye.

"Take care gentlemen, it was a pleasure to have met you. I wish you the best when you get back at your base." He shook each of their hands and said "good day."

By 1000 hours, the boat was mostly emptied of provisions and personnel.

Dominic was aware that modifications were going to be made to Tuna. The refit was to take six weeks. He was not sure exactly what it was, but it was something to help the submarine detect ships and other submarines under the water, something called "ASDIC Sonar."

Before Dominic left the boat, he walked to the seamen's mess and retrieved his crucifix and chain from the peg on the wall. He placed it over his head and under his shirt. The metal felt cold against his skin.

With the submarine now empty and the engineer officers and shore crew starting to prepare the boat, Dominic could begin his leave.

He had not bathed in several days, and the sweat from the last couple of days had made him long for a shower. He couldn't go home smelling this ripe. He walked across the compound and into the main barracks. In the middle of the barracks there were toilets with showers. He hung his duffel bag on the peg and stripped off his clothes. He turned the water on, which warmed up as he stepped in.

The warm water felt wonderful as he grabbed the soap and washed down. When he had finished, there was a small towel he used to dry himself off with.

He had a quick shave before unpacking his duffle bag with his navy-blue dress uniform and cap, and quickly changed into them. When he was changed and packed up, he walked outside again and across the quad to the administration office.

Dominic walked through the front doors towards the to the pay master's office. There was a short line of sailors. He approached the purser who was a senior warrant officer. Bommy gave his name and service number and asked for a travel voucher.

The warrant officer checked the listing, went to a cash drawer, and came back to Dominic with a pay envelope. He was not sure how much he was going to receive; while some guys will have their pay owed calculated down to the last shilling and penny, Dom was just happy to get paid and be on his way. He tucked the pay packet into the front pocket of his pants. The warrant officer asked Dominic, "When do you have leave until?"

Dominic replied, "Until the twenty first of December."

The warrant officer completed the travel voucher and handed it to Dominic.

"Thank you Sir," Dominic said. He placed the slip of paper into his pocket with his pay packet.

A military truck was being loaded to take service men who were starting their leave to the rail station in Plymouth. Dom threw his bag in and jumped in the back of the covered truck. ERA Victor Lammin was already sitting in the truck.

He looked up and asked, "Bommy, are you heading home?"

"Hey Vic, yes, home to Liverpool. It will probably be the longest nine hours home. Where are you heading to?" Dominic asked.

"Bath, I'll be taking the bus, I should be home in two and a half hours."

They both settled in for their trip into the city to the bus and train stations.

When they arrived at the town centre Dominic said goodbye to Vic as he walked towards the train station. He walked into the station and over to the ticket counter, took out his travel voucher and asked, "Can I get a get a ticket and return to Liverpool please?"

The ticket agent prepared four tickets.

"These are your tickets to London Paddington Station, and Euston to Liverpool, and your return tickets." Dominic gave the travel voucher to the ticket agent, picked up his tickets and said, "Thank you. What time does the train leave?"

"At eleven o'clock, so you have a couple of minutes to wait," the ticket agent said.

"Much appreciated," Dominic then walked into the small café. When he approached the tea lady Dominic ordered a cup of tea and a scone with butter. He missed having butter on the boat. The tea lady served the tea in a white earthenware cup and the scone with two pads of butter on a plate. He paid the tea lady and sat down.

There were soldiers and sailors sitting across the café—Dominic was not sure if they were coming or going. He slathered the two pads of butter onto his scone and took his first bite. The salty, creamy butter on his tongue gave him a smile. Nothing like the taste of butter on a scone.

Dominic looked across at the clock in the station; he had five more minutes before his train came. He finished his tea and the last crumbs of his scone, picked up his bag and walked out to the station platform. Track one was going east to London. He put his duffle bag on the ground as he waited patiently. He thought he could hear a train, looked to the right, and the train was coming around the corner and then entered the station.

When the train came to a stop, the conductor opened the door. A couple of sailors and officers exited off the train carriage. Dominic waited for an elderly lady to climb aboard and he followed her into the train corridor. There was an open sitting compartment on the right. He walked in and placed his duffle bag on the rack above his seat and sat down. A couple of minutes later, he heard the conductor say, "All aboard." Dominic had an empty compartment—he was not disappointed; he would be able to get some shut-eye.

The train lurched forward, and they were underway. He watched as the train pulled out of the station. A couple of minutes later the conductor opened the door asking for tickets. Dominic gave him his ticket. The conductor punched his ticket and handed it back to him saying, "Thank you."

He settled back into his seat, closed his eyes, and was asleep in no time. The train travelled east towards Exeter, the next stop.

Chapter 11: The World Atlas

12 December 1942
Crewe

Jack arrived home to the aroma of beef stew with potatoes on the kitchen hob—his favourite meal. Dolly would have been to the shops and the butcher that day, so the stewing beef would be fresh, and he was looking forward to his supper.

Footsteps were heard in the upstairs corridor as Eve ran down and hugged her dad. She had been reading in her bedroom all afternoon since she got home from school, and was happy to see him.

"We're on letter 'T' today," she exclaimed.

Jack had been thinking all day about which of the world cities he would challenge Eve with. Yesterday's letter *S* had been Sao Paulo, Singapore, and Saigon—Eve had found each one. Tonight was the letter *T*, and he had to be prepared. "Toronto, Toledo, and Tofino," Jack said.

Sitting on the settee, Eve opened up her atlas. She knew Toronto was a city in Canada, but not sure which province. She had recently learned that Australia and the United States of America had states and Brazil and Canada had provinces. Because Eve had not heard of Toledo or Tofino, they would be a challenge. She turned to the page showing the continent of Africa, and started to scan as Jack sat down to take off his boots. "I know that Toronto is in Canada, but can you give me a clue on the other two?" Eve asked him.

"Yes. They are all on the same continent."

"Woo-hoo," Eve replied, "They are in North America."

She turned to maps of the United States of America and Canada and started scanning them from west to east. Eve was very methodical with her search, but not every city was shown on the country map. She might have to look at each state or provincial map. "Both the USA and Canada are big countries, with so much to cover," she exclaimed.

"Dinner's ready," Dolly called from the kitchen.

Evelyn's dad said, "We can continue this after supper."

Dolly was taking the white stoneware bowls out of the cupboard when Jack and Evelyn came into the kitchen. Jack gave her a kiss on the cheek. "Sit yourselves down" she said, with a smile.

Eve came into the kitchen with her atlas open to the eastern US states. She knew she was close and only had to search a little more before she found what she was looking for.

"Put that book away," her mum said scornfully. "How was your day, Jack?"

He slumped into his chair at the end of the table and reached for the salt and pepper. He was ready to eat. "Good, thanks. I am back on the fire watch tomorrow night, so I am off until then."

Jack never got used to the changing shifts at the Rolls Royce plant. Work went on 24 hours a day, so he would stay up as late as possible and try to sleep tomorrow.

After clearing the dinner dishes, Eve dove back into to looking for Toledo and Tofino. Since she could not see either city in the Western US States, she was now was looking at the Eastern States. Eve focused on the state lines and cities in Michigan, Illinois, and Ohio. "There's Toledo," Eve said proudly. "It's in Ohio."

"Well done," said her dad. "But you still have Tofino and Toronto to find."

In order to prep for today's letter, Jack had found Tofino on a detailed map of Canada—it was on the Esowista Peninsula, located on Vancouver Island, British Columbia.

Since there were no cities that he knew of beginning with letters U and only a couple of cities with V, he would be prepared for tomorrow and go directly to W with Warsaw, Washington, and Wellington.

The evening settled in, and the blackout curtains had been drawn. Eve was still trying to locate Tofino on the maps in the Atlas. It was tough to find. Starting with the Canadian Provinces, she knew it would be easier to find Toronto. It was a place her Uncle Mike had said he would like to visit in the future.

The radio was on low, playing the BBC as everyone settled into the evening. Suddenly, there was the blaring sound of the air-raid siren on the street corner.

"Evelyn. Come on, get under the table." Her mum said. "Quickly now." Blankets and pillows were kept at the ready just for these raids.

Eve folded the book closed on her finger and bent down to get under the table. Crewe was no stranger to bombing, especially with the Merlin engine factory close by. Not bombed as heavily as Liverpool, but bombed nonetheless. As Crewe was in a valley, bombers attacked predominantly during daylight hours.

Dolly climbed under the table with Eve. Jack laid down on the blanket and said, "Have you found Tofino?"

"Not yet," Eve replied. "Can I have a clue?"

"It's on an island," Jack smiled.

"An island!" Eve had just searched Newfoundland in the Gulf of St. Lawrence, so she flipped the pages to Ontario, finding Manitoulin Island in Lake Huron. "No, not there," she muttered, continuing her search. Finally, she found the Pacific Ocean and the province British Columbia. Scanning the coastline, she chirped, "It's on an island off the west coast of British Columbia, called Vancouver Island. Yeah, I found it."

Jack was falling asleep, remembering that Eve had not announced where Toronto was. "So, where's Toronto?"

"Oh, yeah. What was the province?" she asked. "I'm still looking—is it in Ontario? There it is!" she announced. "Toronto is on Lake Ontario. It has a star in the circle, so it must be the provincial capital."

There was snoring coming from Jack. "So much for staying up late," Dolly said.

Suddenly, there came the sound of distant bombing. Rocking gently, Dolly hunched over with her fingers plugging her ears. Gertie just sat quietly. She had her rosary beads and was saying her prayers.

The bombing lasted twenty minutes, sounding like it was down at the rail yard.

Dolly stayed under the table for ten minutes after the air raid sirens stopped. Gerty stood up and said good night to Dolly as she went up to bed. Jack was sleeping and so was Evelyn. No need to disturb them, Dolly decided. She grabbed her packet of cigarettes and opened the front door. The moon was high overhead and the stars were out.

She took out a cigarette and lit it with a wooden match. If an air-raid warden caught her, there would be hell to pay. She inhaled deeply. Dolly could not stand the sound of bombing. The worry was that a stray German bomber might go off course and bomb their house. There had been much more damage to surrounding neighbourhoods in Liverpool than there was in Crewe. She was grateful that there were not as many air raids here. Since Jack had started at the Merlin factory two years ago, they had been fortunate not to have been bombed.

Dolly thought back to the May blitz, when she and Evelyn had been staying with her sister Eily and Eily's husband Mike on Royston Street in Liverpool. Since Jack was working in Crewe, they decided to move there with him to avoid the heavy bombing.

Jack had voiced how fortunate he felt that because he was a metal worker, and just over the age of conscription, he was spared from being enlisted in the army. His brother Harry was in the army, and Jack was not sure where he was deployed.

Dolly heard the sounds of distant sirens and bells as the fire brigade was being mobilised. Somebody had been bombed. She was well aware of the damage from the bombs and subsequent fires they caused. Liverpool, like London, had been heavily hit.

She put out her cigarette and closed the door. There were no more air-raid sirens for the rest of the night.

Chapter 12: Fire Watch

13 December, 1942
Crewe

Jack woke in his bed to the sound of his alarm clock. It was late afternoon and he was on fire watch that night at the factory. In addition to his regular sixty-hour week, he and his fellow machinists were expected to work as fire watch throughout the sprawling factory complex with a couple of monthly shifts.

After getting himself washed and dressed, he walked down the stairs. Dolly was cleaning up the dinner dishes in the kitchen as Eve was working on schoolwork at the kitchen table. Eve looked up and saw her father and said, "Da, did you have a good sleep?"

"I did. You were nice and quiet, thank you," her dad replied.

Having boiled the kettle, Dolly prepared a cup of steeping hot tea for Jack. Taking it over to him she said, "there you go. I have packed your lunch for you, too."

Jack was sorry that he could not stop and chat further with his wife and daughter. "I am missing spending more time with you both. Between my regular shifts and working on the fire watch it, I have no time off."

"We miss you too, Da," Eve said. "I hope you have a good night at work."

With that, Jack finished that last of his tea and he walked over to the sink. He placed his cup on the counter and grabbed his lunch bag. "I had better get going."

"We had a small roast for dinner tonight, so I have made you a nice pork sandwich and some biscuits for your lunch," Dolly remarked.

"Lovely." Jack smiled as he picked up his lunch pail. He opened the front door and put his jacket on, kissed them both goodbye.

Dolly and Eve stood at the doorway to wave him off.

It was a pleasant evening for the twenty-minute walk to the factory. Jack arrived at the main gate and nodded to the security guard inside the shack as he walked through and onto the factory property. It was a sprawling facility, with many outbuildings and warehouses. He walked in to where the fire watch team was gathered.

As oil and lubricants were stored and used throughout the facility, the fire watch team was assigned to parts of the plant that were not used during nighttime hours. It was a dreary job, walking around the warehouses, but he did not grouse too much about it. He wanted to do his part.

The fire watch ensured buckets of sand and water were there to dowse any fire caused by bombing. Jack had seen his share of unexploded bombs dropped on Liverpool, but it was the greyish cylinders, about a foot long and weighing about two pounds, scared him the most. They were incendiary bombs. Now every fire watch member was trained and instructed on what to do if an incendiary bomb was ignited.

When a canister hit the ground, it ignited. There was time for the fire watch to extinguish it. It had to be smothered, and the perfect agent to do so was sand. The fire watch had placed buckets of sand throughout the facility to use immediately in the event of a bombing.

Jack and workmate Jim Dempsey had spent previous shifts shovelling sand into buckets and using a trolley to deposit them around the warehouses. They both hoped they would never have to use them, but they were prepared in the event that they did.

The weather had turned overcast, with low-lying clouds moving in. This was a good indication that there might not be any bombing that night. That meant that Jack and Jim only had to keep themselves alert. They had prescribed areas to walk through, coming back together to the fire watch muster station, where they would have their lunch and tea.

After Jack had finished his rounds, he put the kettle on the boil. Walking on the concrete floors was hard on his feet, especially while wearing his work boots. He would be glad to get them off when he got home. He made himself a cup of tea and sat on one of the wooden chairs placed in the area. While he waited for Jim who would be joining him shortly, Jack ate his sandwich. He would have his biscuits with his tea.

The large, cavernous warehouse creaked and groaned with the wind, which had picked up outside. He heard Jim's footfalls coming back from his rounds.

"All's quiet?" Jim asked.

"It is," Jack replied. "And the kettle just boiled, too."

Jim walked over to the kettle. "Lovely. I could use a cup of chai."

The men enjoyed each other's company. They had both started as machinists at the plant at about the same time. Jim, like Jack and his family, had moved to Crewe to get away from the bombing that Liverpool was experiencing. He was originally from Ambleside, in the Lake District, and still loved taking his holidays there before the war broke out. As an avid boater, he loved to sail on Lake Windermere and hoped to buy a small sailboat after the war.

"I don't need a big boat, just enough room to be comfortable while out on the lakes," he had said.

Jack, meanwhile, loved history and geography, a love of the latter that was passed on to his daughter.

After their tea break, they started their rounds. "If you want to take the loading facilities in the north, I'll do the southwest warehouse," Jack said.

"Sounds like a plan," Jim replied. "We'll meet back here in an hour?"

"Righto. We'll see you then," replied Jack.

They walked away in the direction of their appointed rounds.

The warehouses were kept dark, to avoid being seen by German bombers overhead. Fire watch wardens carried small battery torches that shone directly onto the floor. This helped them get about without walking into racks or tripping on materials stored on the floor.

Jack's footfalls in the cavernous warehouse echoed off the walls and high ceilings. He made a mental note of where each fire pail was located as he did his rounds. He didn't mind his time serving. The hours could drag on, but the company on fire watch shift made the time go by a little quicker.

He had walked through the second warehouse when he looked at his watch. It was time to head back to the muster area. It was nearly dawn, and the day shift would start shortly. He walked back to find Jim, who had already returned. "Well, Mate, we survived and another night without any fuss," Jim said.

"Aye. I bet with all the walking, we'll sleep well today," Jack replied.

They walked over to the building where their timecards and punch clock were located. It was only a couple of minutes before seven. Daytime workers were shuffling in to start their shifts.

"I am back on the tools tonight. You too?" Jack asked.

"You bet. I'll see you tonight," Jim replied, punching his card and replacing it back in the rack.

As they walked out the double doors, there was a cool breeze. Jack raised the collar of his coat to brace himself against the cold, lit a cigarette, and started walking. His feet were a little sore from last night, so he would be glad to take his boots off when he got home.

When he arrived, he found Dolly and Evelyn up and getting ready to start their day. "Daddy," Evelyn announced, as he walked in the front door and kicked off his boots. "Are you ready for bed?"

"I am, my love. You have a wonderful day, and I will see you later."

He walked into the kitchen and said good morning and goodnight to Dolly. "Would you like a cup of tea?" Dolly asked.

"No, thank you, I'm looking forward to my bed."

Jack climbed the stairs and got washed and undressed before heading into the bedroom. His head had not hit the pillow for more than a couple of minutes before he fell fast asleep.

Chapter 13: Albany Road

13 December, 1942
The train home

The train travelled east towards London, stopping at stations along the way. When they arrived at London's Paddington Station, Bommy grabbed his duffle bag off the rack and exited the train. Many people were getting off the train and onto the main concourse. He followed them, and he looked up for directions to the tube station.

He still had to get to Euston, so he started running towards the underground station. Dominic stopped at the ticket office and paid his fare into the box. Getting on the escalator, he travelled down and ran along the left side. He could hear the train coming. Landing at the bottom, he looked for the right track—to Euston. The train was just pulling in, and he ran to an open door.

"Made it," he muttered.

The journey took about twelve minutes. He stood alongside an open pole, thinking to himself, *not too much further.*

The train travelled on eastward. Euston was the next station. He walked anxiously to the doors waiting for them to be opened. When they did, he ran for the escalator. He started to climb on the left, but the running at Paddington had left him a little winded. *Too close to quit now.* He found his second wind and started climbing again. When he reached the top, he saw the directions to the train station and ran. He entered the Euston Station's main concourse and found the departure board.

The Liverpool train was leaving in five minutes, from platform six. Dominic scanned the station for a reference. There down on the right was his platform so he ran towards the sign.

As he entered, the train was there and people were still getting on. Bommy walked to the last car and boarded the train carriage. It was full of passengers, so he continued walking up, looking for an empty seat. As he walked into the next carriage, he was relived to find a vacant seat. There were two nuns who looked up at Dominic as he walked in to the compartment.

He smiled and said, "Good day, Sisters."

"Good day, Sir." The nuns smiled.

Dominic placed his duffle bag on the overhead rack and sat down. Just then, he heard the guard on the platform call out, "All aboard!" They would now be underway. A smile came to his face. He was very fortunate to have made the connecting train. He did not have to wait in the station for the next one, and he was truly grateful for this.

The train lurched forward as the engine slowly moved out of the station. The nuns had their tickets in hand, so they showed them to the ticket collector as he walked into the compartment. An older gentleman in a bowler hat and cane had followed him in. He too handed his ticket over to the collector and sat down. Finally, Dominic passed his to the conductor, who punched and handed back to him.

After the train had cleared the station, it travelled through districts of London that had been badly bombed. The German bombers were aiming for the railway station and the rail lines; unfortunately, the houses and businesses along the way had sustained severe damage. The train headed northwest through Wembley and then Watford, before the passing view outside the window became the rolling hills of the Midlands countryside.

They continued north-northwest, passing through the West Midlands and the cities of Coventry and Birmingham.

It was dark when the train pulled into Crewe. Was Gertie still there, or had she gone to Liverpool? He was hoping that she was already in Liverpool. They hadn't stopped long when the conductor passed by their compartment. Dominic stood up and asked him, "How much longer before we arrive in Liverpool?"

His Majesty's Sailor *and the Girl in the* Blue Coat

"We arrive at Lime Street station at seven-fifteen," he replied.

"Thank you," Dominic said, and he went back to his seat. He was getting anxious for home. *Nearly there,* he thought to himself. *Nearly there.*

The train departed Crewe for its final destination.

Upon arrival in Liverpool, Dominic stood up, grabbed his duffel bag, and exited the carriage onto the platform. He joined others who had disembarked the train and walked towards the main concourse. People were coming and going, walking through the station and out onto Lime Street.

It would take him one tram ride to get home—or should he take a taxi? He had just been paid, so he had the money, and would get home even quicker. Dominic thought for a second and decided to take the tram. As he walked to the stop, he looked up and saw the clouds had cleared, and the moon was in its first quarter. He missed seeing the night sky. Not having to scan the darkness with binoculars looking for German aircraft and U-boats was a luxury.

He crossed the street as the tram arrived and walked to the top level where he could have a smoke. As the tram pulled out along Fraser Street, it turned right towards. There were many damaged buildings from the bombings. Liverpool has definitely seen its share of misery.

As the tram travelled along, on the right was the Royal Infirmary, where he had had his physical to get into the Navy. They crossed over Low Hill, along Kensington, and then to Prescot Road. He was almost home. He pulled the cord and rang the bell to stop the tram. Dominic walked off the back and onto the pavement as it pulled away. He crossed Prescot Road and walked down Derby Lane to Albany Road on the left. On the corner was an air-raid defence bunker. There were two men in uniform and helmets. "Good evening, gentlemen," he smiled and said. "How are you this evening?"

"Ay-up, mate," one of the wardens said. Bommy smiled and nodded to them as he passed.

Dominic had not heard a Liverpool Scouser accent in some time—it was good to be home. As he approached his mother's house, he noticed that the metal fence was missing from on top of the brick wall. The metal must have been recycled for the war effort.

He walked to the door, stood on the stoop hesitating for a moment. Should he knock? Or just walk in? Deciding it was best to knock, he rapped firmly on the door. He could hear voices inside.

"Dom, it's you," Mary Helen exclaimed, as she opened the door. His eldest sister embraced him and kissed his cheek.

Just then, his mum came around the corner from the kitchen. She looked up with a big smile. "You're home." Wrapping her arms around him, she gave him a big kiss.

"Is Gertie here?" he asked.

Dominic looked up, and there was his wife coming out of the bedroom. They had not seen each other in over three years, since they were married and he had left for submarine training at Gosport.

She hurried down the stairs, threw her arms around him and kissed him repeatedly. "Hello, my love," Dom said, as he lifted her off the floor. "I have missed you."

"Would you like something to eat?" His mum asked. "You must be hungry"

He realised that he had not eaten since this morning. "Please, I'm famished."

"Come sit yourself down. We had bubble and squeak for dinner."

Dominic walked into the kitchen. Nothing had changed. He sat at the table, where his mum placed a steaming hot plate of fried cabbage and potatoes. "Wonderful! Thanks, Ma. It's nice to be served."

"There is a pint of Newcastle Brown if you're interested," his mother said with a smile, knowing the answer. "Mick brought them to our last get-together. You'll be wanting to get to the pub soon, I'm sure."

Dominic smiled. "Ah, it's good to be home."

They talked about the family for the next couple of hours, about how everyone was doing—but Dom did not talk about his time aboard the submarine. His mum updated him on everyone in the family—those serving, and those at home. "John has been a prisoner of war for the past two years. He is now being held now at Stalag 37 in Germany—Dolly and I write to him regularly. David is in East Africa, and Thomas and Charlie Fitzsimmons are at sea. Dolly and Evelyn are coming over for Christmas, but I am not sure about Jack, Eily, and Rose. Mick may be working too."

His Majesty's Sailor *and the Girl in the* Blue Coat

As Dominic sat there, he had a thirst for his daily tot—neat. He would love to walk down the street to the pub for a shot or two, but he wasn't sure that he should leave Gert on his first night home. Dom knew he could, but was worried he wouldn't sleep that night after dozing off on the train.

"What time is the pub open until?" he asked.

"Ten o'clock," his mum answered. "Sorry, we have no rum here, but I am sure you will make last call if you leave now."

"I will be back shortly after I have a wee tot," he smiled at Gertie.

She knew his thirst for the spirits before they married. He was home safe, and she could relax for a couple days. *He's home*, she reminded herself. A visit to the pub was not the end of the world. "Go on, my love. Go have your tot."

Dominic bent over and gave her a big kiss. "Thank you, my love."

He said goodnight and was out the door. It was quite eerie, walking down to the pub with all the houses windows blacked out.

He opened the door to the familiar smell of stale beer and smoke. "Ah." *It was nice to be home.*

He did not recognize the barmaid behind the counter who asked, "Good evening, sailor. What can I get you?"

"Rum, dark rum. I'll take a double please." The barmaid got a tumbler and poured two shots. As Dominic watched, he noticed they were generously poured. Handing it to him, the barmaid heard a low sigh after Dominic had quickly knocked it back.

"Can I have a second, please, if you don't mind?"

The barmaid smiled, picked up his empty glass, poured two more heavy-handed shots, and passed it back to Dom. He stood at attention and said "to the Queen" as he downed half, then the second half. Finally, he let out another long sigh. The rum felt good going down his throat, and the burn in his belly helped him forget the rigours of war. "What time is it?" He asked the barmaid.

"It's ten minutes to ten and last call," she replied.

"Well, I'd better have one more for the road." She poured him a hefty double.

"What do I owe you, my dear?" Dominic asked with a slight slur in his speech.

"Well, the first one is on the house when a service man is home on leave. So, eight shillings."

Dominic pulled a pound note from his pay packet. "Thank you for a wonderful evening. I must be going home now." He placed the note on the counter, saying, "Keep the change."

"Thank you very much, very much appreciated," the barmaid replied.

He walked to the door, stopped and turned around. "What is your name?" he asked her.

"Flo," she answered. "What's yours?"

"Bommy. Pleased to have met you."

With that, he was out the door.

Once on the pavement, he got his bearings. "Here we go."

Dominic retraced his steps back to the house. Along the road, he decided he needed to take a pee. Looking up and down the street, he could see no one. Dom unbuttoned his fly and started peeing on the wall. He had not noticed the air-raid warden walking along the pavement. "Too much at the pub, me old pisser?"

"Bursting, I was. Keep up the good work," Dominic chortled. He buttoned up and started home. Along the way, his walk turned into more of a stagger.

The front door was unlocked, and the lights were on in the upper hall. He kicked off his boots, locked the door and walked upstairs.

Up the apples and pears, he remembered from his childhood—something his mum used to say.

The light was still on, and spilling out from under the second bedroom door. Dom slowly opened it. There Gertie lay, on the right side of the bed. *I guess I am on the left,* he thought to himself. They'd never gotten a chance to establish which side they would sleep on before he was shipped off to Portsmouth.

He pulled off his clothes and laid down beside her.

Gertie stirred "Goodnight, my love." She mumbling.

"Goodnight," he replied, as he switched off the light. He did not lay awake long, and the bed wasn't spinning as it had after previous episodes.

His Majesty's Sailor *and the Girl in the* Blue Coat

14 December, 1942

The sun crept through a crack at the edge of the bedroom black out blinds and into Dominic's eyes. "What the blazes?"

He realised quickly he was at home in bed. Reaching to Gertie's side, he found she was already up and gone. His head was pounding, but not so badly. Not as bad as New Year's Eve, 1939, in Hong Kong—when he had been assigned to the supply ship HMS *Medway*. He'd been an able seaman on eight hours of shore leave. The whole day and evening were spent in bars and taverns in central Hong Kong. He'd missed the midnight curfew and was listed as AWOL. Far too much rum on that bender. It deprived him of his good conduct badge for six months.

Today's headache was not that legendary. Perhaps his mum had some Anadin? He swung his legs out and sat on the side of the bed, testing his sea legs as he stood up. Looking around the room, he noticed his trousers and tunic were gone—replaced with a pair of brown pants, a white shirt, an extra pair of underpants and socks. Realizing they might be Jack's or Mick's, he tried them on and made his way downstairs.

His mum and Gertie were both in the kitchen with the kettle on the boil. They had emptied his duffle bag and his clothes were in the wash.

"Good morning," Dominic said as he stopped in the doorway arch. He then walked over to Gertie, who was bending over to pick up his duffle bag off the floor. As she stood, he grabbed her by the waist and kissed her. Gertie smiled, but there was sadness in her smile. She was upset about last night and him going off to the pub.

"Your uniform and dungarees needed a wash, and your duffel bag smells. We'll give it a Persil wash and hang it on the line," she said. "I see Mick's clothes fit you alright. You can thank Eily for that."

"Do you have any Cephos powder or Anadin tablets, Ma? My head is screaming at me," Dominic asked.

"Sorry, my love, you'll have to go down to the chemist," his mum said.

"Shall we go for a walk?" he asked Gertie.

There was a lot of standing or sitting in place in the Navy, and especially on a submarine. Not much walking about. Guys would get a Rikshaw to take them to the city centre in Hong Kong, but he preferred to walk when he was in port.

"The laundry can wait. Let's go," he urged Gertie.

"You go for your walk, I'll look after the laundry," his mum said.

Dominic took money from his pay packet on the nightstand and put it in his pocket. He was not sure how much the tablets would cost. Being in the Navy for the past thirteen years, he had lost track of how much everything was. He grabbed some shillings and a pound note, just in case.

They walked out of the door. He had a vague idea where the chemist was, and turned left when they hit the pavement.

It was a nice day. There was no need for a jacket. He held her hand as they walked together.

Gertie spoke of her stay in Crewe with Dolly and Jack, and how they lived on strict rations. She wondered how well Dominic ate while on the submarine. He told her of his eating well and helping Cookie make dinners when his watch allowed.

The pair chatted and made small talk as they walked to the chemist. Finally, Dominic opened the door for her, and they walked inside.

"Could I get some Cephos powder or Anadin tablets?" he asked the chemist at the back of the shop.

"We have a twelve-pack of Cephos or Anadin in thirty tablets or fifty tablets. Which would you like?" the Chemist asked.

"I'll take the thirty Anadin, please." Turning to Gertie. "Is there anything you need?"

"No" she smiled.

Dominic paid and they walked outside. Twisting off the lid and shaking out two tablets onto his upturned palm, he opened his mouth tossed them in and swallowed. He already felt better than he had when he got up. The fresh air certainly helped. He still had money in his pocket, so he turned to Gertie and asked, "Fancy some fish and chips?"

As much as she would have liked the fish and chips, they could not afford to spend his pay packet frivolously. "No, we had better not," she replied. "It is probably closed until the dinner hour. Not much call to stay open for lunch."

"Ah, I could have tucked into an order," he said, disappointed.

They started for home.

His Majesty's Sailor *and the* Girl *in the* Blue Coat

If he was back on the ship, he would be waiting to have his daily tot of rum at about this time. That would help remove the headache. *The hair of the dog that bit you*, he thought.

As they walked back to the house, they passed the pub. He thought it looked familiar. "Could we stop for a quick one?" Dominic asked.

"It is after eleven," Gertie replied. "I'm not sure what time it opens."

So, they tried the door, and it opened. There was the familiar smell again, stale beer and cigarette smoke. "What would you like? Lemonade, or a shandy?" Dominic asked.

"A lemonade sounds wonderful," she replied as they approached the bar. Being away for so long, he did not recognize the barman serving.

"Could I get a double Pusser's dark rum and a lemonade, please?" Dominic asked.

The bartender was well aware that the person ordering a double dark rum was a sailor home on leave from the Royal Navy. "Where are you from, sailor?" he asked.

"I'm from Liverpool, home on leave."

He did not want to get into being on a submarine. *Loose lips sink ships.*

The bartender prepared the drinks and handed them to Dominic. "There you go, mate—as a serviceman, the first drink is on the house. All you have to pay for is the lemonade."

"Listen, as much as I would like to take advantage of your generosity, I was in last night. The barmaid, Flo, treated me to a free tot, so thank you very much. What do I owe you?"

The barman told Dominic the amount, and Dom gave him a small tip. He seemed to recall leaving too much last night.

The barman thanked him and wished them a pleasant day.

He walked back with the drinks and sat down beside Gertie, who was sitting on the bench. "Cheers, my love."

They toasted each other as he sipped the dark rum. There was the familiar burn down his throat and into his belly. The Anadin had kicked in, but the rum would help the most to get rid of last night's fog.

There were a couple of patrons in the bar, but they were alone for the most part. It felt nice, having a tot with Gertie. He had looked forward to having a tot every day he was on the boat—now, he was having a tot with his wife. It felt a little surreal, like he was in a dream. He could not remember the last time he'd worn civilian clothes. *His wedding day!*

Dom did not want this moment to end. He looked across the small table and into Gertie's eyes. He took her right hand, and they just sat there, enjoying each other's company, getting to know the person who sat across the table.

Gertie sipped her lemonade as Dominic finished his rum.

They walked back out into the sunlight. Dom squinted as he looked up. He missed the daytime sky.

When they got home, his mum had finished his laundry and was bleaching his duffle bag. It was starting to smell a little. He yawned, and said "I feel like a nap. He kissed Gertie and went upstairs to the bedroom and lay down. In no time, he was fast asleep, and slept the better part of the afternoon.

Chapter 14: Christmas in Liverpool

19 December, 1942
Liverpool

Dominic walked into the house with his mum and Gertie, carrying grocery bags. They had been to the shops and bought the food and fixings for the Christmas party. His leave would end before Christmas Day, so the family were gathering early to celebrate with him. They were expecting a couple of people to come over later. He took the bags he was carrying and placed them on to the kitchen table.

Dom had a nice couple of days while he was home. His leave would end on Monday, when he would be taking the train back to Plymouth.

His mum and Gertie started preparing the dinner, and he asked if he could help. They both said they had everything under control and that he could rest. What his mum did not say was that she had been doing without and hoarding her rations of sugar and flour so that there would be enough for their Christmas meal that afternoon.

He had been resting all week and could not remember sleeping as much as he had these past couple of days. They had picked up the Saturday Echo while at the shops, so he sat in the sitting room and opened the paper. There were only a couple of pages to read, with advertisements on the second page along the sides. Some companies and businesses he remembered from before he went into the Navy. He couldn't recall the last time he had just sat reading the newspaper.

Dom enjoyed reading the newspaper. In particular there were open letters to the Minister of Agriculture and one to Lord Woolton, the Minister of Food, stressing that there would be no food shortages this Christmas.

He looked at the clock. Their guests would not be here for a couple of hours yet. However, he was feeling like a tot. The pub was open. He thought he might pop down before everyone showed up.

Dominic walked into the kitchen, where his mum and wife were preparing dinner. "I'm just popping out for a bit. Won't be long, just going to stretch my legs," he said.

Gertie knew what he was up to. "Go on, stretch your legs. We'll see you shortly. Remember, everyone will be here around three, so don't go too far."

"I'll be good and stay close," he said as he kissed her on the cheek.

Dominic walked out the door and headed to the pub.

Crewe

Evelyn and Dolly had risen early to get ready. Unfortunately, Jack was working nights and could not travel with them to Liverpool.

Eve had on her yellow floral dress and her sky-blue coat. She liked getting dressed up, and today was no exception, especially as she would be seeing her Nana King and family. "Will Uncle Mike be there, too?"

"I'm not sure, Evelyn," her mum replied.

They walked out of the door, and Dolly locked the latch.

It was a beautiful early winter's day. The sun shone as they walked along Gainsborough Road and down Derrington Avenue. They were at the train station within a half hour. Walking up to the ticket booth, Dolly asked for two return tickets to Liverpool. When she took the tickets, she placed them in her purse, and they walked out onto the platform. Dolly had taken this train into Liverpool quite often. It would be there in just a couple of minutes.

Evelyn heard it first. The train was chugging up the towards them. Dolly took hold of Evelyn's shoulder and moved her back from the platform edge.

The train stopped, and they walked towards the front carriage from where the guard stepped out. The platform was quiet, with passengers getting on the carriages. They did not see anyone get off the train, as they climbed aboard. There appeared to be plenty of seats available. So, they easily found an empty compartment. Evelyn took a seat by the window.

The guard was heard to say "All aboard!" and the train gently started moving forward.

After a few minutes, the guard opened the compartment door, asking for tickets. Dolly handed them to the collector, who punched them and handed them back.

"We'll be in Liverpool within the hour," Dolly told Evelyn.

Liverpool

Dominic smiled as he entered the pub. He thought to himself *"It smelled better that a submarine submerged for more than fourteen hours"*. He walked up to the bar, and there behind the counter was the barmaid from the other night.

As he walked up, she noticed Dominic and said, "Hey, sailor, come here often?"

Dominic felt his face go flush. He was not expecting to see her, she had not been there in the couple of times he had come for a drink with Gertie. "What can I get you," she asked, "a double dark rum?"

"Yes, please!" he replied, taken aback.

A moment later, Flo returned with a tumbler filled with the mahogany-coloured liquid and placed it on a coaster.

"There you go. Bottoms up."

"Cheers," Dominic said, thanking her as he picked up the drink. Taking a sip, he could taste caramel on his tongue. Was he getting a more discerning taste? Not likely. He did not drink rum for the taste. He drank for its effect.

Dominic knew he could not be long. Eily, Mick, Dolly, Evelyn and possibly Jack were coming over. He had not seen his family since his wedding day in April, 1938, four and a half years ago. How fast that time had flown.

Dominic sat down at the bar. Flo had gone off to serve someone else. The pub had not changed much in the past few years: it looked much the same as the last time he had been there before the war.

While he sat at the bar, he had a cigarette and continued to sip his tot. There were a couple of older gentlemen chatting while having a pint. He did not mind sitting alone quietly, he simply enjoyed the atmosphere.

He thought, *one more won't hurt*. So, he caught Flo's attention "Could I have another, my dear?"

"Coming right up," she answered. She picked up the bottle of Pusser's dark rum, poured it into the jigger and then into the tumbler. He could tell she was over-pouring it from where he sat. Walking over, she placed it on the counter in front of him and said, "there you go."

"Thank you, cheers," Dominic said.

He could feel the rum starting to take effect, relaxing him. There was not much that really got him anxious, but the tot of rum certainly helped keep his blood pressure in order.

He held out his hands and looked down at them. There was no shaking. His hands were rock steady. Dominic smiled, reached for his drink and took a sip. He should be getting back to the house. Standing, he finished his tot. He remembered how much two double rums were, plus he would leave a little extra for Flo. Taking the money from his pocket, he placed it on the counter.

He started to walk to the door, when Flo called out, "Goodbye sailor! You take care!"

"Thank you, I will." He said. Remembering that Christmas was in a couple of days, he added "Happy Christmas, Flo! I hope you have a wonderful day."

With that he walked out of the door and made his way back home. The rum felt good. It did as it was intended to do. It took his pain away. It was not an ache as much as it was a weight that he felt. He would have to leave tomorrow; his leave was never long enough.

As he approached his mum's house, he saw a lady and a young girl walking up the street towards him. She looked familiar—it was Dolly! He looked at the girl in the bright blue coat. Was that Eve? How much she had grown since he last saw her.

Dolly saw Dominic walking towards them and said to Evelyn, "There's your Uncle Bommy."

She saw him and ran up to his open, waiting arms. "Hello, Kate!" Bommy cried.

His Majesty's Sailor *and the Girl in the* Blue Coat

Evelyn remembered that Uncle Bommy called her Kate. She must remind him of someone called Kate. "Hello, Uncle Bommy. I have missed you so much." She gave him a big hug.

"I've missed you too," Dominic said. "Look how much you have grown."

Dolly walked up and gave him a big hug. She could smell the rum on his breath. "Were you down for a dram?"

Bommy smiled. "You know me too well. How have you been? Jack not able to come?" he asked.

"No, Jack is on nights tonight," Dolly replied. "He was sorry that he couldn't be with us."

As they walked into the house, he noticed Mary Helen and Mick had arrived since he had gone to the pub. He shook Mick's hand, hugged Eileen, and gave her a kissed on the cheek.

"How are you, Eily?"

"We're good, Bommy, thanks! Enjoying being home?"

"I have been well looked-after." Dominic replied. "Wonderful to see you both."

It had been a long while since he had seen Mick. He was taller than Dominic by a couple of inches, with a big barrel chest. Mick was a carpenter. He loved working with wood and used to make cabinets before the war began. "By the way, thanks for the togs while my kit was being washed. What have you been up to, Mick?"

Mick filled him in on his work at the factory where they made Mosquitoes. "My cabinetry experience has come in handy and I am now making the Mosquitoes' wooden frame and fuselage. Jack is a machinist at Rolls Royce working on the Merlin engines used in Spitfires, Mosquitoes and Lancaster Bombers. I'm here in Liverpool, where the carpentry work is."

It was not long before the dinner was ready and everyone was called to the table. There was a brisket of beef, braised red cabbage and pureed parsnip. There was Evelyn's favourite, too: Yorkshire Pudding. Her nana had saved her rations of eggs and flour to make the golden, fluffy dish.

When dinner had finished, everyone looked like they had had their fill and were well satisfied. Topping off dinner was dessert: everyone had a serving of trifle with whipped cream. There was little left, the last serving scraping the bowl.

"That was delicious, Ma," Dominic said.

She knew trifle was his favourite at Christmas from when he was a little boy. It had taken some help from the neighbours to pull it off. *Ellen Moroney pays her fair share,* she said to herself. There would be a few sacrifices in the future to pay them back for the cream and eggs.

After the dinner dishes were cleared from the table and the guests gathered in the sitting room, Eily and Mick had brought out a tin of sweets that were shared. As Eily opened the tin, Eve had her choice of the sugary treats. She reached in and pulled out a Lemon Sherbert and popped it into her mouth. "Mmm," she said. "It tastes so good."

Her nana had left the room and returned with a small wrapped gift in her hands. "Evelyn, I have something for you for Christmas, I hope you will enjoy it."

Eve took the small brightly wrapped parcel and opened the tied paper. She could smell a pleasant aroma coming from the package. Opening the paper, she found a bar of Pears soap. The translucent, amber-coloured oval bar smelled fresh and clean. Her parents used Dove soap at home; she had not tried this type before. She thanked her nana, giving her a bug hug and a kiss for the gift.

Since they were nearing the winter solstice, it was already getting dark as everyone was preparing to leave. "I'll walk with you down to the Prescot tram stop," Dominic said.

"Goodbye and Happy Christmas," Dolly said to the others, as they all embraced.

Evelyn hugged and kissed her nana goodbye. "You take care, my love. Goodnight and God bless," her nana said.

As they were leaving, Dolly found Mick having a cigarette on the stoop. "Take care, Mick. We'll see you soon," she said.

Evelyn gave her Uncle Mike a big hug and a kiss, "You take care, kid," he said.

With that, the three of them—Bommy, Dolly, and Eve—walked down Albany Road towards Prescot. "How is school, Kate?" Bommy asked.

Eve did not want to talk about the caning she had received the other day from Mother Superior. She was still stinging from that whipping. Instead, she told him about her new world atlas and her love of geography. "Where are some of the places you have been?" she asked her uncle.

"Well, let's start with Hong Kong, then Malta and Alexandria. Can you remember how to find them on the map?" he asked.

"Yes, I'll remember," Evelyn said, confidently.

Just then, the Prescot Road tram came. Dolly turned to Bommy "You take care of yourself," she said emotionally, not wanting him to go.

"I will," he said. "And you, Kate, be good fer ya ma." He gave her a hug.

The tram stopped, and Dolly and Evelyn got on. Dolly put the change into the collection box and walked back to where Evelyn had found a double seat. It was a twenty-minute ride to Lime Street station and their train home.

She knew that their train left on the hour to Crewe and hoped she'd planned accordingly. She had their tickets already, all they needed was the platform number.

When they got to the station, there were many people carrying gifts and dressed up for the Christmas season.

As they walked towards the gate, Dolly looked up at the board and found their train on track two. They should make this. *Good news*, Dolly thought.

They walked to the third passenger carriage and climbed aboard. There, on the right, was an empty compartment. "There we go, in yah get," she said to Evelyn as they walked in and sat down.

After a couple of minutes, the familiar, "All Aboard!" came from the guard, and they were on their way.

Jack woke up to his alarm clock. With the quiet house, he had had a good sleep. It was dark out as he walked down the stairs and turned on the light. At that moment he did not realise the blackout blinds where not drawn. A minute later there was a loud rapping at the door.

"Air-Raid Officer Jones," someone bellowed outside.

Jack rushed to open the door. "We are to be in blackout and your front and side windows are not blinded," Warden Jones commanded.

"My apologies, I am just getting up for work. I'll close them now," Jack said as he shut the front door. He walked across the room and drew the blinds.

As Jack got ready for work, he made a cup of tea. Since Dolly was at her mum's, he realized that he would also have to make a lunch for himself today. He looked into the larder and there on the shelf was some cheshire cheese and a couple of cooked rashers of bacon. *"I'll have that tonight"* he thought to himself getting 2 slices of wheatmeal bread for a sandwich.

Dolly and Evelyn arrived home a couple of minutes later. They were both happy to see him before he went to work. "Good bye, and see you in the morning," they chimed.

Evelyn grabbed the atlas and went up to her bedroom to find Hong Kong, Malta, and Alexandria.

Chapter 15: Back to Plymouth

20 December 1942
Liverpool

Dominic woke up to his alarm. He did not want to be late getting back to Plymouth. Gertie was still sleeping when he slipped on his trousers and went to the kitchen. His mum was still in bed too.

They had finished his laundry. It had been folded and placed on the dining room table. His duffle bag had also been cleaned. It hadn't looked that clean since he'd gotten it, all those years ago.

He made a cup of tea and went to the stoop to have a smoke. He watched people walking down Albany Road, making their way to work.

As much as he'd enjoyed being with his family over the past few days, he knew his place right now should be back on the sub. He put out his smoke and walked back into the house.

Dominic changed into his all-blue uniform and packed his dungarees and undershirts into his duffle bag. Placing his sailor cap on the bag, he was ready to leave. Just then he heard footsteps on the stairs. It was his mum.

"Not leaving without saying goodbye, were you?" she asked.

"No, just getting ready to leave," he replied. "I had better go say goodbye to Gertie."

He walked up the stairs and opened the bedroom door. Gertie started to stir. Dominic walked over to her. "Goodbye, my love. I have enjoyed every minute at home with you."

Gertie threw her arms around him. "You take care and come back to me in one piece, ya hear?"

"I will." Dominic said smiling.

Gertie followed him down the stairs to where his mother was standing at the bottom. She wore a thin smile as she tried to hide her sadness. She patted Dominic's chest with her right hand, and could feel the crucifix that lay around his neck.

"I made you something for Christmas," she said, passing him a small gift wrapped in the same colourful paper and twine that had been on Kate's present the other night.

Bommy opened the parcel and found a pair of knitted socks. "Brilliant, thank you," he said. "You can never go wrong with a pair of comfy socks." Dominic stuffed them in his bag and turned to give his mum a hug and a kiss.

He put his hat on and threw his duffle bag over his shoulder. Opening the door, Dominic walked out onto the front pavement. He turned around to see his mum and wife in the doorway. Smiling, he waved one last time. He'd had a wonderful visit with his family, with plenty of rest.

The train pulled out of Liverpool on the way to London, where Dominic would arrive at Euston Station and go to Paddington to get back to Plymouth. It should take just over nine hours to get back to the base. Dominic closed his eyes, thinking about the day he joined the Royal Navy. He had been seventeen and had needed his parents' permission to sign on.

1930
Liverpool

His mum took him to the Royal Navy recruitment centre on Tabley Street by the Liverpool Docks.

His dad had been a private in the East Lancashire Regiment, and had told his son that it was no disgrace to be in the service. Dominic had thought long and hard, deciding which of the armed services he would join. He remembered at fifteen wanting to join the Royal Navy, only his mum had said he was too young to enlist. He had seen the training ship HMS *Indefatigable*, which had both funnels and masts, that was moored in the Mersey on the Birkenhead side.

His brothers each had a preference for which service they would enter when they came of age. John and David said they would go into the Army. His youngest brother Tom said he, too, was going into the Navy.

It was a cool morning when they set off to the Recruiting Office; Dom had to wear his coat. Waiting at the tram stop, he stood by his mother—they nearly saw eye to eye. There was a sadness on his mum's face, it was in her eyes. Her eldest boy wanted to join the Navy.

Several people were already on the tram when it had arrived. His mum paid the conductor and they walked up the aisle. Two seats became available, and they sat down. As tram travelled, his mum watched for the street corner where they would get off. After about twenty minutes, his mum stood up and grabbed his hand as though she did not want to lose him.

They got off and started along the pavement. Walking briskly, they passed some open shops—others were boarded up.

Walking towards the Royal Navy Recruiting Office, Dominic noticed the front poster, stating, "A man's life in the Royal Navy."

Dominic's pulse began to rise. They walked up a couple of steps and in through the front door.

There were other lads his age with their mothers, so Dominic did not feel alone. There were two men in black jackets with gold braids on their sleeves, and a sailor in dress blue uniform with three stripes on his sleeve. One of the men in the black jackets introduced himself. He was a Sub-Lieutenant. "How can I help you?"

"I would like to join the Royal Navy," Dominic said proudly.

"Well, let's get started," the Sub-Lieutenant replied. They walked to a desk with two chairs, and he and his mother sat down.

Reaching for an application form, the Sub-Lieutenant repeated, "So you want to join the Royal Navy. We are pleased that you have offered your service to the naval defence of this great land. And your name, please, Ma'am?"

"Ellen King."

"And your son?" he asked.

"Dominic King," he replied.

"Your date and place of birth?"

"The fourth of September, 1913, Mitchelstown, County Cork, Ireland."

"And your address?" the Lieutenant asked.

"40, Albany Road, Liverpool," Dominic replied.

"That's fine," he said as he stood. "I will be right back."

Just then, the sailor in the uniform with the three stripes, and a red anchor and rope wound around like an "S" on his sleeve, came over to the table where they were sitting.

"Hello, son. What is your name?"

"Dominic," told him.

"Pleased to make your acquaintance, young man. So, you're interested in joining the Royal Navy? My name is Leading Seaman Parks. I most recently served aboard the *Oberon*, one of the newest Odin Class submarine. Being deployed on a submarine is known as 'the silent service,' where a complement of crew and officers of about fifty all work as a single unit. We have a strong comradery, where you trust everyone aboard with your life."

Dominic listened intently as Leading Seaman Parks told him about life aboard a submarine. All the exotic ports of call, through the Mediterranean and the Far East, could be visited.

"You will not be disappointed if you opt to become a submariner. But first, you must start your training and career aboard HMS *Indefatigable*, which is moored in the Mersey. There, you will learn about the rigging of sails and how a naval ship operates. So, if you are interested in submarines, get started and work towards where you want to be."

"Would the Royal Navy choose me to serve aboard a submarine?" Dominic asked.

"No, you have to request the assignment. Suppose you are successful and are chosen from the applicants. In that case, you will have a three-month training at the Royal Navy's HMS *Dolphin* at Fort Blockhouse, Gosport, in Portsmouth. There you will learn everything about the submarine. The day starts at 0500, with calisthenics in the morning and in the classroom for theory in the afternoon. You will also practice with the Davis Submerged Escape Apparatus using a buoyancy bag to float from a submerged chamber and up through a 100 foot cylinder—simulating the escape from a submarine. I can tell you—secretly—that if you pass the escape tower, you pass the course."

Just then, the Sub-Lieutenant arrived back with some paperwork and a pamphlet.

"We are nearly done here. You will take this paperwork with you to the Royal Infirmary on Tuesday next week at 1000 hours. There you will be given a physical to see if you have the right stuff to become a sailor." The Sub-Lieutenant placed all the paperwork into a brown envelope and handed it to Dominic. "I would like to congratulate you on your application to join the Royal Navy. Welcome aboard."

As they both stood up, the Sub-Lieutenant saluted Dominic, who stood at attention saluting back.

Ellen was so proud of her eldest son that there was a tear in her eye, which she wiped away with her handkerchief.

"Come, Dominic, your brothers and sisters are going to be excited to hear all about our time here today."

They rode home in silence. Dominic's head was spinning with everything he had heard that day. He always thought he would be stationed on a battleship or a destroyer, but the thought of being on a submarine interested him.

They got off the Derby Lane tram and walked up to Albany Road. In front of their house, his brothers David, Tom and John were playing rounders with a stick and ball with their friends in the street.

David, who was about to bowl and Tom who was catcher noticed his mother and brother walking up the street.

"Hey, Dom, are you off to sea?" he yelled.

Joined by John and Tom, who came running over to meet them.

"How did it go?"

"I'll tell you all about it inside," Dominic said.

As he turned up the walkway, his sisters Dorothy and Rose were at the door. They all walked into the parlour. Dominic placed the envelope on the table. When he turned around, his brothers and sisters were all looking at him.

"So, how did it go?" David asked again.

"I go for a physical at the Royal Infirmary next Tuesday," Dominic said. "I think that I will also try to be a submariner."

"Submariner? What? Are you barmy?" John said. "Why the heck do you want to go underwater?"

Dolly heard what John had just called him. "Barmy, Dom is Bommy?"

"There you go, Dominic. You must be Bommy to go into a submarine."

His brothers and sisters all laughed. They were not making fun of him—he'd just gotten a nickname that would be with him for the rest of his life.

The following week, his mum took him to the Navy doctor. He grabbed the envelope, and they were out the door. It was a long walk to the Royal Infirmary. They left early for the over two-mile walk.

They walked to the front door, and approached the nurse who was at the desk.

"Can I help you?" Dominic stepped forward and handed the nurse the envelope. "Ah, you're here for a physical. You're joining the Royal Navy. Congratulations, you will make your family proud."

The nurse stood. "Your mum can come with us to the next area, with seats where she can wait for you."

They walked up the stairs and along a long corridor to a waiting room on the left. "This is where your mum can sit," the nurse pointed out. "And you can come with me." There were other ladies in the area, waiting on their sons to be screened.

The nurse and Dominic walked to a nurse's station, where there were men in black uniforms like at the recruiting centre, and other men in white smocks. They must be the doctors, he thought. The nurse indicated that he could be seated until his name was called. His heart was beating in his ears. He was so excited.

He took deep breaths. *It's all right,* he said to himself.

A second nurse came over. "Dominic King? Please follow me." They walked through a set of doors. "You can take your coat, shirt and trousers off and hang them right here," she said. "Once your shoes are off too, you can then walk through these doors when ready."

She pointed to a set of doors and exited through the way had they entered. Dom did as he was told and walked through the double doors in his underpants. Another nurse instructed him to stand until his name was called.

"King, Dominic. Examination room number two," the nurse bellowed

Dominic walked in. There was an examination table and a poster with letters of different sizes on the wall.

A man in a white smock walked in the door and closed it behind him, "King, Dominic?"

"Yes, Sir." he replied.

"I am Doctor Barker and I will perform a physical on you today."

It was his first time, and he did not know what to expect. The Doctor started by taking his weight and height when he stepped onto the scales. "Nine stone, eleven pounds," The doctor stated as he raised the ruler to record Bommy's height. "Five feet, nine inches." And he noted it on his chart.

The Doctor then asked him to sit on the examination table. He listened to his chest, back, and heart and asked him to breathe in and out deeply. Then again. The doctor continued to listen to his chest. "You have sinus arrhythmia, but that should not affect your application," he said, making a note on the chart.

The remainder of the examination consisted of poking, prodding, bending over, and coughing.

The doctor checked Dom's vision, making him look at the eye chart with the different size letters, covering one eye at a time. Then, when the doctor was finished, he said he should wait and the nurse would come in.

The nurse came back with a syringe and a glass bottle. She took a vial of blood, and he used the loo to give a urine sample. She said he could get dressed and leave. Once Dominic was ready, walked to where his mother had waiting.

"How did it go?" she asked.

"Good," he replied. "I can go home now."

A couple of days later, a letter from the Admiralty arrived to say that he was accepted and where to report. He remembered his mum had cried.

"Your Father, God rest his soul, would have been proud of you," she'd said.

1942

Dominic arrived at Plymouth after sunset and walked into the dining hall. They were still serving supper. He took his plate to the table and sat down. He hadn't eaten all day, and was hungry for his dinner.

When he finished, Dominic walked over to the barracks. He would not be sleeping on the submarine while it was being retrofitted. He found an open bunk and sat down on the side.

It was several hours before he could have his daily tot. Wondering if he would fall asleep, Dominic laid back. There were echoes in the fairly empty hall. Some of his crew mates had already returned. Everyone had a different number of days they were entitled to for leave—Dominic was due back tomorrow, so he would enjoy his last night off.

He closed his eyes, and, with his belly fed, fell asleep in no time.

Chapter 16: Christmas in Crewe

24 December, 1942—Christmas Eve
Crewe

Dolly and Jack were cleaning up after dinner when Evelyn bounded into the kitchen, "I am looking forward to seeing Sonny tomorrow. What time are they coming?" she enquired.

"Your Aunt Rose and the boys will be here after ten," replied her mum. "Now, Santa Claus doesn't come unless you're asleep, so go get yourself ready for bed."

Evelyn walked past the sitting room that was decorated with colourful paper garlands. Strips of paper pasted in links hung across the archway. Climbing the stairs, she remembered when last year Sonny stayed over Christmas Eve. They tried to stay awake to see Santa, but both ended up falling asleep on the settee.

Back a couple of weeks ago, Dolly and Eily had gone Christmas shopping at T.J. Hughes department store in Liverpool. The store was all decked out with festive decorations and a Christmas Grotto that included a manger scene. The sisters had conspired to get Evelyn a doll for Christmas.

Mrs. Sullivan across the street made girls' dresses, so Dolly had asked if she would make one to fit a doll 14 inches in length. She had picked up the dress the other day. Dolly was so pleased, showing Jack how beautiful it was before hiding the bag in their bedroom wardrobe.

Eily and Mike were spending the day with her mum in Liverpool, not wanting her to be alone. After putting on that big dinner last week, her mum would be short, so they brought her their rations. Rose and the boys, meanwhile, would take the train out to Crewe to spend the day with Dolly and family

Evelyn was changed into her pyjamas and had crawled into her bed. As she was pulling the blanket up, her mum and dad walked into her room. "We'll see you in the morning, sweet dreams," said her mum.

"Good night, my love. Have a wonderful day tomorrow," said her dad, as he leaned over to kiss her good night.

"I will miss you, Daddy," she said, giving him a big hug.

Dolly had wrapped the gifts with coloured paper and ribbon. It was after eleven when she pulled the gifts out and placed them on the dining room table for Evelyn to open in the morning. Jack was already asleep when Dolly slipped into bed beside him. *He has to work tomorrow, Christmas Day,* she thought to herself. *Poor soul!*

25 December, 1942

Eve woke up after her dad had left for work. She threw her covers off, jumped out of bed and ran down the stairs. On the dining room table were three presents. There were also a couple sprigs of green holly with bright red berries that her mum had been able to get in town the other day. She knew she had to wait for her mum to be up before opening her gifts. Aunt Gertie was with her parents in West Derby, so all she was waiting on was her mum. She listened, and heard her stirring in bedroom.

It was only a couple of minutes later when her mum walked down the stairs and into the sitting room. "Happy Christmas, Evelyn, and thank you for waiting for me. You can open your presents now," said Dolly.

Eve picked up her gifts and took them to the settee. She opened the largest of them: it was a doll with a green dress. "That's from your Aunty Eily and Uncle Mike." her mum said. "Aunty Eily was sorry to have had to miss your surprise." Eve reached for the second parcel and opened it. It was a little mauve dress made for her new doll. Evelyn was so enthralled that her mum had to remind her that there was still one more gift to open. "Don't forget this one too," she exclaimed, handing it to her daughter.

Eve unwrapped a box of Peek Frean biscuits—her favourite—and a bar of Cadbury milk chocolate. Opening the wrapper and smelling the aroma of the chocolate, she took a corner off the bar and placed it on her tongue. "Mmm," she said, as she savoured the chocolate melting in her mouth.

Dolly went into the kitchen to make a cup of tea. Rose and the boys would be there shortly. They would have an early dinner so that they could go back to Liverpool later in the day.

Eve must have changed the doll's dresses a half dozen time by the time her aunt arrived with Sonny and Dave. There was a box under Sonny's arm. "What's that?" she asked.

Sony opened the box that contained a board, coloured pieces and a die to roll. "I got it for my birthday," he exclaimed. "Snakes and Ladders, but we call it 'Night Raiders'. It's the best. You go up the search lights and down the anti-aircraft fire. Would you like a game? Dave can play too."

"Sure," said Eve, as they set the board up on the floor.

Dolly and Rose started to prepare for an early supper in the kitchen as the children played their games. Between them and their rations, they were able to have a small pork roast and potatoes. Dolly had put a pot on the boil yesterday for mushy peas. They were Jack's favourite.

When everything was ready, the kids were called to the table to tuck in. Rose prepared Dave's plate, while Dolly made one for Jack to have when he gets home. For dessert, Evelyn shared her biscuits and a piece of chocolate for each of their guests.

Shortly after their dinner, Rose looked at the clock. "Time to go, if we want to catch the train." Sonny packed up his game.

"That was good fun," Eve said. "Thanks for bringing it over to play."

"Sure thing" he replied.

It was dusk when they opened the door to leave. Rose hugged Dolly and Evelyn goodbye. "See ya," Sonny said to his cousin.

Eve had had a wonderful time playing with her cousins that afternoon. In addition to Sonny's board game, Dave enjoyed playing with her post office set—that included letters and a date stamp—that she had received as a gift last Christmas. She gathered up her new doll and toys and took them to her room. *No more chocolate for me if I want to sleep tonight,* she cautioned herself.

When Jack arrived home after work, he took off his boots and coat and headed to the kitchen. Dolly brought him his dinner, "Oh how nice, you made mushy peas," he thanked her. Eve came downstairs and gave her dad a hug. "I had so much fun with Sonny and Dave, we played games and had chocolate. Glad you are home," she said yawning.

"Your eyes are making button holes," her mum said. "It's time for bed, night-night."

Eve turned to climbed the stairs. "I really enjoyed Christmas, thank you," she said, on her way up to her room. She climbed into bed and when her head hit the pillow, she was asleep in no time.

Her parents had a quiet moment together, telling each other what their day was like. Dolly stood and brought out a small, wrapped gift and handed it to Jack. "There you go, you have been working so hard."

Jack opened his gift and found a pair of knitted gloves. "Perfect," he said trying them on. "They are very comfortable, and will keep me nice and warm. But I have not gotten you a gift," he said.

"You have worked so hard, and it was such a nice day with Rose and the boys today. That's enough for me," Dolly replied.

It was not too much longer before Jack started yawning. "Good night," he said as he toddled off to bed. "I may miss you again in the morning, but I hope to get a day off shortly."

Dolly would have a smoke before going up to bed. She opened the back door and stood on the stoop. She had lit her cigarette with the match and blew out the flame. It had been a nice day today with her sister. Looking out, she saw there was heavy clouds. *Good weather for us, but bad for the Germans. They cannot find us in the valley.*

Snuffing out her cigarette, she threw the butt in the waste bin and closed the door.

She was ready for bed herself. She turned off all the lights and climbed the stairs. Peeking into Evelyn's room, she found her fast asleep, clutching her doll. Opening their bedroom door, Dolly saw Jack fast asleep on his right side, lightly snoring. If she could only fall asleep herself now.

About 15 minutes later, there were rhythmic snores from all.

Chapter 17: Back to It

21 December 1942
Plymouth

Dominic wandered down to the submarine moored at the dock.

The boat's signalman, William Huthwaite, was chatting and having a smoke with a Naval Engineer. Dominic walked up to them.

"Hey, Bommy," Signalman Huthwaite said. "Did you have a nice leave?"

Huthwaite had not been able to get leave when they returned to Plymouth as Dominic and some others had. He was working with the Naval Engineers to install the new system on the *Tuna*.

"I had a smashing time." Bommy replied. "You'll get leave next time. What have you all been working on?"

The engineer piped up, "It's called ASDIC Sonar RDF."

"What does it do?" Dominic asked.

"It's a range and detection finding system." Huthwaite replied. "I'll let Theadore Edwards, the engineer here, give you the run down on it. Teddy?"

Teddy was used to explaining it.

"It is like seeing underwater with sound. A sound wave is generated, and when it hits something, it bounces back to a receiver on the submarine. Depending on how long it takes for the sound wave to return, we can calculate the range and motion of the vessel. We will also install an improved amplifier on the ASDIC that should increase the subs' ability to detect German submarines."

"Doesn't the submarine have a hydrophone for listening underwater too?" Dominic asked.

"Yes, and because the sonar is generating a pulse of energy or noise, the problem is when the submarine or another naval vessel generates the sonar 'ping', ships with a hydrophone can hear them too," Teddy agreed and added. "In addition to the Type 710 hydrophones already installed, *Tuna* will be fitted with a special amplifier too. Apparently Sparks here and other signalman reported hearing grunt and groan in the North Sea, this will help them determine what they are hearing."

"Your signalman has been learning how to both operate and understand the information coming into the receivers on the submarine," Teddy explained. "He will also get some training on the ASDIC at Portland. I believe your submarine will be getting some sea trials once it has been fully installed."

In addition to the instalation of the ASDIC-RFD and hydrophone upgrade, the retrofit included a 20mm Oerlikon gun and an aft torpedo tube.

Tuna was certainly challenged while conducting sea trials before her next war patrol.

5 January, 1943
Crewe

Eve was washed and dressed and looking forward to school this morning. Having had her breakfast, she was all ready to go. She called from the front door to say goodbye to her mum and aunt in the kitchen, and she ran out the door and up the path.

She travelled down Valley Road to Langley Drive to meet with Maureen so they could walk together. As Evelyn reached her house, Maureen walked out her door.

"Good morning," Eve smiled and said "how are you?"

"Good, but I was thinking about the mathematics we were doing at school yesterday. I just don't get geometry and angles."

"I will try and help you," Eve suggested. "Let's see if we can get together after school one day."

Maureen had been struggling with mathematics all year. She enjoyed reading and writing, but numbers always confused her. Eve understood basic geometry and could follow along with the teacher as she did sums on the blackboard.

As they walked towards the school, children were playing in the yard. There, playing with a football, was Arthur Emmett who was in their class. He had blonde hair that fell over his eyes. According to Maureen, he was quite cute. Eve agreed, and thought he was a good footballer too. She smiled as they walked into the playground.

Just then, the football was kicked over to where Eve and Maureen were standing. Arthur ran over to retrieve the ball. He looked up when he saw Evelyn, and he smiled. She smiled back. No words were exchanged.

Evelyn thought he must be a little shy, because Arthur would never try to talk with her. She would be willing to speak with him, but didn't she know what to say.

At the main door, one of the sisters started to ring the morning bell. It was time for class.

They walked through the school doors and down the hall. Their classroom was on the right. Eve and Maureen took their seats, while Arthur sat down two rows over, near the back of the class. All the children were at their desks when their teacher Sister Mary Margaret entered the classroom.

"Good morning, class," she said.

"Good morning, Sister," they responded.

"We will start with geography this morning," the sister announced. "We have been discussing continents and today we will review Europe and Asia."

A large map of the world was hanging over the front blackboard. Sister Mary Margaret had a pointer that she used to describe the boundaries of the two continents.

Eve not only knew the continents, but the different countries in each of them. The teacher described how it was one large land mass but was divided, with Asia being the larger of the two.

Eve had extensively searched Europe and Asia when playing their game of finding cities with her dad—and she noticed that the teacher had not mentioned Germany or Japan. She knew it was because England was at war with them.

Evelyn remembered a couple of years before the war, while she was at St. Hugh's in Liverpool, when her teacher was talking about Japan. She had asked the class if anyone knew anything about the country. Evelyn remembered putting up her hand and saying, "It is called The Land of the Rising Sun." Her teacher, Miss Williamson, was very impressed that she knew this. Her dad had told her about that fact, and she was proud of herself for remembering it.

When she had recently been playing the world atlas game with her dad, Eve remembered that Kyoto was one of the cities she had looked up. It was in Japan too.

Sister Mary Margaret spoke of the divide between the two continents, and that Turkey was a transcontinental country in Asia and Europe. Evelyn had not heard that before.

After their geography class, Sister Mary Margaret made an announcement. They would have an art class after the lunch break. Then Sister Mary dismissed them and they all rose to leave. Evelyn walked to the end of the row and met up with Arthur standing beside her. He looked over and smiled. Evelyn smiled back and said hello.

"Are you all right?" Arthur asked.

"Great, thank you," Eve replied.

They walked out of the classroom together and into the hall. Just then, Arthur remembered he had forgotten his football and walked back for it. Evelyn wasn't sure if she should wait for him while he retrieved his ball, so she stood at the side of the hall as other pupils left for lunch.

When Arthur came back out with his ball, he saw Evelyn standing in the hall. Walking up to her, he realized that she must have waited for him.

"Where do you live?" he asked.

"On Clydesdale Road, number two," Eve replied.

"I live on Jesmond Crescent, number fifteen," said Arthur.

They walked out the school door and out to the playground. Arthur saw his mates, said goodbye and ran over to join them. Maureen had seen Evelyn walking with him. "Chatting up Arthur?" she said, as she approached her.

"I think I have finally said two words with him," Eve smiled.

"Well, he loves his football," Maureen said, and they started to walk home for lunch.

After their lunch break, Evelyn met with Maureen and headed towards the school.

"What do you think about the art class?" Maureen asked.

"I don't know," Evelyn said. She had tried drawing in the past but had not been very good at it.

They arrived at the school playground just before the bell. Evelyn noticed Arthur playing football with his mates. His back was towards the girls. Maureen noticed Evelyn looking over in Arthur's direction and said, "Ev-vee, something interesting to look at?"

Evelyn dropped her eyes; she felt her cheeks blush. The school bell rang and the children lined up outside the door. The girls walked down the hall towards their classroom. When they walked into the room, they noticed that Sister Mary Margaret had placed a sheet of white paper on each desk.

Maureen turned to Evelyn and said, "Looks like we will be drawing today."

Eve took her seat and waited for the class to start.

Sister Mary Margaret stood at the front of the class and welcomed everybody back from lunch.

"We will be drawing today." She said. "Either a portrait or perspective, your choice. I want you to work together in partners, so we will go alphabetically. Please, take out your pencils." She picked up her attendance sheet and called out, "Arthur, you will work with Evelyn. Francis, you'll be drawing with Gregory."

As the sister went down the list, she paired everyone off. Harry and Joan, Maureen was to draw with Norman. "Okay, children," she said. "Join your partner."

Evelyn turned around and saw no one sitting beside Arthur. As she stood up, she picked up her paper and pencil, and she walked over to his desk.

"You can draw the person you are with, or an inanimate object," Sister Mary Margaret further clarified for the class. "It is your choice."

"What would you like to draw?" Arthur asked, as Eve sat beside him.

"I am not a good drawer." Evelyn answered. "Tell you what, I'll draw your football," Arthur's reached down under his seat and placed the ball on his desk.

"There you go," he said.

"What will you draw?" Eve asked.

"I would like to draw you," Arthur replied.

He took his paper and pencil and started sketching Evelyn as she sat there.

Eve wasn't sure where to look. She took hold of her pencil and paper and studied the football on Arthur's desk.

Everyone in the class was now starting to draw something of their choice. Sister Mary Margaret began to walk around to see what everyone was drawing. She stopped beside Arthur's desk and commented, "You're very talented, Arthur. You have certainly captured Evelyn in your drawing."

Eve wanted to look over and see the portrait, but she focused on the football. She drew the lines of the stitching on the ball and the shadows from the sun coming through the window.

"I like your shading." Sister Mary Margaret commented. "Good work."

The sister allowed everyone about twenty minutes to continue with their drawing. When the time was up, Sister Mary Margaret asked everyone to return to their desks.

Eve started to stand up when Arthur offered the portrait, he had just drawn of her. "Would you like it?" he asked.

Evelyn looked over at his drawing. She could not believe how well it was done. Taken aback by the offer, she was unsure what to say. "Thank you, you did a smashing job. Wouldn't you want to keep it?" she asked.

"No, it's all yours," he answered.

Just as Evelyn was about to reach for the portrait, she asked, "Would you please sign it for me Arthur?" Arthur smiled. He signed the sheet of paper with a flourish, and gave it to Evelyn. "Thank you." Evelyn said, as she stood up and walked back to her desk.

The teacher announced that they would be reviewing their mathematics. "We started with geometry and angles the other day. We will continue where we left off."

His Majesty's Sailor *and the Girl in the* Blue Coat

Eve found it hard to concentrate on the lesson. Her eyes were drawn back to the portrait of herself. The afternoon dragged on for her. She could hardly wait for the class to be finished, wanting to show Maureen the portrait that Arthur drew.

Then, finally, the lesson came to an end. Eve was unsure if she could remember what the teacher had just reviewed with the class.

Sister Mary Margaret said that the class could pack up and that she would see everyone tomorrow morning. Evelyn noticed Arthur running for the door with his football. He was gone in a flash. "I still don't get geometry!" Maureen said as she approached Evelyn.

Evelyn had nothing to say to her. She had not been concentrating on arithmetic, as she was still thinking about the portrait. Maureen had not brought up art class, so Evelyn decided she would not boast about the picture. She placed the artwork in her notebook and started walking towards the door.

They walked home together in relative quiet. Maureen was lost in thought about geometry. Eve was thinking about the art class.

She said goodbye to Maureen at the corner of Valley Road and Langley Drive and walked towards Stewart Street and Gainsborough Road. She decided not to show her mum the portrait Arthur had drawn of her. Instead, she would keep it her secret.

That evening, Jack was preparing to leave the house for his next night shift at the Merlin engine factory.

"I had better be going. I do not want to be late," Jack announced as he walked down the stairs. Dolly had made his lunch and prepared his tea caddy. "Here's your lunch box." She said. "You're all set."

"Thank you! Very much appreciated," said Jack, and he gave his wife a hug and a kiss. Just then, Evelyn opened the door to her bedroom and came running downstairs, "Have a good night at work, Daddy."

"I will, and I'll see you both in the morning," Jack said with a smile.

He walked out the door and down the pathway.

It was a lovely evening. Nice to walk to work without getting rained upon. It was about a twenty-minute walk to the factory. As Jack neared the complex, he noticed other workers from his group heading his way.

Jack had been more at ease since they moved from Liverpool to Crewe. The blitz bombing was getting to Dolly, and she was struggling. Jack thought of his two sisters: Doris, still in Liverpool and Florence, in London. Jack hadn't seen since before the war and would have liked to write to them, but what time did he have with all the shifts and fire watches? Any day off was spent catching up on sleep.

He crossed over the railway tracks and headed towards the security gate. At the main entrance, sandbags were stacked around the gatehouse with the gate open for Jack and the other workers. There were many buildings in the compound. Jack worked primarily in the east wing, also known as the Engine Shop.

Workers were working on shifts around the clock to manufacture Merlin engines used in the De Havilland Mosquito, Hawker Hurricanes, Handley Page Halifax, Avro Lancaster Bombers, and Supermarine Spitfires. Jack was proud to be working making the engines, which were fitted for aircraft protecting Britain.

He walked into the front doors of the two-storey brownstone building. The punch card rack was on the left of the main hall. He found his card, punched it and placed it in the rack to the right of the time clock, walking a little further into the men's changing room. Their cubby holes were a place to put their lunch box and to hang their overalls. He removed his coat and hung it on the hook, and he lifted his faded blue overalls. They were loose-fitting and comfortable to wear over his clothes.

Once ready, he walked out onto the shop floor. With the shift change, most of the machine noise had quietened down. The factory was laid out in rows with lathes and milling machines lined up in different production areas.

Since starting at the Merlin factory, Jack had worked on several machines, depending on the parts produced on the shift. He walked down the main aisle to the production office in the middle of the factory floor. At the start of each shift, workers would gather outside the office and listen to the superintendent outline what were going to be the shift's priorities.

Standing in amongst the workers for the shift was Jim Dempsey. Jack walked over and greeted him.

"Hello, Jack," Jim said as he turned and saw his workmate approach. "Fancy meeting you here."

"So, what do you think we will be working tonight?" he asked.

"I guess it depends on how the day shift went," Jack replied.

The shift superintendent and area supervisors exited the office and started the meeting. The superintendent stood on a small crate and asked for everyone's attention as he outlined the shift's priorities. Jack and Jim were in group B and would be working on the lathes tonight.

After the production meeting, they wandered down to the line of lathes. Twenty machinists were in their group, and over half were now women. Although when Jack first started it was mostly men in his group, the number of women had steadily grown over the past couple of months. Most of the workers had a particular piece of machinery that they were used to.

Both men walked across to their lathes. Many parts were manufactured on the lathes, but the primary item was the pistons, one of twelve in the Merlin engine. The piston heads were first turned to size, and then the compression ring slots were added before being sent to the milling department.

Jack did not mind working on the lathe. He was familiar with the machine and the accuracy needed when turning the pistons. On a good shift, he would finish about five or six.

The women working in his group had been instructed on how to use the lathes and milling machines. He was impressed at how quickly they had learned the operation of the tools. They had the patience for the precision needed to manufacture the engine components.

In addition to wearing the same overalls as the men, women had to wear their hair tied up in a bun and covered with a handkerchief or piece of fabric. There had once been a most unfortunate accident: A female worker had a tress of hair hanging over her face. It got caught on the lathe and yanked her head into the chuck. It pulled out her hair and part of her scalp—she survived, but there was blood everywhere. Since then, all women have had to keep their locks undercover.

Jack was concentrating on his task at hand. He had just placed a solid blank into the lathe's chuck, getting it ready to turn the piston to the required 6 inch, 152.4 mm diameter, when a gentleman in a brown smock approached him. It was his supervisor, Allan Bates, who was a few years older. As was the practice, those in authority were always addressed formally. Jack noticed his supervisor walking over to him, "Good day Mr. Bates," he said. "How are you today?"

"Fine, Jack," Mr. Bates replied "We have been going over the group shift rotations and fire watches and determined you have more than done your part. Therefore, I would like to offer you take your next shift off tomorrow. You won't need to be back in until the night after. How is that?"

"That is very good news," Jack said. He had been wondering when he was going to get a shift off. "Thank you, Mr. Bates, much appreciated. My wife and daughter will be pleased to hear it."

"Righto, keep up the good work, Jack." He replied as he walked away towards the office

Just then, the horn sounded. It was lunchtime. Jack switched off his lathe and went to the changing room to retrieve his lunch box. The coolant used on the lathes was oily to the touch. He didn't want to eat his sandwich with dirty hands, so stopped to wash them.

Jack walked into the lunch room. There, sitting at their usual table, was Jim, who had already started to eat.

"I got some good news, Jim. I get a night off tomorrow," Jack said.

"Good for you. I know you have earned it." Jim replied. "I should be getting one off too shortly,"

Jack went to fill his cup with hot water from the urn for some tea. They only had a half hour, and he hoped for a bit of rest before returning to the shop floor.

He opened his lunch box and removed the condensed milk and sugar caddy. He liked his tea not too strong, milky with a bit of sugar. Jack unwrapped the wax paper and tucked into his sandwich. Ah, the mutton tasted good.

He finished up with the biscuit and the last drop of his tea, and looked at the clock on the wall. There was just enough time to put his lunchbox back in the change room before he went back to work.

By the time the horn went off to announce the end of the shift, Jack had completed three more pistons on the lathe. Walking into the change room, he removed his overalls and put on his coat. He grabbed his lunch box and headed to the punch clock. He met up again with Jim Dempsey, who was also ready to leave.

"Well, Jack, have a great day off." Jim said. "Try not to spend the whole day sleeping,"

"I hope not to, have a good one," Jack replied as he punched his card and walked out the door.

The sun was rising on the horizon as Jack walked home. He was trying to decide what to do with his day off, as it had been almost a month since his last one. When he arrived home, Dolly and Gertie were both up and in the kitchen with Evelyn still in bed. He took off his boots and joined them.

"Good morning. Guess what?" He announced. "I get a shift off tonight."

"Good for you," Gertie said.

"What would you like to do? Stay up or have a sleep for a couple of hours?" Dolly asked.

"I think I'll have a couple of hours, and then I can spend some time with you all," Jack said.

"Go on then, I'll come for you a little later with a cup of tea," Dolly said.

Jack went upstairs and changed into his pyjamas. He laid down, put his head onto the pillow and pulled up the covers. Finally, he was ready for a bit of sleep.

Chapter 18: Working out the Bugs

26 January, 1943
Plymouth

Dominic had spent the last three weeks helping with the retrofitting. The plan now was to conduct sea trials in the waters off Plymouth to see if there were any bugs in the system.

When the day arrived, the crew had reassembled and were ready to return to sea. Everyone was in good spirits when *Tuna* left the dock.

While submerged, the boat went back and forth in a grid pattern, pinging as she went through the water. There was a new screen installed in the already-cramped wireless compartment. The boat was listening for the echoes to return, and the signalman could see the distortion they created on the new screen.

Bommy and Willie were back together on the helm. It was like no time had passed since they were both at their posts.

The sea trials went so well that Captain Lieutenant Raikes announced they would travel up to Holy Loch with an escort from HMS *Cutty Sark*.

They slept in the submarine that night, in Devonport.

The following day, a shipment of food for the sub came to the dock. It was enough to last them a few days and get them back to Holy Loch. That morning, at the break of dawn, they met up with HMS *Cutty Sark* as they left on a heading of 250 degrees. It was a two-day passage to get up to their destination.

Two days later, the submarine arrived late in the day. They came up beside HMS *Forth*, which was moored in the loch and tied off against the supply ship.

Tuna started her exercises in the waters of the River Clyde the following day. The submarine travelled back and forth along a grid pattern just like it had off Plymouth, pinging as it went through the water.

A day later, Bommy and Willie were tasked to take the troop boat to the Glasgow docks to pick up their allotment of food and provisions for at least the next two weeks.

With a cold wind blowing in from the north, they were glad that they wore their white-knitted jumpers. Dominic's hands were cold from the raw wind, so he kept them under his arms to keep them warm.

They arrived at the dock where, nearly 2 months before, they had picked up the Marines and their canoes for the Bordeaux harbour operation. Bommy often wondered how the Marines had made out on their mission with one team missing.

After loading the food and rations onto the troop boat, they returned to the supply ship. Since they were going that way anyway, they loaded some extra equipment to take back to the *Forth*.

For the next six days as the submarine practised with its new ASDIC Sonar. Signalman Huthwaite was learning as he went.

Submerged targets were used, and when a ping hit an object, there would be a beep. This information would be transferred to the control room to determine the next course of action. The beep could also determine if the craft was closing in on its location or opening up its range.

The ASDIC Sonar could also listen for the cavitation sound of a ship's propellers, even though slow-moving submarines could still hide undetected underneath the water's thermal layers, virtually silent.

Tuna continued conducting exercises for another week in the Clyde River. Following that, for the next two days, the submarine proceeded to Campbeltown on the Kintyre Peninsula. When the manoeuvres had finished, they returned to Holy Loch.

By that time, the boat required maintenance that could not be conducted at Holy Loch.

The submarine had to travel north to Gairloch, on Strath Bay, Wester Ross in the Northwest Highlands of Scotland. Their boat was at the floating dock for two days while the repairs and adjustments were made to the ASDIC Sonar housing.

Tuna returned to Holy Loch, where they were to conduct speed trials over a measured mile. It was found to have a top speed of 15 knots, or about 17 miles per hour, on the surface and reached 9 knots or about 10 miles per hour when submerged. Lt. Raikes was pleased with *Tuna*'s performance. The crew learned that when HMS *Triton* first sailed in 1940, she registered 16.9 knots or 18.75 miles per hour which was the top speed of any of the T-Class submarines.

After the final day of conducting exercises in the waters of the Clyde River, the submarine moored again at Holy Loch for the night.

23 February, 1943

Tuna had been conducting nearly a month of exercises and sea trials, testing the ASDIC Sonar, when it was called upon to start its 17th war patrol. This time it was ordered to patrol off the Norwegian coast.

Tuna left Holy Loch and travelled south through the Firth of Clyde. It met up with the trawler HMS *Scalby Wyke*. The *Scalby Wycke* was to escort the submarine to Lerwick—a sheltered harbour on the east coast of the Shetland Islands.

Force 7 and Force 8 gales were recorded, with 30-to-45-mile-per-hour winds while they passed Cape Wrath on the north-westerly corner of Scotland. The *Tuna* and the *Scalby Wyke* sailed to Lerwick, where *Tuna* stopped for 24 hours to make more minor repairs to the ASDIC Sonar System.

25 February, 1943

Tuna was on a heading of 30 degrees, travelling towards the Shetland Islands, where Lt. Raikes and crew would patrol in the Norwegian Sea.

The submarine had the ASDIC Sonar active as she searched for U-boats which would surface during the day. The trick was being at the right place at the right time to spot them.

Tuna surfaced at midnight to charge her batteries for a couple of hours and to cook the crew's dinner. The diesel motors were notorious for making plumes of black smoke and they had to be careful not to be detected.

Because of German airbases in Trondheim and Narvik Norway, which provided them with reconnaissance of the area, there was always the chance of being detected while on the surface—the charging was better done at night. Also, the Kriegsmarine has sonar detectors installed in Norway at Stadlandet and Obrestad that could detect British Submarines sonar beams.

11 March, 1943

HMS *Tuna* was finishing her 17th war patrol in Lerwick, Shetland Islands, and had not encountered any German submarines while on patrol in the Norwegian Sea. The crew had a 24-hour layover in Lerwick while they waited for submarines HMS *Simoom* and HMS *Sportsman*. They were also expecting the Norwegian HNoMS *King Haakon VII*, which would escort the ships to Holy Loch.

14 March, 1943

Tuna arrived in Holy Loch late that evening and moored beside HMS *Forth*.

Dominic was sitting in the seamen's mess with Willie, who was nursing a cup of coffee. "Rumours are that we are in Holy Loch to conduct training exercises in the Clyde," Willie said. "We're going to be in the area for a wee while."

Dominic did not mind that the submarine was not on a war patrol. "We are certainly being well tested by the Admiralty." He said. "I guess they'd know best."

The crew still had to perform their regular watch duties; however, they did not have the rigours of searching for German submarines, dodging mines, or avoiding detection. "I'll take this respite any day," Willie replied.

"No arguments here," Dominic said.

21 March, 1943

A week later, Dominic woke up before his watch began. He had been able to sleep quite well over the past week. It had been a nice break to be in Holy Loch, but it was all about to change.

As red watch was currently on duty, Lt. Raikes called the submarine's lieutenants and petty officers together in the control room for an announcement.

"Gentlemen, it has been my pleasure to have served as your captain over the past seven months. I have been notified that your new commanding officer will be Lieutenant Desmond Samuel Martin, who is a Canadian from Vancouver Island. He has had a storied career in submarines while in the Royal Navy for the past two years, serving aboard HMS *Una*, *Ultimatum*, and *Seadog*. I wish you all the best, as you have been a superb crew while under pressure. It has been a privilege to have worked with you all."

Raikes had already packed his duffle bag. "Lieutenant Martin will be here shortly," he said, as he shook the hands of each of the officers. "Please afford him the same courtesy and hard work you did for me. Lieutenant Travers, you are the officer of the watch until Lieutenant Martin arrives."

With that, Raikes grabbed his duffle bag and climbed up the ladder topside.

Willie turned to Bommy and said, "We're getting a new skipper."

"Yes, we are Willie." Bommy replied. "Yes, we are."

That afternoon, a troop boat arrived from Glasgow harbour and put alongside *Tuna*. On board was a tall, slender man in a Lieutenant's coat with a duffle bag over his shoulder. He thanked the three sailors who brought him across and climbed aboard the outer hull. Standing on the freeboard to greet him was Lt. Travers. "Welcome aboard, Sir," he said, saluting as he introduced himself.

Lt. Martin climbed up to the freeboard, returned his salute, and shook Travers' hand. "Good to meet you, Lieutenant. I have heard from the Admiralty that the *Tuna* is a well-run submarine. I am looking forward to meeting the officers and crew." Martin said.

"Won't you come this way, Sir?" Lt. Travers asked as they walked to the fore hatch and down into the torpedo room before walking into the Control Room. There, gathered were the submarine's lieutenant and petty officers as well as the red watch seamen.

Lt. Travers introduced Lieutenants Brown, Fletcher and Blake, ACPO Alfred Mallett to the new skipper. Then Lt. Travers took the him for a quick tour of the boat, he was introduced to the current artificers and radio communication personnel on watch. When they returned to the bridge, he asked the officers to join him in the ward room.

Lt. Martin asked them to take a seat as he outlined the plans. "*Tuna* is to conduct exercises in the Clyde area for the next 12 hours. Then we will proceed down to Campbeltown tomorrow and return to Holy Loch the following day. This will give me an indication of the handling and trim of the submarine, as well as how the crew reacts. Any questions?" The group shook their heads. "Then you are dismissed."

The officers filed out of the ward room.

Tuna was set to traverse the length of the Clyde in a grid pattern for sixteen hours a day. Ships with sonar and hydrophones would track the direction of the boat. They would also run under the thermal layer at 150 feet, where the water was colder and submarines with a slow propeller speed were virtually silent.

After the exercises in the Clyde River were concluded, the boat headed down to Campbeltown, which took the better part of the day. When they arrived, there was a training exercise: Trainees were assigned to the sub to learn and understand the new range and detection capabilities of the ASDIC Sonar from Signalman Huthwaite. He instructed them on how to interpret the sounds from the earphones and the images on the sonar screen.

The following day, *Tuna* left Holy Loch for Kames Bay in Loch Melfort, on the Isle of Cumbrae. There, a floating dock was used to make quick adjustments to the ASDIC Sonar. The sub returned to Holy Loch that evening.

With the galley filled with food and provisions, the 18th war patrol was about to begin. The sub left Holy Loch for a patrol area in the Norwegian Sea. *Tuna* made passage through the Firth of Clyde with HMS *Stubborn* and HMS *Universal*. Their escort ship was HMS *Tadoussac*, a Bangor Class Minesweeper.

Chapter 19: Trouble and Change

3 April, 1943
Liverpool

Dolly and Evelyn had spent the day in Liverpool, visiting her Nana King and Aunt Rose with her two sons, Sonny and Dave. Eve had played with her cousins in the backyard, enjoying the unusually warm spring day. It was now time to take the train back to Crewe.

They had purchased their tickets and were walking towards the train that had just pulled into the station. Climbing aboard the carriage, they took their seats in the first compartment and waited for the train to depart.

There was the familiar call of, "All aboard!" from the guard as they both settled back in their seats for the hour ride home to Crewe. Just then, a group of soldiers came in and sat down. The carriage compartment soon filled, and Eve had to sit on her mum's lap. One of the soldiers, who had sat across from them, smiled at Dolly and Eve.

"And how are you today?" he asked.

Usually, Dolly was very protective of Eve, not wanting to talk with strangers. But she had a soft spot for soldiers, as her brothers were all in the services.

"Good day," Dolly replied. "We're fine, thank you for asking."

"I am on my way home to Birmingham on leave." The soldier said, clearing his throat. "I can hardly wait to see everyone." He continued—he started coughing, losing his breath and barely able to finish his sentence. "I'm sorry, sore throat. Must have a bit of the grippe," he said, coughing again.

"You may want to rest your voice," Dolly said, noticing there was quite a rattle in his cough.

"Yah, you don't want to hear me cough the whole trip," he replied, sitting back in his seat.

As the train pulled into Crewe, Dolly and Eve stood. The soldier had fallen asleep and they did not want to disturb him, so they opened the compartment door and left quietly.

It was another 30 minutes later when they arrived at their house. Jack was at work, on nights again at the plant, but Gertie was sitting quietly in the kitchen when they walked in.

Eve said she was going to her room as Dolly walked into the kitchen.

Ten minutes later, Evelyn came down in her pyjamas and dressing gown. "I'm off to bed," she said, and kissed her mum and Aunt Gertie goodnight.

Lerwick

Tuna travelled to Lerwick on her way to the next patrol area or billet. HMS *Forth* parted with *Tuna* and they made passage through The Minche, between Lewis and the Western Isles off the mainland of Scotland. They travelled by Pentland Firth through very poor conditions, with visibility down to 100 yards. Navigation was by radio direction finder and soundings.

The signal operators training on the new sonar system left the submarine, before the submarine departed for waters southeast of Jan Mayen Island.

Tuna travelled north on a heading 330 degrees in a direction of north by northwest and a speed of 10 knots. The skipper peered through the for'ard periscope, scanning the horizon for German U-boats sitting on the surface.

4 April, 1943

Evelyn woke to the sunshine streaming into her bedroom. It was Sunday morning, and she had planned to go to church. She sat up, swinging her legs out and suddenly felt dizzy.

It alarmed her—she was not used to the sensation. She put on her dressing gown and slowly went downstairs.

Jack was in the kitchen. He had just arrived home from the plant and was getting a cup of tea before going to bed himself.

"Hello, my love, did you have a nice visit yesterday at your Nana's?" he asked Evelyn.

"Yes, thank you," she said.

She did not mention anything about the dizziness to her dad, because she did not want him to worry.

He picked up his cup of tea and walked towards the stairs. "Have a nice day, good night," he said, toddling off to bed.

"Have a nice sleep. I'll try to be quiet for you," Eve said. Her mum would be down shortly, Eve thought to herself as she got her breakfast. She had better not dawdle in getting ready. Maureen would be here in a few minutes to walk with her to church.

Evelyn had her sky-blue coat and her Mary Janes on when there was a knock at the door. It was her friend, right on time.

They started walking to church. Evelyn noticed a pain in her throat. She did not get a sore throat too often, and wondered if she would be able to sing today at the service. As they arrived at the church and sat down in the pew, Evelyn's throat was getting worse. It hurt her to follow along with the mass. She thought she had better rest it and just listen.

When the service ended, they were walking back to Eve's house. She told Maureen she was not feeling well—they said goodbye, and agreed to see each other in the morning. With that, Evelyn walked up the path and into the house.

Her mum was in the kitchen. Evelyn was about to say something, but the pain in her throat stopped her from speaking. Her mum noticed something was wrong. "Are you all, right?" she asked.

With a squeak in her voice, Evelyn said, "I have a sore throat."

She informed her mum that she also felt dizzy when she woke up this morning. Dolly put her hand on Eve's forehead. "It feels like you have a bit of a fever. You had better take it easy today. Go get yourself back to bed. I'll bring some salt water up for you to gargle. That should help you with your sore throat."

129

Evelyn went back up to her bedroom and got changed into her pyjamas. She crawled in under the covers and waited for her mum to come up with salt water.

Dolly walked up the stairs and called for Eve to enter the bathroom. Eve came in holding her throat—it was really starting to burn. "Here," her mum said as she handed her the glass of salt water. "Gargle with this."

Evelyn started to gargle and spat it out. "Do it again," her mum said.

"My throat already feels better." Evelyn said after the second gargle.

"Good," Dolly replied, leading Evelyn back to her bedroom. "You had better take it easy today. Rest up, and we'll see how you are later."

With that, Evelyn climbed into her bed and opened her Rand McNally Atlas.

5 April, 1943

Evelyn had not slept well. Her mum had given her Cephos for her throat the night before, but she was still in pain the next morning.

Shortly after, her mum came into her room and asked, "How are you this morning?"

"My throat is still sore, and it hurts to swallow," Evelyn said.

"You're staying home from school today. I'll bring you up some tea, and we'll see if that helps," her mum said.

All day long, Evelyn rested in her bed and read a couple of her stories over again. It was not fun, being sick.

That evening her dad came in to see her. He bent over and touched his lips to her forehead and said, "You have a fever!"

"My throat is still sore," she told her dad. "But the medicine worked a little bit, and the tea helped too. What letter are we on?" she asked him as she picked up her atlas. "I think it's W."

Having checked the day before, Jack was prepared. "Warsaw, Washington and West Port," he replied. "That should keep you busy."

"Any hints?" Evelyn asked.

"Don't be fooled by Washington," he said. Jack kissed her forehead, and said goodnight as he went downstairs to get ready for work.

The Norwegian Sea

That day, Signalman William Huthwaite received signal for the patrol. The orders stated that U-boats had been sighted from Jan Mayen Island and from air patrols disposed in a line approximately 150° from the island waiting to intercept Russian convoys.

Arctic convoys of ships from the United Kingdom, Iceland, and North America made perilous trips carrying millions of tonnes of supplies for the Soviet army fighting against the German army on the Eastern Front. The patrol was to be established between 69°N 04°W and Jan Mayen Island. The submarine was instructed to keep clear of ice and not to approach the island in poor visibility. Due to the short hours of daylight, they were to spend the maximum amount of time diving and on the lookout for U-boats.

For two days, the weather in the area was abysmal, and the submarine had to slow down. The CO acknowledged that they would be late arriving at their patrol position. The submarine had to dive twice daily to clear the ice that covered everything. They took special precautions to keep the number 1 main vent, the telegraphs, and voice pipes clear.

There was a dispatch from Rugby at 0400 hours. Along with the signal came an announcement that Able Seaman Dominic King was being promoted to Temporary Acting Leading Seaman. Lt. Brown was officer of the watch, and was handed the information from central command.

Dominic was still sleeping when the signal was recorded in the log. He would be told when he woke up for his shift on the white watch, starting at noon.

Later that morning, Dominic woke up, hungry for breakfast and a cup of coffee. Since being reassigned to the white watch, he had not had much time to help Cookie with evening dinner, and he hit the bunk before dinner had finished. But Cookie always had something to eat if a crewman found himself unfed. He returned to the control room, where Lieutenant Brown was still on duty.

"Able Seaman King. I need to discuss something with you at once." Lieutenant Brown said firmly.

Dominic thought to himself, *Oh, shit, what have I done?* "Yes, Sir," he replied.

"It has come to the Admiralty's attention that you have acted in a most distinguished manner, so it is my pleasure and privilege to inform you that, effective immediately, you have attained the rating of Temporary Acting Leading Seaman." Lieutenant Brown exclaimed. "Congratulations, Seaman King," He continued, "you have certainly earned it. Well done."

Bommy was gobsmacked and completely caught off guard by the news. As Temporary Acting Leading Seaman, he would outrank ordinary and able seamen. He never really thought of the day when he would be promoted to an acting rating. He smiled as he walked back to he returned to his mess, pleased when he realized he was entitled to a raise in pay.

"Welcome to the club, ma boy," Willie said, as Dominic walked in. He had also received his Temporary Acting Leading Seaman rating recently. "That means one of us will be moved," Willie concluded. "They have no need for two of us in the same submarine."

Bommy had been on the helm as coxswain and on the same watch with Willie for a little over a year. Willie was right, one of them would be on the move.

That night, the submarine had surfaced to charge the boat's batteries. The blue watch was on duty and had sighted a flashing Aldis lamp signalling 'PPP' approximately three miles away. The officer of the watch turned towards the light and sounded the night alarm. The weather was overcast with snow squalls, winds of force 5-to-6 and a sea state of 45.

About five minutes after seeing the Aldis signal, it was expected that they would hear the hydrophone effect of the U-boat.

Unfortunately, the signalman operator reported that he could not hear any hydrophone effects, but only water noises ahead. Commanding Officer Travers gave the order to dive deeper, to get clear of the water noises.

Thirteen minutes later, after diving to 75 feet, the diesel hydrophone effect was reportedly heard.

Lt. Travers altered the course to starboard and ordered them to rise to periscope depth. The signalman operator reported that the hydrophone effect was closing in on the starboard side, but that it eventually faded out. It was estimated that the U-boat passed at 10 knots, about 1500 yards on the submarine's starboard side. Travers then gave the order to surface, where they gave chase. However, after twenty minutes, no further sighting or contact was made.

6 April, 1943
Crewe

Evelyn woke up early. She had had a fretful night with her sore throat and fever. It felt like her neck had swollen, too.

She sat up in bed. Her legs felt numb, like they were asleep when she'd knelt on the ground for too long. Evelyn swung her legs out to the side of the bed. Perhaps they just needed to get the blood back into them. She waited a minute to see what would happen. There were no pins and needles like when her legs went to sleep, they just felt numb. Eve needed to use the toilet. She put her feet on the floor, but could not feel them touching it. Trying to stand up, her legs buckled underneath her and she fell hard to the floor. Eve was scared. What was wrong with her?

"Ma'am!" she called out. There was no answer. Evelyn called out again, "Ma'am, help."

With that, she heard footsteps as her mum entered her bedroom and saw her in a heap.

"What's wrong? What's the matter?" Dolly asked, who was frantic seeing her daughter on the floor.

"I can't walk," Evelyn cried. "My legs feel like jelly, and I can't stand."

Dolly started to panic. Eve told her mum that she needed to use the toilet.

Dolly bent over and picked her daughter up with all her might. She could not remember the last time she had to carry Eve. Probably not since she was a little girl.

When Eve was finished Dolly carried back to her bed, where she placed her gently. Her mind was racing. What to do?

By this time, Gertie had woken up with all the commotion. "Can I help?" she asked.

"What time does Doctor Edwards' Surgery open?" Dolly inquired. The family had been seeing Doctor Edwards since they moved to Crewe.

"I think the receptionist starts at eight-thirty," Gertie replied.

"Right," Dolly told Evelyn. "We'll take you then."

Dolly helped Eve get dressed, and Gertie helped carry her downstairs, where they sat her on the settee. Having gotten washed and dressed, Dolly looked at the clock. It was after eight and getting Eve to the doctor's surgery would take some time.

Dolly put on her coat as Gertie helped Evelyn with hers. Her mum bent over and lifted her up into her arms as Eve wrapped herself around her neck. Dolly found she could carry Evelyn, even though she must weigh at least five stone. "All right, let's go," Dolly said.

Gertie opened the front door and they walked out and down the path.

It was a long way to the doctor's surgery, and Dolly had to stop several times to adjust Eve in her arms. Finally, she could see the doctor's surgery as she turned the final corner. They were going to make it.

She opened the front door and walked in.

The receptionist looked up. She had come to know the Jackson family since they arrived in Crewe. "What's wrong?" she asked.

"My daughter's legs are numb," Dolly answered. "She can't walk."

The receptionist showed them into the examination room, where Dolly sat Eve down on the reclining table. "Doctor Edwards will be right in," the receptionist said.

Evelyn looked at her mum. She was scared, and so was Dolly.

Doctor Edwards walked in and looked over his glasses.

"What seems to be the problem here?" he asked.

"Eve has had a fever and sore throat for the past two days. She cannot walk this morning. I'm worried she will not walk again," Dolly said. "She has had little to eat and is only drinking tea."

"Let's take a look," Doctor Edwards said as he took out a tongue depressor from the dispenser. "Say ah," he said, and Eve opened her mouth.

"Did the paralysis start today?" the doctor asked.

"Yes," Dolly replied.

"We will have to run a blood test to confirm," the doctor said as he checked Evelyn's throat. "But I believe your daughter has diphtheria."

"Will she walk again?" Dolly asked nervously.

"That I cannot promise you," he replied. "Evelyn will have to be admitted to the hospital immediately, where she will receive antibiotics to help fight the virus she has been exposed to."

Dolly thought back to the soldier coughing on the train the other day. Could Evelyn have gotten sick from him? "What should I do now, Doctor?" Dolly asked.

"For now, take her home. We will call Cottage Memorial Hospital and arrange for the ambulance to pick her up at your house."

"Thank you, Doctor, for seeing our Evelyn so promptly," as she picked up her daughter. "Let's get you home," Dolly said.

By the time they arrived home, Jack had heard the news about Evelyn from Gertie.

Dolly opened the front door as he walked up to the hall to greet them. He took Evelyn out of Dolly's arms and carried her into the living room, where he sat her down on the settee.

"How are you feeling?" he asked.

Evelyn was a little concerned about the trip to see the doctor. "I'm all right, but I cannot walk. My legs don't work." There was worry on her face.

Jack turned to Dolly and asked, "Are you okay?"

"Yeah, I'm fine. I'll survive," Dolly answered.

Jack saw she was exhausted from carrying Eve to and from the doctor's surgery.

"Here, you rest. What can I get you?"

"I'd love a cup of tea," she replied.

"Right. I'll get right on it," Jack said. "Would you like a cup of tea too, Evelyn?"

"Yes, please, Da," she replied.

They had just finished their cups of tea when there was a knock at the door. Jack opened the door and found two ambulance attendants in white uniforms.

"Good day. We're here to take Evelyn Jackson to Crewe Cottage Memorial Hospital," said one of the attendants, carrying a stretcher.

"She's in here," Jack said.

The two attendants entered the house and walked over to Eve sitting on the settee. "Miss Evelyn S. Jackson?" asked the first attendant. "We're here to take you to Crewe Cottage Memorial Hospital."

"Can I pack her some clothes?" Dolly asked him.

"Whatever clothing she's wearing will be incinerated when she gets to the hospital," he replied. So don't bother. You should know that your house will be fumigated and you will need to find accommodation while they spray."

The attendant bent over and placed Evelyn on the stretcher. Then both attendants picked her up and walked to the front door. There was no time for goodbyes. Everything happened so fast.

Dolly grabbed Jack's arm when they lifted Eve. "They're taking our little girl," she said.

The first attendant walked over to Jack and Dolly after putting Eve in the back of the ambulance. Closing the door, he said, "She'll be well looked-after at Crewe Memorial. They're good people. There is a list of patient's names with their status posted daily on the main gate."

As the ambulance drove away, Dolly turned to Jack and asked, "how long will our little girl be gone?"

"I don't know, I just don't know," said Jack, as they went into the house and closed the front door.

Chapter 20: Crewe Memorial Cottage Hospital

6 April, 1943

The ambulance arrived at the hospital and drove up to the accident and emergency entrance. The driver opened the back door to step into the cabin, to where Evelyn was now sitting up.

"We're here, Miss Jackson," he said. They carried the stretcher through the doors, where a nurse instructed them to take Eve into examination room three. There, they transferred her onto a hospital bed.

"You'll be well looked-after here," the attendant said, as they walked back out to the ambulance.

A moment later, a nurse walked into the room. She had a white cotton facemask on. Eve could not see her mouth, but she could tell by her eyes that she was smiling. She was carrying a chart with paper on it. "Your name is Evelyn S. Jackson?"

"Yes." Evelyn nodded.

"You live at two Clydesdale Avenue, here in Crewe?" the nurse asked. Again, Evelyn confirmed.

"Doctor Edwards called and told us to expect you," the nurse explained. "Let's get you prepared," she added.

As she helped Evelyn get out of her clothes, she placed them into a large paper bag, closed it, and put it aside. She then helped Evelyn put on a faded pink hospital gown.

"We'll leave it open so that the doctor can examine you," she said as she unfolded a white cotton sheet and placed it over Evelyn.

"The doctor will be here in a couple of minutes," she added, picking up the paper bag and left the examination room.

Eve was listening to sounds coming from the emergency room when the doctor walked in. "Hello, Miss Jackson," he said. "I'm Doctor Crawley. Let's have a look and listen, shall we?"

He gave her the same examination that Doctor Edwards had, looking at her throat, and listened to her chest and back with the stethoscope. "We will be swabbing your throat and sending you for a chest x-ray. You are going to have to stay in the hospital while you get better. Hold on while I get the nurse," he said as he walked out.

The same nurse wearing the face mask returned and put the caddy she was carrying onto the table. She took a white swab from its protective cover and took a throat sample.

"We will send that to the laboratory," she said "And in the meantime, take you for your x-ray."

A couple of minutes later, an orderly walked into the room with a hospital bed on wheels.

"Miss Evelyn Jackson?" he asked.

"Yes," Evelyn answered.

"I'm here to take you for an x-ray," he said. "I'm going to pick you up and place you on the bed. Is that okay?"

"Okay," Eve said.

The orderly put his arms under her legs and around her back. He then lifted her onto the wheeled bed and smoothed out the top sheet.

"Ready?" he asked.

When she nodded, he wheeled her out into the emergency room and along a hall to where the x-ray department was located. He opened the door. It was cold inside. An x-ray technician took the chart from the bed and asked, "Miss Evelyn Jackson?"

"Yes," she answered.

"We will need you to move over onto the x-ray table."

Evelyn could not use her legs, but she could slide over onto the table. Unfortunately, it was very cold.

The technician put a plate into a holder, sliding it under the table. "I need you to lie back and keep still while we take the picture." He said as he adjusted Eve's position.

"Okay. Now take a breath, hold it and keep still."

The technician walked out of the room. There was a sound like a motor winding up, and then it was quiet again.

"That should do it." He said as he walked back towards Evelyn. "Let's get you back to your ward now." Shortly after, the orderly returned to the room.

"Okay, Miss Jackson, back onto your chariot." He said with a smile.

Smiling, Eve slid back onto the wheeled bed. She was getting used to this way of moving around.

The orderly pushed her out of the x-ray room towards the lift. The doors opened, he pressed the button for the second floor.

The nurse's station was in front of the lift door. "Which room is Evelyn Jackson in?" he asked.

"Ward two." The nurse replied.

Following her directions, he wheeled Evelyn through the door. There were several girls in beds, and an empty one beside the window.

"Here we go, you will be well looked-after here," he said, as he turned to leave the room.

There were wheeled screens placed around some of the beds. Evelyn could not see who was in each one from where she was lying, but she could hear voices that were muted and distant.

Shortly afterwards, a white cotton–masked nurse entered the room. She walked over to Evelyn's bed.

"Hello. I'm Nurse Elyse. I work in this ward. If you need anything, I am here to help. First, we will set up with an intravenous in your arm to get the antibiotics you need to make you better."

"I have to go to the toilet," Evelyn said shyly.

"We'll get you a bedpan," the nurse said as she walked to the cupboard and brought a white metal pan over to her. Evelyn had never used a bed pan before. "If you need any help, just ask. But let's see if you can manage it on your own," the nurse said. She opened up the wheeled screens and placed them around Evelyn's bed for privacy. "When you've finished, just leave it at the end of your bed." As she handed her a couple of pieces of tissue.

When the nurse had left, Evelyn picked up the bedpan. It was cold to the touch and she knew it would be cold to sit on. Moving it to her side, she carefully climbed upon it. When she had finished, she placed the bedpan at the end of her bed as she was instructed. Please with herself for not making a mess, she lay back against the metal headboard and rested.

Nurse Elyse returned to the ward with a wheeled stand. It had a glass bottle hanging from it with a tube attached. She took a device that looked like a needle out of a paper wrapper.

"I'm going to place this needle into a vein in your arm. There will be a small prick, but there should be no pain."

Evelyn steadied herself as the nurse swabbed her skin with a wipe. It didn't hurt too badly when she stuck it in. "Well done," the nurse said. She adjusted the drip that was going into the tube. Eve could feel the cool liquid seeping into her vein. "This will help us administer the antibiotics you need to get better. Now, try to keep your arm still," the nurse instructed. "You should rest," she said as she walked away.

Evelyn laid back on her pillow and pulled the sheets over her body. As she listened to the sounds coming from inside the hospital, she soon drifted off to sleep.

Chapter 21: U-Boats in the Norwegian Sea

7 April, 1943
Norwegian Sea, southeast of Jan Mayen

At 2100 hours, Signalman Huthwaite reported engine noises on the hydrophones. "Sounds like a U-boat running on diesel motor, bearing 190°."

Lt. Martin called for the sub to go to periscope depth and prepare for action stations. ERA Fourth Class Wilfred Jarvis raised the periscope once the sub came just below the surface. Lt.David Brown as Pilot confirmed the submarine was at a depth of 35 feet.

Lt. Martin took hold of the controls for the forward periscope, searching for a submarine travelling on the surface. The skipper scanned the horizon and sighted the 750-tonne German submarine. "There he is. Speed 11 knots at a range of 500 yards on a bearing of 280°." Martin said. "Load six torpedoes."

"Six torpedoes are loaded, and the bow doors are open." confirmed Lt. Gordon Fletcher. "The tubes are flooded."

"Helm, come left to 250°, steady at 9 knots," said Lt. Martin.

Bommy turned the helm to port until the boat was in a position to take the shot. Temporary Acting Leading Seaman John 'Willie' Wilband was on the hydroplanes, keeping the sub steady at a depth of 35 feet.

When the skipper gave the order to load, the Torpedo Artificer Gerald "Boomer" Watson and his team assembled in the for'ard torpedo room. The loading ramps were stored below the starboard racks along with the block and tackle to physically move them into the for'ard tubes. It took a team of four up to 15 minutes to load each of the 2,000-pound Mark VIII torpedoes into the tubes and to close the breach hatch.

A firing solution was reached after considering the bearing, course and speed estimated via the periscope. The periscope also had a stadimeter that consisted of an optical range-finding device. The information was then fed into the Submarine Torpedo Director MK1, calculating the moving target's position and compensating for the ship's own movement by Torpedo Officer Lt Gordon Fletcher. The data from the Director was transmitted continuously before the launch, primarily by the Gyro-Angle. The Gyro-Angle told the torpedo which direction to turn as it left the tube. The launched torpedo then travelled to the desired interception point.

The Submarine Torpedo Director also called the 'Fruit Machine' referring to the one-armed-bandit gambling machine it looks like, selects multiple torpedoes, with varying solutions. Each fired within a few degrees difference, to compensate for any evasive manoeuvres by the targeted ship.

Lieutenant Martin continued to watch the U-boat on its heading. "Steady as she goes. Fire all six torpedoes with an interval of seven seconds."

The range was now 1200 yards with a spread of torpedoes, half the target length, to secure two hits. There was a rush of air through the submarine as the torpedoes were fired.

"Five torpedoes launched." Confirmed Torpedo Officer Gordon Fletcher. "Torpedo six did not fire."

"One explosion heard." Announced Signalman Huthwaite. "And now breaking up noises are coming from the U-boat." A moment later, he called out again. "Three more torpedoes exploding at the end of their run, Sir."

Lieutenant Martin ordered the submarine to surface. "Take us up, Mr. Travers."

The submarine breached the surface.

"Blue watch topside." Lieutenant Travers ordered. "Let's see what we have,"

Seamen Jones and Walker climbed the for'ard man hatch ladder. Opening the hatch, they went up and onto the freeboard. They were followed by the Lieutenant.

In the fading sunlight, about 300 yards away, were floating debris and an oil slick. "Looks like there is a survivor!" Seaman Walker called out.

His Majesty's Sailor *and the Girl in the* Blue Coat

He pointed in the direction that he had last seen the sailor in the sea.

"He was right there!" He exclaimed

By the time Travers could focus on the area, the sailor was gone.

In the end, they found two bodies on the surface.

"It does not look like there were any survivors after all." Travers concluded.

Seamen Jones was instructed to retrieve debris samples to confirm the hit and sinking. An officer's cap and a piece of clothing were gathered up as proof.

"Okay, gentlemen, we're done here. Let's go below," Lieutenant Travers said as they climbed down the hatch, securing it behind them.

Lt. Travers updated Lt. Martin in the control room. ACPO Mallett took note of the findings in the boat's log.

Lt. Martin enquired as to the battery charge. ERA Fourth Class Wilfred Jarvis confirmed 40 Ah in both the fore and aft batteries so the submarine could dive for another a couple of hours before needing to be charged.

"Take us down to 100 feet," Lt. Martin commanded. "On a heading of 170° at 10 knots."

Bommy and Willie, still at their station on the helm, manoeuvred the submarine down to the desired depth and heading.

It was quiet on the submarine for the rest of the watch. They were proud of their achievement, but they also knew that there was a crew just like them on the U-boat that had just been sunk. As they had been at their positions for the past eight hours, Bommy and Willie were relieved shortly after.

The skipper made an announcement in the control room. "In recognition of the excellent work that our officers performed during the sinking of the U-boat, they are entitled to join you in a tot of rum to toast our good fortune." The Lieutenants all smiled, they would look forward to partaking tomorrow when the rum was distributed.

Bommy was exhausted, but his heart was still racing after the sinking of the U-boat. He could have really used his tot of rum right then, but would have to wait for another thirteen hours.

He laid back on his bunk and closed his eyes. It was not long before he drifted off to sleep.

There were no more sightings of German U-boats that night.

8 April, 1943

A fair quantity of small drift ice was observed in the area, and large icebergs could be seen on the horizon to the north—therefore, the decision was made not to go any further north and risk a collision with a growler.

For about two minutes, while *Tuna* was at periscope depth, Lt. Travers had observed twelve feet of another periscope at approximately 4000 yards. However, when they altered their course towards it, the U-boat could no longer be seen. Signalman Huthwaite had not detected anything on the hydrophone and there were no other sightings.

Lt. Martin, now on duty, decided not to give chase. As there were calm seas, he did not want to give away his location to the U-boats and laid "doggo," keeping the sub as quite as possible. The visibility was excellent, so he would wait for them to resurface within shooting distance before the day was over.

In the distance, he could see the 7,675-foot peak on Jan Mayen Island, approximately 73 miles away—however, the weather started to worsen, and visibility deteriorated with passing snow showers.

There was poor weather for the next two days, with limited visibility from snow storms. A fire on the auxiliary drive control panel caused the submarine to fill with smoke, forcing *Tuna* to surface. It ran on only one engine for ten minutes to clear the smoke.

Lt. Martin estimated that the U-boats patrolled 150° from Jan Mayen Island, approximately 25 miles apart. He decided to cover the area to the southern end of the patrol line as he thought the enemy at the northern end would become a bit suspicious of them. They may be more successful if they return in a couple of days.

Over the next three days, the weather improved, and the visibility was excellent.

On the morning of April 12, Lt. Martin could see the peaks on Jan Mayen Island, approximately 80 miles away. However, the weather started to deteriorate again, so they had to patrol at a depth of 60 feet and turn south to avoid the ice that was closing in.

His Majesty's Sailor *and the Girl in the* Blue Coat

13 April, 1943

Signalman Huthwaite informed the skipper that he heard hydrophone effects.

Lt. Martin ordered the for'ard-looking periscope to be raised. He soon spotted the conning tower of a U-boat approximately 9000 yards away. He altered their course and closed in on the U-boat at full speed. In order to get within 5000 yards, he had to alter their course twice more.

He then ordered all torpedoes to be loaded: two external and six internal. After Lt. Gordon Fletcher confirmed they were ready, Martin commanded, "Fire all eight torpedoes."

They tracked at 122°, with a firing interval of eight seconds. The point of aim was one and a quarter length ahead. The estimated course and speed of the U-boat was 068° at seven knots. The torpedo spread was half the target's length apart to ensure two hits. The estimated range was 5,000 yards.

Before firing, Lt. Martin realised that he could only afford to be off by one degree on either side of his bearing dead ahead. The speed of the U-boat would be the deciding factor. The ASDIC estimated the U-boat's speed was 240 revolutions or 9 knots. Speed by plot was 5 knots based on one shaky range and a series of true bearings. The signal operators reported that the U-boat was on electric motors and not on her diesels, so he decided on a speed of 7 knots. He had to fire then because he was starting to lose both bearing and distance, and it would not have been long before a shot was impossible.

All torpedoes missed their mark. Lt. Martin considered that they must have missed just astern, the U-boat speed being 9 knots. Or that she saw the tracks of the oncoming torpedoes in the oily, calm sea and took evasive action. Martin did not see more than the conning tower at any time except once, when he saw the deck gun. That enabled him to get a good re-estimate, he thought, of the angle on the bow.

The U-boat, being on her electric motors, would have been able to keep a good listening watch on her hydrophones. They probably heard the torpedoes running a long time before they reached her. Their hydrophone effect was not heard again after 0736. It was presumed that she had submerged as was not seen again.

Chapter 22: Getting Better

17 April, 1943
Crewe Memorial Cottage Hospital

Evelyn had finished the breakfast that was delivered to her in bed. Her throat was starting to feel a little better. The antibiotics must be starting to work. She tried to lift her legs, but there was still no feeling in them. Her feet felt like rocks.

Nurse Elyse walked over to Evelyn's bed, "Good morning, Miss Jackson," she said bringing a wheel chair over to the side of the bed. "Now that you have finished your breakfast, we can start you on your physiotherapy. Can you swing your legs over the side of the bed?"

Eve picked up her legs and managed to sit up.

"Good. Now hold on to the armrests and sit on the wheelchair seat," the nurse instructed.

Eve sat down on to the wicker seat and placed her feet onto the footboard.

"Right. You hold on to the IV stand, and I'll push you." Evelyn grabbed hold of the stand, and they were off.

There was a large room down the hall with gymnastics equipment and mats on the floor. There was no one else in the room at the time.

"I want you to sit on the bench and try lifting your legs," Nurse Elyse said. Eve climbed over and onto the bench with her legs hanging along the side.

The nurse picked up her leg. "Now, try to raise your foot," she said. Eve tried with all her might. She could barely feel it lifting at all.

"Good. Now let's try the other leg."

It felt the same, but Nurse Elyse seemed happy with her attempts. "It may not feel like you are getting very far, but before long, we'll have you walking between the balance bars," the nurse said.

It was almost lunch time when she had finished her physiotherapy, and Eve was wheeled back to her ward. With the screens moved back, she could see the other children, who were all about her age.

It was a bright, sunny day, with the sun streaming into the hospital ward when her lunch was brought in. She sat up in bed and started to eat. The food was somewhat tasty. Not as good as her mum's cooking, though.

When Nurse Elyse returned, Evelyn asked her if there were any books to read. "I'll go get the trolly," she said. "Maybe you'll find a suitable book there."

A couple of minutes later, she arrived back. There had to be about a hundred books on the shelves, with a couple of books—titled *Stories for Girls* and *School Friends*—that interested Eve. She thanked the nurse, settled back into her pillow, and started reading.

Back at home, Dolly got herself dressed and ready to go to the hospital to see what Evelyn's status was. She grabbed her purse and locked the door.

It was a good fifteen minutes to get to the Crewe Memorial Cottage Hospital. There was a bricked wall with wrought-iron fencing around the perimeter of the grounds.

There, hanging on the gate, was a board with a piece of paper listing the patients in the hospital and the care they were receiving.

She scanned the list. Evelyn S. Jackson was listed as *Quarantined*.

Beside other names were *In Care* and *Ready to Discharge*.

Dolly was optimistic that Eve's status would change, so that she could come home soon.

As she looked around, she saw a wicker basket on the ground with instructions written on a piece of paper.

> When leaving a package for a patient, be sure to write on it the person's full name.

Dolly thought she would pick up some items and leave them for Evelyn. She was unsure how long Eve would be in the hospital, but she thought a small care package from home would help make her feel better. She made her way home to inform Jack and Gertie of Evelyn's status.

When Dolly got home, there was an envelope on the hall floor from the Health Department. She took a pair of scissors and opened the formal letter. It was from the Government Ministry of Health stating that due to the detection of diphtheria, the premises had to be fumigated. They were instructed to make arrangements to be out of the home for 24 hours on Friday the 23rd of April.

Dolly thought for a moment—she could go to Liverpool and stay at her mum's. But where would Jack stay while he went to work? Perhaps with Mrs. Turner, the widow, she had a spare room. It would also depend on what shift Jack was on.

In the meantime, she walked out the door and locked it. Dolly was going to the shops to buy Evelyn some treats and comics. She would probably like a doll to play with, too—but for that, Dolly may have to wait until she visited Liverpool to see what was available at Woolworth's there.

19 April, 1943
Lerwick, Shetland Island

HMS *Tuna* arrived at Lerwick and ended her 18th war patrol. She departed later that day for Holy Loch. She made passage with submarine HMS *Severn* and HMT *Hayling*, an Isles Class minesweeper trawler.

The flotilla arrived at Holy Loch on Wednesday afternoon, then *Tuna* travelled across to Rosneath on Gare Loch to have its propellers repaired

20 April, 1943
Crewe Memorial Hospital

Evelyn had been wheeled down the hall for her physiotherapy every morning with Nurse Elyse. On the days when her nurse was off, Nurse Marjorie would help her with her daily exercises.

Evelyn was starting to feel better. Her throat was not as sore as when she first entered the hospital. The daily physiotherapy was also progressing. She was now able to lift her legs, but she was still unable to stand.

One day, after a particularly gruelling physiotherapy session, Evelyn was wheeled back to her room. There, in her bed, was a brown paper bag with her name on it. As she climbed onto the bed, she noticed the printing on the bag looked like her mum's. The head of a doll was sticking out of the top of it. As she opened it further, there were comic books and a package of Macintosh toffee—her dad's favourite. She did not recognise the doll; it looked like it was new. *I'm going to have to think of a name for her,* she exclaimed to herself. *Melissa,* she thought. *That's the perfect name for my new doll.*

Crewe

As the fumigation day approached, Dolly walked over to Mrs. Turner's house and knocked on the door. A couple of moments later, the door opened.

"Hello, Mrs. Turner, how are you today?" Dolly asked.

"I am fine," Mrs. Turner replied. "What can I do for you?" she asked. "Won't you come in?"

"Thank you," Dolly said.

They walked into her small but cosy living room. "Please, have a seat."

With Mrs. Turner sitting across from her. Dolly started by telling her about Evelyn, who had been in the hospital for the last couple of weeks with diphtheria, and their house needing fumigation. Mrs. Turner listened intently as Dolly recalled to her how Evelyn's legs had become paralysed, and how she had to be carried to and from the doctor's surgery.

"Could we impose on you and ask if Jack could spend one night?" Dolly asked.

"Where will you go?" Mrs. Turner enquired.

"I'll go and stay at my mum's in Liverpool. Gertie will probably stay with her family in West Derby. With Jack working at the engine factory on all shifts, we must find him a place to stay locally."

"By all means, Jack can stay here. When is your house being fumigated? You are welcome to stay here too," Mrs. Turner suggested.

"That is awfully kind of you," Dolly answered and she filled her in on the details.

"I hope that Evelyn will be able to come home soon," Mrs. Turner said. "I am sure you miss her dearly."

"We do, and thank you so much for your generosity, Mrs. Turner," Dolly said as she stood up.

"Please call me Elizabeth," Mrs. Turner added as they approached the front door.

"Well, thank you again, Elizabeth," Dolly replied. "We'll be in touch."

"Yes, we will. Take care now."

Dolly walked down the path and turned to towards her house. She wondered how Evelyn was doing and what her status was. She was anxious to see what was written on the chart, but first she had to pick up a package from home. Her sister Rose and Rose's son Sonny had put together a care package for Evelyn, which Dolly had brought home from Liverpool after visiting her mum.

It was a lovely spring day. She would take advantage of it as she walked up the street towards the hospital.

21 April, 1943

Evelyn was sitting quietly on her bed, reading her books. Nurse Elyse had removed the intravenous from her arm the other day. The physiotherapy was progressing, too. She was able to do a leg raise now by herself.

Nurse Elyse walked into the ward and over to her bedside. It was the first time Evelyn had seen her without a mask. Evelyn smiled at the nurse as she approached her bed.

"We have some good news. You are no longer contagious, and don't need to be in quarantine any longer. Also, we will get you up and walking with the balance bars today."

Nurse Elyse walked out of the room and brought back in a wheelchair. Evelyn was getting much better at getting in and out of it. She grabbed the armrests, swung herself over, and sat on the wicker seat. The nurse wheeled her out and down to the physiotherapy room.

It had only been a couple of weeks that she could not walk. But she was a little scared to be trying the balance bars. Nurses Elyse and Marjorie had been working with Evelyn to get her legs stronger by moving them—It was a very slow process.

Nurse Elyse rolled the wheelchair up to the end of the balance bars. Evelyn took her feet off the foot board and put them on the ground. She was wearing socks, but the floor still felt cold.

"Now reach up, get a good hold of the bars and stand up. I'll be right beside you." Evelyn took a deep breath, raised her two arms, grabbed the horizontal bars, and stood up.

Her legs were very shaky as she raised herself and tried to put her weight on them.

"You're doing great," Nurse Elyse said. "Just stand there and get used to feeling your legs again."

Most of her weight was being supported by her arms. She could feel her feet on the ground and her weight on her legs as she stood there.

"Very good, Evelyn. Did you want to try to take a step?" Nurse Elyse asked.

Evelyn steeled herself. She lifted her right foot off the ground and placed it in front of the other one. She was very pleased with herself.

"Well done," Nurse Elyse said enthusiastically.

Evelyn took another step with her left foot. She was now standing inside the balance bars.

"You are doing great," the nurse said.

The standing was starting to take its toll. Evelyn's arms were getting tired from supporting her weight.

"Okay. Now, can you walk back to the chair?" Nurse Elyse asked.

Slowly Eve turned herself around. She was amazed at how far she was able to walk. She took a couple of steps back to the wheelchair and sat down.

The physiotherapy session continued. Evelyn was using all her muscles today. Her arms and tummy muscles were particularly tender, but she was feeling stronger.

"You have made great progress, Evelyn." Nurse Elyse exclaimed, "You should be very proud." Evelyn was both pleased and exhausted after her day on the balance bars, but she thought the sooner she learned to walk again, the quicker she could get home.

"That's enough for today; let's get you back to your room now." The nurse stated as she wheeled her around.

Dolly arrived at the gates of the hospital and scanned the list. There, beside her daughter's name was *In Care*. She was no longer in quarantine. Evelyn was getting better.

Dolly smiled, thinking that Eve might not be in the hospital that much longer. She bent over and placed the package that Rose had prepared for Evelyn into the wicker basket. With the good news of her not being in quarantine any longer, Dolly walked back home excitedly to tell Jack and Gertie.

22 April, 1943

Evelyn was sitting on her bed when Nurse Elyse walked up to her. She had a smile on her face.

"Eve, your family has been so very kind to you in providing packages from home—Penny has not received any treats, and she has been here as long as you have. I know you're a good girl because you share with the other children. Do you think you could share the whole bag with her this time?" the nurse asked.

It was true. Evelyn had received plenty of parcels from home. There were comics that she still had not read and more than enough toffee.

"Okay," Evelyn said, reluctantly. "She can have my package." It was especially hard to share when the package was really meant for her.

"Thank you, Evelyn. I know how hard it must be, but I believe this will help to cheer Penny up!" Nurse Elyse said, as she walked out of the room.

A couple of minutes later, Nurse Elyse walked back into the room with the bag and gave it to Penny, who did not say anything. Not noticing that Evelyn's name was on it, Penny quietly opened the package and pulled out comics and sweets. There were liquorice and jelly babies, which were Sonny's and Eve's favourite.

Penny opened the sweets and had a couple of bites. She scanned the comics and made a funny face. They looked strange to her. *The package must have been from my Aunt Rose, Sonny and Dave,* Evelyn thought to herself, as Penny opened the *Buster* and *Beano* comic books. She remembered they were Sonny's favourite.

Penny ate the sweets piece by piece, quietly sitting there for the rest of the day. She was eating them much faster than Evelyn would have, who liked to savour her sweets. Penny did not offer any to the other children in the ward, nor did she say thank you to Eve. Perhaps she didn't know how to read, or maybe didn't notice that the name was not hers.

Eve reached over and picked up her book. She rolled onto her side, and started reading. She was a little disappointed, after all, that her package was given to Penny—who did not even seem to be grateful for it. However, she reminded herself that Penny had not received any packages from her family, so Eve counted her blessings. She had been well looked-after.

Evelyn found the page she had last been reading and buried herself in her book. She was looking forward to going home soon—just not sure when that would be.

Chapter 23: Time to Go Home

23 April, 1943
Holy Loch

The day after Tuna returned to Holy Loch, the Captains of the Third Submarine Flotilla convened a meeting aboard HMS *Forth*.

Lieutenant Martin's log, where appended, included the comments of Captain (S) Third Submarine Flotilla:

> *"Never a dull moment in this patrol; which was Lieutenant D.S.R. Martin's first in command of HMS Submarine Tuna. I have always considered the Tuna as one of our most efficient and well-run submarines, and the success was very well deserved by all.*
>
> *Recommendations for awards will be forwarded in due course.*
>
> *I am more than pleased that Lieutenant Martin has had this chance against the enemy and has seized it so ably as he has been in this flotilla in various capacities for a considerable time and has always shown a particular interest in Torpedo Control problems."*

24 April, 1943
Crewe

Dolly was awake before the alarm clock went off. They had spent the night at Mrs. Turner's house while their house was being fumigated. She had decided not to stay with her mum in Liverpool because she didn't want to be too far from Evelyn, who could be released soon. Dolly thought she would let Jack sleep until it was time for him to go to work. Hearing Mrs. Turner, she made her way downstairs.

The hall was dark as she descended downstairs.

In the kitchen, Mrs. Turner was making a cup of tea. "Good morning, Elizabeth!" Dolly said, cheerfully.

"Good morning, Dolly!" Elizabeth replied, as she turned around. "Did you sleep well?"

"Yes, very well, thank you," She replied. "Jack will still sleep for a few minutes more. His alarm is set."

"Could I make him a sandwich for his lunch?" Elizabeth asked. "I have some old Cheshire cheese if you think Jack might like that?"

"That would be very kind of you," Dolly said.

A short time later, the sound of Jack's alarm was heard in the kitchen.

"Would Jack like a cuppa tea to start his day?" Elizabeth asked.

"Yes, he would. Thank you." Dolly replied.

Jack came down the stairs for breakfast. He was very grateful to have been able to stay there last night.

"Will you go back to your house this morning?" Elizabeth asked.

"We were told we only had to be out for the night." Dolly replied. "The fumigators said they would leave instructions for us to follow. I will go see how it went, after Jack leaves."

Jack went back upstairs to get ready for work. When he was ready, he thanked Mrs. Turner for her hospitality and his lunch. As he put on his coat and shoes, he said his goodbyes and made his way to work.

Dolly went upstairs to make the bed and then tidied up the room before coming back down.

Having gotten herself dressed to leave, she thanked Mrs. Turner again. "Your hospitality was very much appreciated!" she said.

"No trouble!" Replied Elizabeth. "It was nice having your company."

Dolly started walking back towards their house.

As she approached it, she noticed there were no lights were on, and that the windows were closed. There was a sulphur smell, like after a match had been struck. Dolly walked up to the door. The odour was much stronger.

She opened the door and the smell hit her. It was like inhaling pepper. It caught the back of her throat and made her cough. She walked into the kitchen and found the anticipated instructions on the table.

They called for her to open all the windows and air out the house. It was suggested that she wash the plates, cups and cutlery as an added precaution. There was a thin white film on the worktop and furniture where the fumigation fog had landed.

Dolly knew she had her work cut out for her. She planned to work on the house in the morning and then go to the hospital to see Evelyn's status later that day. She hoped her little girl would be coming home soon.

She took off her overcoat and started cleaning.

Crewe Memorial Hospital

Evelyn was eager to go for her physiotherapy. The previous day, she had been able to get up and walk with the parallel bars and she wanted to get back to them to practice.

Nurse Elyse entered the room with a wheelchair. Evelyn's legs were still a little wobbly, but she had more strength with each day's therapy.

"Good morning, Nurse Elyse," she said. "I am ready to go today."

"You had such a good day yesterday. Let's build on that today, shall we?" The nurse replied.

Evelyn hopped into the wheelchair for the short journey from her ward to the physiotherapy room. She was eager to get started. She had to be able to walk before she could go home. Nurse Elyse wheeled her into the therapy room and over to the balance bars.

"Okay, Evelyn, get a good hold and up you get," she said.

Evelyn was confident. She reached up to the balance bars and stood up. She took a step and then another. Her legs held her up as she walked carefully back to her wheelchair.

"Evelyn, would you like to try to stand on your own?" the nurse asked.

Eve took a deep breath and let go of the balance bars. She was standing without holding onto them. Her legs were feeling much stronger now. She took a step over towards the wheelchair and did not lose her balance as she stood there.

"Well done, Evelyn." Nurse Elyse exclaimed. "The doctor is going to be pleased with your progress today. We'll see what he says about letting you go home."

Eve was excited. *That is very nice to hear,* she thought. *I might be able to go home soon.*

"Let's keep practising," she said out loud, as she turned around. Evelyn started walking between the balance bars with only her hands lightly touching them. She knew she needed to walk unaided. Pushing herself, she continued back and forth several more times until she was too tired. Finally, she sat back in the wheelchair. Her legs felt much better after that morning's therapy.

"Perhaps we could come back again in the afternoon?" she asked Nurse Elyse.

The nurse sensed Evelyn's enthusiasm, "Absolutely, we can." She replied, wheeling Eve back to her room.

Just after lunch, Doctor Crawley came into the room and walked over to Evelyn in her bed.

"Miss Jackson, I have been hearing good reports from Nurse Elyse that your physiotherapy going well. Are you able to stand on your own?"

"Yes, Doctor," Evelyn replied.

"All right, let's see how you are doing. Would you please stand up beside your bed?" the doctor asked.

Eve swung her legs out to the side of the bed and slid down until her feet touched the ground. She was in thin stockings, and the floor was cold to stand on. She reached beside her and then stood up on her own.

The doctor took her hand.

"Now, can you take a step?" he asked

Eve did not wobble too much as she took a second step. She didn't have the balance bars to give her the confidence she felt she still needed, but the doctor looked quite pleased with her progress.

"I don't think you have to be here much longer," he said. "We can send you home tomorrow. After that, you will be able to recuperate at home. All right, now, can you climb back up?"

Evelyn gingerly walked back and climbed into her bed. She was pleased that she might be going home tomorrow, and beamed as the doctor made notes on her chart.

"We'll let your parents know that they can come and get you tomorrow. How does that sound?" the doctor asked.

"Wonderful, thank you, Doctor!" Eve exclaimed. She was going home.

Crewe

Dolly had been cleaning the house all morning, and the sulphur smell was dissipating with the windows open. She washed all the cutlery and dishes and cleaned most of the surfaces. Then, she decided to take a break to see Evelyn's status at the hospital.

She locked the door and started walking the fifteen minutes it would take to get to the hospital. It was a lovely April day, with the birds singing as she walked along the road.

When Dolly arrived at the gate, she looked at the posted sheet with all the patients' names and statuses. She scanned down the list. Half way down was *Evelyn S Jackson: Discharge 25 April, 1943.*

Dolly could barely contain her excitement in. *My little girl is coming home tomorrow,* she thought to herself as she headed back home.

On the way, Dolly wondered what clothes she would pack for Evelyn to return in. Remembering how much Eve liked them, she decided on her yellow dress and blue coat along with a pair of shoes and some clean knickers.

Dolly almost started to run. She was so happy Evelyn was coming home tomorrow, and Jack would be pleased to hear it too. She continued the rest of the way with a big smile.

25 April, 1943

Evelyn woke early in the morning, raring to go home. Suddenly, she realized that there were no clothes for her to go home in—perhaps her mum would think to bring her what she needed.

She would leave the comic books she had received for the children remaining in her ward. Evelyn bundled up her newest doll, Melissa, and sat quietly on her bed, waiting to be discharged.

Dolly folded Evelyn's clothes and shoes and placed them in a brown paper bag. Then she grabbed her coat, locked the door, and went to the hospital.

She arrived in no time and walked up to the main door, where she was met by a nurse.

Dolly approached her, "Good morning." she said. "These clothes are for Evelyn Jackson, who is to be discharged today."

"We will get Evelyn dressed and bring her down to you." The nurse said. "Won't you have a seat while you wait?"

"Thank you, I will," Dolly replied as she sat down on the chair.

Eve was waiting in the ward as Nurse Elyse came to her bed with a paper bag.

"Your mum brought a change of clothes for you to wear home."

Evelyn took the bag as Nurse Elyse wheeled the screens around her bed for privacy.

She opened the bag, and there was a strong odour coming out of it. All her clothes smelled. Oh well, she thought, the most important thing was that she was going home.

Evelyn got dressed and was ready to go when Nurse Elyse walked back into the room with the wheelchair.

"I don't think I will need the wheelchair," Evelyn said.

Nurse Elyse smiled. "Hospital rules, we take you as far as the front door, then you're on your own."

Smiling back at the nurse, Evelyn took a seat and lifted her legs onto the footboard. "All right, let's go," she said.

Dolly was still sitting on the chair when Evelyn, with a big smile on her face, was wheeled over to her.

She stood up and gave her a big hug and kiss.

"We have missed you so much. Are you able to walk?" she asked.

"Yes, I can," Evelyn answered.

Eve grabbed both armrests and stood up.

"Wonderful. How do you feel?" her mum asked.

"A little wobbly, but I am okay to go home." She replied.

"You were a very good patient, Evelyn." Nurse Elyse said. "It has been a pleasure. You are a lovely young lady and I am sure your parents have something to do with that," she added.

Eve could feel herself blushing. "Thank you, Nurse Elyse. You and Nurse Marjorie were very kind to me."

Evelyn took her first step outside. She was holding on to her mum tightly. "We'll take it nice and slow home." Dolly said. "Rest whenever you need to."

Evelyn waved goodbye as she walked out the door and down through the main gates. "Make sure to stop whenever you need to rest." her mum stressed. "Promise me?"

"I will," Evelyn replied as they started to walk home.

It took them a little over an hour; Evelyn had to stop to catch her breath every so often. Dolly was very patient as she slowly got her daughter home.

When they arrived at their house, Evelyn could smell the same odour as had been on her dress and coat.

"What is that smell?" Evelyn asked.

"We had to have the house fumigated. We'll keep the windows open to air out the rooms," Dolly added. "I hope it won't be too long before it goes away." Dolly hated the smell herself. "Your dad is on days, so you will see him tonight, and your aunt Gertie is in West Derby staying with her family. Your dad and I stayed with Mrs. Turner the other night while they fumigated."

"Do you mind if I have a lay down?" Evelyn asked. "I am a little tired from the walk home."

"By all means, you should," her mum answered. "Your linen was changed, so you can have a nice rest on your bed."

Evelyn started to climb the stairs. It was harder than it looked: she had to rest twice before getting to the top. Finally, she made it to her bedroom. Eve had missed it these last three weeks at the hospital.

Chapter 24: Back on Her Feet

27 April, 1943
Crewe

Eve had been home from the hospital for a couple of days. She was getting stronger each day with her mum looking after her. She had yet to start back to school, but was anxious to see her friends again. Dolly would allow her to go outside for fresh air as long as she stayed close to their house, which still had the lingering smell from the fumigation that permeated everything.

Evelyn wanted to get back to her studies, too. She'd been away for nearly four weeks, and wondered what subjects her classmates were studying.

"Ma'am, I have a question." she said.

"What is it, dear?" her mum asked.

"Could you ask Maureen to come by? I would like her to bring me some schoolwork so I do not get too far behind."

"Of course, I will. She lives on Langley Drive, doesn't she?" Dolly enquired.

"Yes, number 22," Eve replied. "She could bring me some schoolwork to keep me busy."

"What is Maureen's last name?" her mum asked.

"Yates, Maureen Yates," Eve said.

"I'll pop down now to see her."

Eve had a big smile on her face. She was looking forward to seeing her school friend again.

"Will you be all right to be here alone while I am away?" Dolly asked.

"Sure, I'll sit on the settee until you get back," Evelyn replied.

"Okay, I'll go now, then," Dolly said. "See you in a bit."

She grabbed her purse, walked out the door, and locked it behind her.

It was early afternoon when Dolly went to ask Mrs. Yates if Maureen could help Evelyn catch up. She did not want to go to the school directly to deal with Mother Superior.

It was only a short walk down Valley Road, turning onto Langley Drive. Their house was on the left side. Dolly went up the path and knocked on the door.

A moment later, the front door opened. "Hello, can I help you?"

"Yes, Mrs. Yates. My name is Dorothy Jackson. I'm Evelyn's mother," Dolly replied.

Mrs. Yates smiled. "Hello, pleased to meet you, Mrs. Jackson. How is Eve doing?" she asked.

"She is getting stronger by the day." Dolly said "We hope she can get back to school in a week or so. I am here to see if Maureen would bring some schoolwork home for Evelyn to work on in the meantime."

"Certainly, I can ask her when she gets home."

"Well, I won't keep you any longer, Mrs. Yates." Dolly said. "We really appreciate Maureen helping us out like this."

"I'm sure she would be happy to help, Mrs. Jackson," Maureen's mum said. "I'll speak to my daughter when she gets home. Nice to have met you! Hope to see you again soon!"

"Thank you so very much. It's been lovely to meet you as well!" Dolly replied, and she turned and walked home to give Evelyn the news.

Later that afternoon, there was a knock at the door. Dolly walked from the kitchen and opened it to find Maureen and another girl she did not know.

"Is Eev-vee home? Can we see her?" the girl, who Dolly did not recognize, asked.

"Eev-vee?! Her name is Evelyn, you silly girl. She will be right down." Dolly replied.

Maureen had several books in her hand. "I went back to school after my mum said Evelyn would like some schoolwork." she said. "So I asked Sister Mary Margaret what I should bring."

"That was very kind of you, Maureen. Won't you both come in?" Dolly asked. "Evelyn, you have some friends at the door," She called.

Then, at the top of the stairs, Eve came into view. "Hello, I'll be right down."

She was still a little wobbly and had to take her time holding the handrail as she came downstairs.

She smiled when she saw Maureen and Joan Foley, another friend from her class. "Hello," Evelyn said as they went into the living room.

"We've missed you," Maureen said.

Joan chimed in. "Are you coming back to school soon?"

"Hopefully, in a week or so. What did you bring me?" Eve asked.

"We started a new topic in arithmetic, and I don't understand it. Sister Mary Margaret thought you would enjoy doing some geography and science. We started botany, which is the study of plants. Sister would like you to read your textbook, starting on page twenty, about the different parts of the plant—and then she wants you to draw them." Maureen said. "In geography, we started to study our colonies in Africa."

"This is very much appreciated, you bringing schoolwork home to me." Eve said. "I do not want to get left behind."

"We'll bring it to you for as long as you need." Maureen replied. "I hope you get better soon!"

The girls stood up to leave. "Thanks for your help! I'll get started right away." Evelyn added.

"TTFN," Joan said.

"Ta-ta for now," Evelyn replied, as she opened the front door.

"We'll see you soon."

As both girls walked down the pathway, Evelyn closed the door. She was happy that she had something to occupy her time. Walking back into the living room, she opened her science book.

"Botany," she muttered. "What's that all about?"

Eve sat down and started reading her textbook.

29 April, 1943
North Scotland and the Norwegian Sea

Tuna travelled from Holy Loch to Rosneath on Gare Loch. She immediately docked on a floating drydock and had a propeller change.

With the propellers replaced, the boat returned to Holy Loch the following day. The submarine conducted exercises in the Clyde area, travelling back and forth in a grid pattern at various depths.

After the Holy Loch exercises, *Tuna* travelled to Campbeltown to participate in ASDIC Sonar testing.

The sub returned to the Clyde area and participated in ASDIC Sonar exercises with the armed yachts HMS *Tuscarora* and HMS *Spaniel*. Upon completion of these exercises, the submarine returned back to Holy Loch.

Tuna was preparing for her 19th war patrol, where she was ordered to patrol the Norwegian Sea. She had taken on supplies and departed Holy Loch for Scapa Flow with an escort from HMS *Bryony*, a Flower Class corvette, and submarines HMS *Stubborn* and HMS *Seadog*.

Bommy and Willie were back together, on the white watch at the helm.

The sub arrived at Scapa Flow, where she spent 24 hours before being joined by the submarine HMS *Ultimatum*. The submarines met and travelled with the escort ship HMS *Bryony* to Lerwick.

The weather for the first week was excellent with good visibility, allowing the submarine to patrol eighteen hours a day at periscope depth. The ASDIC/Sonar was operating perfectly.

Clear weather provided Sub-Lt. Ronald Blake to take 0800 Sun sextant readings of the height and angle above the horizon. He relayed the readings to ACPO Alfred "Jimmy" Mallet through the voice pipes . Who then recorded the position after reviewing tables where the sun and stars position should be above the horizon at the specific time and date.

Readings are taken at noon and midnight to determine the submarines latitude and longitude.

4 May, 1943

Rear Admiral C B Barry, Admiral (Submarines), Northways London, reported:

> "The patrol was most ably carried out by HMS Tuna; the plan of operations mentioned in the report shows careful forethought, which was deservedly rewarded by success. With a little more fortune, a second U-boat might have been added to the bag. From

further evidence from the commanding officer of HMS Tuna, it is most probable that the U-boat sunk was of the 500-tonne type and not 750-tonne since only one gun was visible on the casing.

The enemy is now probably aware of the loss of this U-boat, and the U-Boats will probably exercise greater caution while on patrol. There is little doubt that the employment of our submarines on anti-U-boat patrols will have a morale effect out of all proportions to the results obtained. Recommendations for awards are being submitted to the Admiralty only in my letter of 1st May 1943."

On 15 June, Lieutenant Martin would be awarded a DSO

5 May, 1943
Crewe

Evelyn was playing out front. She had started back to school again and was enjoying the warm spring weather. Dolly would allow her to go to school, but she had to come right home. She was allowed to play outside, near their house.

Maureen was with Evelyn in the front garden. She had a length of rope that she was learning to skip with. They were taking turns when Dolly came out of the front door.

"How are you feeling?" she asked Evelyn.

"I'm okay, Ma'am," Eve replied. "It's lovely and warm out here."

"You stay close," Dolly said as she closed the door.

It was nearly noon when the girls' heard planes in the sky overhead. Eve stopped what she was doing and looked up at a plane high above them. It was dark grey, and did not look like a plane she had seen before. Suddenly, it started turning over their house.

Eve had a bad feeling. She had come to recognise the sound that a Spitfire or Mosquito made, but this was different.

Just then, the air-raid siren started to wail. The strange plane that was overhead started banking left as it came closer to the ground. A red van had turned on Clydesdale and was driving past the house.

Dolly approached the front door just as the plane dropped again in the sky. It was right over their street when it started firing at the van going up the road. The girls saw the bullets strafe the pavement, just missing the van. Dolly grabbed the two girls by their arms and whisked them into the house, shutting the door behind them.

"Quick, get under the table," Dolly yelled at the girls, and they all scrambled to get under it.

Jack, who had been asleep upstairs, heard the air-raid siren and the plane overhead. He came down to see if everyone was all right.

There was the sound of bombing in the distance.

Evelyn was still catching her breath when she told her dad, "There was this grey plane. It started firing at a van on our street."

"The girls were outside the front when this happened." Dolly told Jack.

Jack, who was still half-asleep, hugged Eve. "But you're okay, that's the main thing." he said.

They could still hear explosions from the bombing. "It sounds like they are after the Merlin factory," Jack exclaimed. "I'm going to get dressed and see what's happened."

A couple of minutes later, the air-raid siren stopped.

Jack came down the stairs, dressed. "I'll go check to see how the factory fared." He said as he bent over to put on his shoes. "See you shortly." He said, and walked out the door.

"Maureen, your mum will be worried about you." Dolly said. "I'll walk you home now. Evelyn, do you want to join us?"

"Okay!" Eve replied. "Do you think it's safe now?"

"Well, the sirens have stopped, and we wouldn't want Mrs. Yates to be worried about her daughter." Dolly said, and they walked towards Maureen's house.

Jack had walked at his usual pace. It only took him fifteen minutes to arrive at the Merlin Plant. There were fire brigade sirens travelling in the direction of the factory—he was wondering if it had been hit.

There, in the distance, smoke was rising into the sky. As he got closer, he noticed that bombs had been dropped on the east side of the factory. Jack worked in the central part, just beside where it had been hit.

There was a small group of people standing outside the entrance gate. He noticed his workmate, Jim Dempsey, standing in the crowd.

"Hello, Jim. That could have been us in there today," Jack said.

"Aye, you're right," Jim replied. "I hope no one from our unit was hurt?"

They had both been previously scheduled in, but there was a shift change. They could have easily been in the factory when it was bombed.

Jack walked up to the guard who manned the gate. "What do you think, will there be a shift tonight?" he asked.

"I dunno, mate. There will be a lot of checking on the building before shifts are allowed back in. I wouldn't count on it," the guard said.

Walking back to Jim, Jack said. "I don't think there will be a shift tonight. I'll come back, but we may be sent home."

"Well, I'll see you later, one way or another. Ta-ra, mate." Jim said, and he turned and walked away.

With nothing left to see, Jack thought he might as well head home. His head was full of what-ifs. The plane firing at the van on their street—the girls could have been easily been hit. What if he had been on shift today? He could have been there, at work in the factory. Dolly would not be too pleased to hear that the plant had been bombed.

He took out his pack, lit a cigarette, and started walking home. He did not travel as fast as he had on his way there. He hoped none of his workmates were injured, or worse. As he walked home, his head was down and his shoulders were slumped. It had not been a good afternoon.

When Jack arrived home, Dolly and Evelyn were already back. Eve had gone up to her bedroom. He walked into the kitchen where Dolly was making a cup of tea. She turned and asked him, "How was the plant?"

"The factory was hit, in the area right beside where I work." Jack replied. "I met Jim Dempsey while I was there. It looks like I could be off tonight. I'll go in, but I may be sent home," he added.

A cold chill passed over Dolly with the news of the bombing. She knew that Jack had been scheduled for the day shift but that it had changed at the last moment. She grabbed his hand and squeezed it.

They sat quietly in the kitchen, waiting for their tea to brew.

Chapter 25: *Tuna* at War

20 May, 1943
Norwegian Sea

Acting Temporary Leading Stoker Arthur Wilkinson called out from the engine room, "Up spirits!"

He was followed by a chorus of voices from the mess area and control room. "Stand fast the Holy Ghost!"

Bommy, who was sitting in the seamen's mess, had joined in the chorus. He stood up and walked back to the petty officer mess, where the tots of rum were being dispensed. He was the first in line for a tot today.

Acting Petty Officer Alfred Mallett and Stoker Petty Officer Spencer Watkins were preparing the grog for the crew.

As he recorded it in the rum ration log book, Watkins passed Bommy a glass tumber with a tot of rum in the grog.

Dominic raised the glass to give cheer and proclaimed, "To the Queen!" He took a sip and then downed the glass, warming with the slight burn on his throat. It was a sensation he could handle. He then placed the glass back on the table, to be refilled for the next sailor.

Dominic followed Willie back to the control room, with a belly full of food and rum. There, Sid the Kid and Jimmy Wray, who were at the end of the red watch, were waiting for their relief and the chance to get their tots.

"Okay, lads! Your replacements are here. Time to go get refreshed," Dominic said.

They both said "Cheers," as they walked to the mess area.

Bommy and Willie took their positions at the helm while the Lieutenant continued his search through the periscope. As he sat there, Bommy stretched out his right hand to try and hold it still. There was a slight shake. He quickly made a fist so that no one could see him checking on his nerves. Recovering, he vowed that no hand-shaking was going to affect his performance at the helm.

At midnight, *Tuna* experienced a piston disintegration in the port engine. This caused major damage which required repairs.

30 May, 1943

Travelling just below the surface, Lt. Martin peered through the for'ard-looking periscope. He had been hunting for German U-boats since dawn, trying to find them while they were on the surface charging their batteries and prowling for convoys.

Signalman Huthwaite announced he heard diesel engine sounds on a bearing of 008°. Swiftly, Lt. Martin brought the periscope around, sighting the conning tower of a German submarine at approximately 9,000 yards.

"I can barely make it out, but it looks like U-341. Load all eight torpedoes!" he commanded.

Torpedo Officer Gordon Fletcher confirmed when all eight torpedoes were loaded and ready to fire.

Lt. Martin ordered Tuna to a heading of 010° as they closed in on the target. Bommy turned the helm to match the direction of the German submarine. "Steady." Martin ordered. "Steady, we're at 8,000 yards. Fire all torpedoes."

There was the familiar rush of air as the control room went silent. Lieutenant Martin continued to watch through the periscope.

Signalman Huthwaite announced he heard an explosion on the hydrophones. "I can see black smoke at the stern of the submarine." Lt. Martin confirmed. "There. The bow is raising up. It is sinking stern first and at an angle of 10 degrees," he stated. "I'm officially declaring the hit and the sinking of the submarine."

A cheer went up in the control room.

"Down periscope," he said. "Good work, men. We'll take that as a kill."

Lt. Martin called the ship's Lieutenant and petty officers into the ward room. He discussed with them the status of their provisions and their

His Majesty's Sailor *and the Girl in the* Blue Coat

remaining torpedoes. Finally, it was decided that they would return to Lerwick and end their war patrol. Lt. Martin also instructed Lt. Travers to record in the ship's log all those on duty and watch, who had played a role in the sinking of the German U-boat.

"I'll look after that, Sir," Lieutenant Travers confirmed.

They all emerged, with Lt. Martin announcing a heading of 190°.

Lieutenant Martin cleared the area quickly, because he wanted to start a long slow charge on one of the batteries. By 2130 hours, the recharge was completed.

At midnight, he gave the order to leave the patrol area. They were heading back to Lerwick.

Tuna arrived at Lerwick on Thursday, 3 June 1943, ending her 19th war patrol.

The following day, she departed Lerwick for Holy Loch with submarines HMS *Stubborn* and HMS *Ultimatum*, along with the armoured yacht HMS *Cutty Sark*. The group was joined by the submarine HMS *Syrtis*.

Three days later, they arrived in Holy Loch.

On 7 June 1943, the Captains of the Third Submarine Flotilla convened a meeting on HMS *Forth* and appended the following report to Lieutenant Martin's patrol log:

> "*The final disappearance of the submarine attacked on 30th May was in plain view of Tuna with the periscope fully extended and the submarine at a shallow depth. Her bow was seen to loft, and she was seen to sink stern first. I consider there is no doubt that she was destroyed. A hit at the near-extreme running range is lucky, but nonetheless, it demonstrates that the torpedo fire must have been most accurate.*
>
> *Recommendations for decoration and awards will be forwarded in due course.*
>
> *A week later, a detailed analysis was carried out on 13th June of Tuna's attack with running times of torpedoes and explosions. The*

173

> *upshot was that everyone agreed that the attack was successful and the U-boat had been destroyed."*

Tuna conducted exercises a few days later in the Clyde area, and then proceeded to Larne, Northern Ireland, for further exercises. She stayed for two days, and then departed Larne for Holy Loch, where they conducted exercises. *Tuna* received a signal from the Admiralty on 19th June saying,

> *"We congratulate Tuna on the destruction of the U-boat on May 30th 1943."*

Monday, 21 June 1943: HMS *Tuna* conducted special ASDIC/Sonar exercises in the Clyde with HMS *Ambuscade*, a prototype Class Destroyer.

Wednesday, 23 June 1943: HMS *Tuna* departed Holy Loch for the west coast of Scotland, where she conducted exercises with her escort HMS *Ambuscade* and HMS *Kingfisher*, a Kingfisher Class patrol vessel.

On 24th June, the Commander and Chief, Home Fleet wrote,

> *"I am much impressed by the way in which HMS Tuna conducted her two last patrols. The destruction of two German U-boats is an example of her general efficiency and of the skill and initiative of her commanding officer. I am very pleased to send my congratulations."*

Four days later, HMS *Tuna* returned to Holy Loch.

On the 30th June Admiral (Submarine) Rear Admiral C.B. Barry forwarded the C in C's letter to the Captain (s) Third Submarine Flotilla with the following comments:

> *"The destruction of the two U-boats on consecutive patrols is an outstanding performance and reflects great credit on the Commanding Officer and crew of HMS Tuna. It is requested you inform Lieut. Martin accordingly."*

Lieutenant Martin was awarded a bar to his DSO on 27th July 1943.

In early July, HMS *Tuna* was docked in Auxiliary Floating Dock #7 at Holy Loch. Three days later, she departed for her 20th war patrol and was

His Majesty's Sailor *and the Girl in the* Blue Coat

ordered to the North Atlantic, north of the Azores, with submarines HMS *Truculent* and USS *Haddo*, while escorted by HMS *Cutty Sark*.

On Friday, 23 July 1943, HMS *Tuna* ended her 20th war patrol. She returned to Holy Loch with HMS *Truculent* and HMS *Scimitar*, an Admiralty S-Class Destroyer and two weeks later, they proceeded to Campbeltown.

Thursday, 12 August 1943: *Tuna* conducted exercises in the Clyde area with HMS *White Bea*r, an armoured yacht. These included night exercises on 13 August 1943.

Sunday, 15 August 1943: *Tuna* departed Holy Loch on her 21st war patrol to the Bay of Biscay. She made passage through the Irish Sea with the submarine HMS *Truculent* and HMS *Loch Monteith*, an Anti-Submarine Warfare Trawler.

Thursday, 19 August 1943: 0001 Hours, *Tuna* had more than hunting German submarines to deal with. She also had to dodge French fishing boats. The high and large moon gave good visibility at night and clear visibility at periscope depth in daylight.

22 August, 1943
Bay of Biscay

There came a call for the Engine Room, Artificers Mess: "Up Spirits!"

Lt. Martin was at the periscope. "Belay that request," He ordered. "We're going to hold off on the grog for the time being. There are five masts of minesweepers."

"Are they using sonar?" Lt. Martin asked Signalman Huthwaite.

"No, Sir, but I hear hydrophone effects of two submarines on a course of 025° degrees," the signalman replied.

Lt. Martin thought that perhaps they were not escorting, but carrying out minesweeping activities. He couldn't see any U-boats, but he assumed they would be astern of the centre minesweeper. This, he found to be the case. He then gave the order to press on through the screen, watching that the periscope did not foul the sweep wires.

"Load all torpedoes and sound action stations," he ordered.

The attack was carried out almost entirely by eye, and what followed required the courage, skill and coolness of the helmsman and crew.

Lt. Martin steered between the centre and the starboard wing escort. He could just see the tops of the conning towers of the two U-boats, but couldn't tell whether they were in line abreast or astern.

Realising the U-boats were in line abreast, he intended to fire at both of them. Unfortunately, he miscalculated his speed of approach and stayed at periscope depth. On reaching the firing position, one minute before firing, he found himself 100 yards off track of the starboard wing of the U-boats and ahead of the starboard stern escort, at 1500 yards. This meant he had to be content with one U-boat as the target. The submarine on the port wing was a 540-tonne type and painted white.

At 1206 hours, Lieutenant Martin was looking through the forward-looking periscope and preparing his approach, when a U-boat passed at 80 yards directly in front of the *Tuna*—blocking sight of his targets.

"Torpedoes are loaded," Torpedo Officer Gordon Fletcher confirmed.

The U-boats were now at 3000 yards and tracking at 075°. The firing intervals were five seconds and the point of aim was three-quarters of a length ahead, torpedo speed was 45 knots and the depth setting eight feet for 1 to 6 tubes; ten feet for 7 and 8 tubes.

Lt. Martin gave the order. "Fire all torpedoes and dive to 150 feet, below the thermal layer."

Willie turned the hydroplane wheel down 30°, and Bommy stayed steady on the helm.

At 150 feet, the submarine levelled off. Lt. Martin was expecting a counterattack. However, nothing followed. After five minutes, he reduced to "Slow Group Down" on both motors.

A minute later, Signalman Huthwaite confirmed there was a small explosion. Another minute afterwards, he announced, "The sound of two more heavy torpedo explosions, four seconds apart".

Lt. Martin noted that two of the last torpedoes had hit and that the enemy's speed must have been about 12 knots, and he gave the order to stay at 150 feet.

One escort U-boat attempted to follow for fifteen to twenty minutes, but no depth charges were dropped, and *Tuna* remained unscathed.

At 1500 hours, HMS *Tuna* came to periscope depth. There was nothing in sight.

However, there was a grating noise from the conning tower when the periscope was raised. It sounded like the submarine had snagged on something.

After staying submerged for eight hours after the attack, the Tuna came up to periscope depth once more.

ERA Fourth Class Wilfred Jarvis attempted to raise the periscope. "There appears to be a problem raising the periscope, Sir," he announced.

"We'll wait until dark to surface and check it out," Lieutenant Martin replied.

At 2200 hours, Lt. Martin decided it was dark enough to rise safely. "Let's take us up now, and see what the problem is." Lt. Martin ordered.

The main ballast tanks were blown, and the submarine came to the surface.

"White watch, topside," Lt. Travers announced. "See what the issue is and report back to me."

Seaman Wray was first up the ladder to the bridge, followed by Seaman Sidney Griffith. A metal cable was across the top of the conning tower and between the periscopes.

"It does look like it's a cable from one of the minesweepers we were tracking," Lt. Martin concurred. At the end of the 60 feet of cable was a paravane—a device that is towed behind a boat so that the cables attached to mooring lines of submerged mines can be cut. "Let's get it untangled and see what damage we have on the periscopes."

Seamen Wray and Griffith untangled and cut the cable. There was some damage to the equipment on the conning tower; Lieutenant Brown noted the damage and repairs that would be needed—many parts of the periscope and conning tower had been damaged.

With the cable removed and the repairs made, the submarine submerged again.

Lieutenant Martin called the senior officers into the ready room and said, "Though we heard a couple of different explosions from the torpedoes, there is no indication we hit a U-boat or minesweeper. In the log, we will record the hits and let the Admiralty sort it out."

177

23 August, 1943

HMS *Tuna* was in her patrol area, when, at 0030 hours, four destroyers or escort vessels were sighted at four miles away—silhouetted against the moon. Lieutenant Martin thought they were searching for *Tuna*. He increased to full speed to open the distance, but the port engine failed.

The destroyers turned away, which was a great relief—*Tuna*'s batteries were low, and she now only had one engine.

24 August, 1943

The next day, HMS *Tuna* arrived at Holy Loch ending her 21st and last, war patrol.

Her Jolly Roger flag now hoisted as the submarine sailed into port. Now adorned with 4 U-boat sinking, 3 scimitars for their 'cloak and dagger missions, 2 Merchant ship sinking and 1 lighthouse. Their 11th War Patrol the submarine was used as a navigation Beacon.

Along with other T-Class submarines, HMS *Tuna* was built by Scots. The *Tuna* had engine problems, which was the reason they were based in home waters for the duration of their years of service. As new submarine construction became available, *Tuna* was assigned to training duties.

Chapter 26: Buckingham Palace

27 November, 1944
Crewe

Evelyn was awakened early when her mother burst into the room. "Rise and shine!" Dolly said, with a song in her voice. "We must get ready quickly so we can catch the train to London."

Evelyn had not been to London before and was excited to be going.

"Pack your pyjamas, two clean pairs of knickers, and your dressing gown." Dolly said. "I have a small suitcase for you to pack them in."

"I'll be ready before you know it," Evelyn said, and she jumped out of bed.

Once washed, dressed and packed, she walked downstairs into the kitchen, where her Aunt Gertie was sitting having a cup of tea.

"Good morning, Eve. Big day today, going to London."

"How long will the train ride take?" Evelyn asked

"It should take about four hours to get there," her aunt replied with a smile.

Her mum had made toast, and Eve took a slice off the plate and bit into it. "Mmm." She liked her toast with butter. It was such a treat to have butter, with all the rationing of food. She was grateful when it was available.

Dolly came downstairs with their suitcase.

"Are we ready to go?" she said, as she opened the front door. "We have thirty minutes to catch the train."

It was a twenty-minute walk to the train station.

"Do you have the envelope from the Admiralty with our passes?" Dolly asked Gertie.

"Yes, I do. It is in my suitcase." she replied, picking the case up off the floor and walking out the door.

Dolly handed their case to Evelyn, "Can you hold this?" she asked.

She braced for the weight and thought, *not too heavy*, as her mum locked the door and put the keys into her clutch purse. Evelyn thought she could manage the case, so she decided she would carry it all the way. She had her atlas in her one hand and the suitcase in the other.

They walked at a good pace, with no time to stop and chat with any neighbours who might be out on their stoops.

They arrived at the station. Dolly approached the ticket office and asked for two adults and one child return for London. The agent prepared the tickets and handed them to Dolly with her change. She put everything away into her purse.

"The train will be on track one in about ten minutes," the ticket agent said.

Dolly nodded and thanked her.

Evelyn and Gertie found an empty bench on the platform and they all sat down together.

"Good timing," Dolly said. "The train will be here in ten minutes."

While they waited, Dolly went over how they would negotiate London once they arrived at Euston Station. "Your Aunt Florence sent us directions in the mail, with a map and instructions on how to get their house. We can ask for further assistance from the warden posts once we get there."

They heard the train sounding its horn off in the distance. It would be pulling into the station in moments. Evelyn and Gertie stood up hastily. "Keep back until it passes and stops!" Dolly warned.

As the train pulled into the station, the forward carriages looked empty as they passed by. They walked over to the steps where the train guard placed a step at the bottom to help them climb up into the carriage. They walked down the aisle and found an empty compartment.

"Here we go," Evelyn said, walking in and sitting down.

They lifted their two suitcases onto the overhead racks. Evelyn sat beside the window. Although she had travelled to Liverpool by train, this was a whole new adventure—they were going to London!

They settled into the journey, with Dolly and Gertie chatting about their trip. They would be staying with Eve's Aunt Florence and Uncle Denis in London. Her mum was discreet when talking about her Uncle Denis—who was a communist, and conscientious objector. Evelyn had not heard those words before and wondered what they meant. Her Aunt Florence was four months pregnant, expecting their first child. Uncle Denis was a warden with the local civil defence.

Evelyn watched the countryside pass by as the train travelled towards the city. Both her mum and aunt dozed off after a while, but she was not able to sleep when there was so much to see with each passing view.

As the train finally entered Euston Station, all the carriage compartments were nearly full. It was crowded. Dolly and Gertie grabbed their suitcases off the rack and they exited the carriage with all the other passengers who had boarded since Crewe.

Holding Evelyn's arm tightly, Dolly warned, "Do not leave my side, do you hear me? I do not want to lose you in London!" she said firmly.

"Yes Ma'am." Eve replied. "I'll stay right beside you."

Dolly took out Aunt Florence's directions to their house from her purse. "Take the underground to Arsenal tube station. Then take the number twenty-three tram east on Gillespie Road. There is a warden post right beside the tram stop. Florence said we would get further directions there."

They left the railway station and caught the Euston tube station across the street. It was early afternoon, and there were many people out and about.

Evelyn's eyes were wide open with the sights and sounds. She looked up and saw a big balloon tethered to the ground.

"What's that?" she asked.

Both ladies looked up. "They are called barrage balloons." Aunt Gertie answered. "They are there to protect the train station from German bombers."

When they entered the station, Dolly walked across to the underground map on the wall. She located Arsenal Station and where they were. Then, more importantly, she found how to get there. "It's only a couple of stops to Arsenal." She said. "It should not be too much longer before we get there."

Dolly reached into her clutch purse, took the money out for their fare, and put it into the collection box. The female guard waved them through as they approached the escalator.

Evelyn looked down the escalator. She had never been on such a long one before. Finally, when they reached the bottom, Dolly spied the required platform and started walking towards it. As they walked onto the platform, Evelyn was amazed to see that all the walls and ceilings were round.

She heard the rattle and screeching of the tube train entering the station. When the train stopped, they approached a cabin door to an open compartment.

"Mind the gap," Dolly said to Evelyn. There was one between the train car and the platform. She stepped over the gap and into the carriage where they found a bench. "We are getting off at the next station and transferring onto the Northern line." Dolly said.

They pulled into the Kings Cross, St Pancras Station in time to make their connection. They followed the signs to Northern line and took the escalator. As they arrived to the platform, their train pulled in.

"Arsenal Station is in three stops." Dolly announced.

When the next train arrived, Evelyn knew to mind the gap and stepped over it as she boarded the train. A couple of seats were open, and all three of them sat together.

When they pulled into Arsenal Station, they stood up and walked over to the doors as door were opened. Evelyn noticed that the gap was not as wide as the previous ones, and she stepped over it easily.

They walked over and onto the up escalator. At the top, Dolly found the signs directing them to the trams. As they got outside, she noticed the 23 Tram and started to run for it. She was waving her hands to signal the driver, who stopped to let them on. Dolly placed the fare into the box as Gertie and Evelyn went to sit down.

"Could you please announce when we will arrive at Avenell Road?" She asked the tram operator.

"Righto, ma'am, I'll let you know," the operator replied as the tram lurched forward.

The windows on the tram were open, and a breeze was wafting in. Evelyn had noticed a smell in the air since arriving in London. She turned to her mum and asked, "What's that smell?"

Dolly took a sniff and nodded. "I smell it too."

Eve asked, "What is it?"

Her mum was a little reluctant to say, but she told Evelyn, "It smells like burned timbers and domestic gas. Not a pleasant smell."

Evelyn scrunched her nose and said, "No, it isn't."

"Avenell Road, next stop." The tram operator called out.

They stood up and Dolly thanked him as it stopped and they clambered off.

Evelyn had been looking out the window and noticing the damage to the houses on the block. Houses, stood shattered with bricks fallen into the street. It must have been a recent bombing, as people were still picking them off the road and walkways. In between bombed-out houses stood others that had been untouched. She also noticed the black Xs on the windows and wondered what they meant.

When the tram pulled away, Dolly noticed the warden post across the street. She took out her page of directions from her purse and they all headed in the general direction.

As they approached the post, there was an elderly gentleman inside with a civil defence helmet on. He was bending over a hot plate, making what looked like a cup of tea.

Dolly spoke first, "Good day Sir. Could you help us, please?"

"Certainly, ma'am. What can I do for you?"

"We are trying to get to Gillespie Road, could you point us in the right direction?" Dolly asked.

He took down a local map that was hanging on the wall.

"Let's have a look, shall we?"

As Dolly and the civil defence warden perused the map, Evelyn noticed that all the posts had been removed from the street corners in the area and were propped up beside the warden's hut.

When Dolly emerged from the hut, she had a good idea of which way to go. She thanked the warden, and they set off again.

When they arrived at the next post, the warden was standing outside.

"'Ello, 'ello. How can I help you?" he asked.

"We are looking for 19 Gillespie Road, please?" Dolly replied.

"Right you are. You're nearly there, my dears. Two blocks down on your right." the warden directed them and said "Cheerio".

All three had smiles on their faces, knowing how close they were to their destination.

Dolly thanked him and started down Gillespie Road. When Gertie had asked her if she would accompany her to the ceremony at Buckingham Palace, Dolly wrote to her sister-in-law, asking if they could stay at their home in London for a couple of days. Florence said she would be delighted to have their company.

They turned onto the street indicated by the warden and started looking for street numbers. There, on the left, was number nineteen. They quickly walked up the pathway and knocked on the door.

A couple of moments later, Aunt Florence opened the door. She wore a yellow frilly apron over her already-showing tummy.

"Hello, welcome, come in, come in!" she announced. "How was your trip?"

"There was not too much ado, but a comfortable trip nonetheless." Dolly replied. She introduced her sister-in-law, and the ladies embraced.

"You must be very happy to see your husband tomorrow." Florence remarked to Gertie.

"Ah, I am, and I pray this will all be over soon." She answered as she made the sign of the cross.

"How are you feeling?" Gertie asked.

"Not bad, thanks. The baby's a real kicker," Florence replied "Evelyn is getting so tall, too. You were just a little girl when we last saw you."

"It's my first time in London, and there are a lot of people here." Evelyn said smiling.

"Yes, there are," her aunt replied.

To the left of the hall was an open door. Inside the parlour stood what looked like a hut, with woven wire along the sides. "Welcome to our 'Morrison shelter'." Florence said. "If you hear an air-raid siren, you must take cover in there immediately."

Evelyn noticed an X on the window as she walked into the room. "Aunty Florence, why are there Xs on your windows?"

"It's tape, in case the window breaks from the bombing. It should help stop the glass from shattering." Hearing that sent a cold shiver down Eve's spine.

"Also, if you hear anti-aircraft guns firing, make sure you take cover in the shelter as well." Florence informed everyone.

Eve looked at her mum's face. She could see her mum shaking her head. Evidently, her mum would have a difficult time in the shelter. She bent over and peered into the wire and wood door. Her aunt and uncle had set up their beds on the left.

"You'll be on the right, Eve. Do you want to go in first?" her aunt asked.

When she crawled inside, there was enough headroom for Evelyn to sit up.

"I'm going to have to sleep next to the door." Dolly said to Gertie.

"Not a worry, I'll muddle here in the middle." She replied as she crawled in beside Evelyn.

"I'll go in there when I have to." Dolly said nervously. "Until then, no thank you!"

When the Morrison shelter was installed, all the chairs and settees had to be removed, but there were a couple of tables with lights on them left. The windows had heavy black curtains on rods, like they had in Crewe.

There was a light right beside the wire wall of the shelter so Evelyn would be able to read her atlas before going to sleep.

Her mum was giving an update to Aunty Florence on her dad. She told her about the number of hours he worked at the factory and that he was also assigned to three nights a month on the fire watch.

"We only see him one day a month!" Dolly bemoaned.

Florence felt badly for Jack, and sorry for Dolly when she had to tell her that Denis would be home shortly. He only worked about 35 hours a week as an area warden.

The ladies entered the kitchen, and Evelyn listened to her aunts and mum getting caught up.

A couple of minutes later, the front door opened. It was her Uncle Denis. Eve remembered meeting him a couple of years ago—he had a long look on his face and did not seem too happy. He walked into the kitchen and greeted his wife and guests.

Since there were no chairs to sit on, Evelyn listened to the adults as she sat quietly in the Morrison shelter.

The conversation soon turned to the war and its effects on everyone's morale. Her Uncle Denis was upset at the Emergency Powers Act that had turned England into a military camp. He said that there should not be any food rationing either.

"The Ministry of Food is controlling everything we eat!" He said angrily. "One egg per week per person is ridiculous. There is plenty of food grown in Britain, nothing should be rationed! And beyond that, the coal shortages are affecting every household. We are all suffering because the government can't get their act together," her uncle said in frustration.

Now, Dolly, who had brothers in the service and her husband working at the Spitfire factory in Crewe, felt that Britain had to go to war to stop the Nazis from taking over all of Europe. "Everyone must do their part to help Britain through these dark days of this war!" Her mum said passionately.

While the conversation was underway, her aunt had quietly prepared the evening supper. Eve was called into the kitchen and they all sat down at the table. Like her mum, her Aunt Florence had to improvise on making evening meals tastier. There was a small pork roast, carrots, parsnips and turnips, which Eve enjoyed, and reconstituted potatoes that looked like sludge, which she did not. She had never been fond of the taste of wheat-meal loaf bread or powdered milk, either, but that was all they had.

"We have been saving our rations for your visit—not that we're doing without," Florence remarked. "We just ate a little less."

Gertie said that she truly appreciated them for their invitation to stay.

After supper, the dishes were washed and put away. The blackout curtains had been drawn over the windows. In the distance, the wail of the air-raid siren was heard. Aunt Florence instructed everyone to get into the shelter.

"We have been besieged between aerial bombings and V2 rockets, and we are glad of the Morrison shelter," She declared. "At least we do not have to go to the Anderson shelter down on the corner. It smells of urine."

They all crawled in and made themselves as comfortable as they could. Aunt Gertie asked, "Do the air-raid sirens last all night?"

"Not usually." Florence replied. "We can get some relief at times and so we do get some sleep."

There was the sound of anti-aircraft guns in the distance. Dolly was sitting on the floor with her fingers in her ears. She did not like the sound of the guns.

A short while later, the air-raid sirens ended, along with the anti-aircraft fire.

"If you want to get ready for bed, now would be a good time." Aunt Florence told Evelyn. Evelyn clambered out of the shelter. Their suitcases had been taken upstairs, where she got changed into her pyjamas and dressing gown.

Eve was tired from all the travel today and had been yawning for most of the evening. She was ready for bed when she came back downstairs.

While her aunts and uncle continued their conversation in the kitchen, Evelyn got comfortable on the small mattress and blankets in the shelter. She missed her dad asking her to find the world cities in her atlas, but she closed her eyes and soon fell asleep.

It was dark when she woke up in the middle of the night to the sound of rhythmic snoring. Her aunt was lying beside her, while her mum had her head near the shelter door. She wished there had been a light on. It felt like the shelter ceiling was right on top of her. She rolled over and, luckily, fell back to sleep.

Eve did not wake up again until morning.

Michael D Gilston

27 November, 1944
Plymouth

Dominic was out of breath, running to the ticket counter at Plymouth train station. He had had just enough time to change into his all-blue uniform at the barracks that evening, where he caught a lift from another sailor. He was there just in time for the last overnight train to London. After getting his return ticket, he walked quickly out onto the platform and did not have long to wait before the train arrived.

The train was not crowded so he found an empty compartment and sat down. Dominic was still panting when they pulled out of the station.

The guard came by asking him for his ticket. As he punched it and handed it back,

Dominic asked him, "Listen, mate, I have a rather special day in London tomorrow, where I will be meeting my wife. I did not get a chance to shower before I left. Is there a wash basin where I could freshen up?"

The guard smiled and said, "Yes, but let's get underway first, and then we'll look after you."

"Much appreciated!" Dominic replied gratefully.

A couple of minutes later, the guard returned. "Follow me." He said.

They started walking through to the back of the train. There, near the end, was a postal carriage. The guard opened the door where, on the right side, was a small water closet with a toilet and basin. "You can get yourself cleaned up in here."

The conductor opened a cupboard, picked up a towel, and handed it to Dominic. "You can take your time. Just leave the towel here when you're finished."

Dominic was extremely grateful and thanked the conductor, who started returning to the passenger carriages. Dominic went in and closed the door.

When Dominic finished washing up, he felt much better about meeting Gertie—he was smelling fresher than before. He walked back to his carriage, sat down, and watched as the train sped by the darkened countryside on its way to Paddington Station.

The total travel time to London was just over eight hours. He should arrive with plenty of time to take the underground tube to Victoria Station and then walk to Buckingham Palace. He had received notification of the investiture last month when it was published in the London Gazette, on Friday 29th. The chits came from Buckingham Palace, and he forwarded them on to his wife in Crewe. Gertie could bring a guest as a witness, so she asked her sister-in-law Dolly to attend with her.

Dominic was unsure where to meet up with his wife and sister. Since they had the chits, he realized they would probably go right in and wait for him in the palace. He had his, along with the papers the Admiralty had sent which included a notification that he would receive the Distinguished Service Medal. He should find Gertie and Dolly waiting inside.

Dominic slept while the train parked overnight on a spur. That morning, as the train travelled east into London, a few more passengers got on and his compartment filled. They slowed down as they entered the city, and all along the railway corridor there were damaged buildings.

Finally, the train arrived at Paddington. He exited and walked onto the concourse, following the signs for the tube to take him to Victoria Station.

Dominic had some money from his pay packet to cover any costs for his travel. He paid for the tube ticket and walked into the station where he took two escalators down to the platform. He had a smoke on the way down the escalator, where he felt a rush of air from the trains pulling into the station. Walking to the southbound platform, he waited for the train to arrive. It wasn't long before he could hear it coming around the bend.

28 November, 1944
London

Dolly had asked Florence if she could set the alarm for the morning. Denis was on the early shift and had to get up at four-thirty so Florence woke up with him. She reset the alarm for seven-thirty and laid back down. To get out, Denis crawled over her and around Dolly's head by the door.

When the alarm went off later in the morning, Dolly was already awake and wanted to leave the confining shelter. Gertie and Evelyn stirred with the sound of the alarm, yawned, and stretched.

They all crawled out of the shelter. Dolly told Gertie that they didn't have much time to prepare for the investiture, so she suggested that

Gertie get ready first. While they waited, Dolly and Evelyn walked into the kitchen, where Florence had filled the kettle for tea and placed it on the hob.

Evelyn was in her housecoat when she stepped into the kitchen, and her Aunt Florence asked her if she would like some toast. "Yes, please," Evelyn replied.

Before the war started, Evelyn had loved white bread, lightly toasted with butter. Since the war, the only bread available was a National Wheatmeal loaf, which was not very appetising. Her aunt opened the larder and brought a saucer of butter and a small jar of jam. Evelyn noticed it was gooseberry, which she was fond of. The kettle had boiled and a couple of cups were set out for Dolly and Gertie to get their tea before they had to leave.

Aunt Florence instructed Dolly on how to get to Buckingham Palace on the tube.

"It should not take you too long, but there might be delays, and I would hate it if you were late."

Gertie came into the kitchen, dressed in a pale blue dress and white sweater. She had a smile on her face.

"All right, Dolly, your turn." She said.

Dolly got herself ready in a couple of minutes and came back downstairs, "We should think about leaving soon." She announced.

Gertie had had her cup of tea and a slice of toast.

"Do you have the investiture chits?" Dolly asked her.

Producing them from her clutch to be sure she had them, Gertie answered, "Yes, I do. I'm all ready to go."

"All right, then we will be on our way," Dolly said.

She gave her daughter a hug and a kiss and told her to be good for her aunt.

Eve said she would, and Dolly and Gertie walked out the front door and down the pathway to the pavement. Dolly got her bearings from coming in the previous afternoon. The two ladies walked together at a reasonable pace and arrived at the Arsenal tube station. Paying their fare, they walked in and across to the escalator.

Many people were in the station, both commuters going to work and London residents who had taken shelter on the platforms. As they walked out, they saw the elderly and mothers with children sitting on bundles of blankets, with presumably no place to go. Florence had said that people taking shelter in the stations could not enter them until seven-thirty at night and then had to be out by seven-thirty the following morning. Residents, still sheltering, had moved back from the platform edge to within four feet of the wall and didn't look like they were leaving anytime soon. Both Gertie and Dolly tried to refrain from walking on their bedding as they passed by them.

"Do they not have anywhere else to go?" Gertie wondered out loud.

"Poor souls!" Dolly cried. "Perhaps their houses have been destroyed."

The train was heard screeching in the tunnel as it entered the station. It was almost full, so they would have to stand in the carriage.

"We take the Piccadilly Line south, which is a short hop on the southbound Northern line." Dolly stated, "So we won't be standing long. Then we transfer onto the Metropolitan line to Westminster Station," She added.

The train carriage stayed full on their journey south. As they passed through each station, they noticed that people remained sitting and were not moving from the platforms.

"So many displaced people," Gertie noted.

"There are." Dolly agreed.

They finally arrived at the Metropolitan line and the Charing Cross station. "We just have one more stop and then we're there!" Dolly exclaimed, with excitement in her voice.

Gertie got a flutter in her stomach. She couldn't wait to see Dominic again after all these months.

They were so excited, though, that it seemed to take forever to get there. The train finally arrived at St. James Park station, where they stepped off the carriage and headed for the escalator up.

The clock at the top of the escalator showed nine-fifty so they still had plenty of time to get to Buckingham Palace by ten-fifteen.

Walking out of the station and turning left, they saw St. James Park a little further up on the right so they knew they were heading in the right direction. They could see the Victoria Memorial and Buckingham Palace as they passed the park. Gertie looked around and saw sailors and servicemen everywhere. She was not sure if they would see Dominic outside before they went in.

Dolly led them both directly to the front gates of Buckingham Palace.

The wicket gate was open as they approached and a palace guard was stationed there. Gertie said they were both there for her husband's investiture and handed over the two chits to him.

"Just head on over through that arch and onward to that side door on the right." He directed them. "They will look after you there."

Gertie took the two chits back and they walked across the outer courtyard to a large wide arch. Then they went into a second courtyard where people were entering the palace under a canopied arch.

As they walked in, the grandeur of the building was not lost on them. They approached the guard who was date stamping chits, and Gertie handed theirs over to him. He stamped and returned them back to her, and indicated to the ladies where to wait for an escort into the palace. A small group of people had already arrived for the investiture. They were waiting there, as instructed by the guard.

A footman in a red and gold tunic walked over to the small group.

"Would you please follow me?"

He directed them to a grand staircase, which they all ascended. Walking along a wide corridor, they entered a gilded reception room. There was a small dais at the head of the hall with chairs set up in front. The footman indicated where everyone should sit.

As they sat down, Gertie looked around the room for Dominic.

More people were seated and they waited for the ceremony to begin. Naval officers and sailors filed in and took their places in front of the platform.

Dolly smiled when she saw her younger brother in his dress uniform—but then she frowned when she noticed he was wearing a pair of scruffy old boots!

Gertie stood up. Almost running over to Dominic, she threw her arms around him. "Hello, my love!" She cried, "I have missed you so much!"

Dominic stepped back to admire his pretty wife in her cotton dress. "You look beautiful. How was your trip down?" he asked.

Gertie smiled, "It was good." She answered. "We stayed at Dolly's sister-in-law's last night."

They both walked over to where the women had been sitting. Dolly stood up and gave Dominic a big hug and a kiss on the cheek.

"It is wonderful to see you." She said. "Congratulations on your award."

"Ah, I was in the right place at the right time, I guess." he replied.

Dominic looked over to where he would be seated and saw John Wilband sitting amongst the other sailors.

"There is someone I would like you to meet." He said to Gertie as they walked over to where his friend was sitting.

Willie stood up when he saw him approaching and held out his hand.

"How are you, Willie?" Dominic asked.

"*Rhyfeddol*," he replied. "Just wonderful, Bommy."

It had been over fifteen months since he had seen Willie, after he had been transferred off the *Tuna*.

"Are you still on the Tuna?" Dominic asked.

"Yes, I am training new recruits in Blyth. I told you they would not keep us both together on the same boat," Willie replied.

"I would like you to meet my wife. Gertie, this is John Wilband, or 'Willie'. We have been through a lot together on the *Tuna*. Was your wife able to attend?" he asked him.

"Nah, she could not get anyone to look after the brood and the farm," Willie answered.

Just then, a palace spokesperson asked everyone to take a seat, as the ceremony would start shortly. He instructed everyone to stand when it was announced that the King had arrived.

Dominic said a quick *see you later* to Willie and kissed his wife for good luck as he left to find his seat. Gertie walked back to where she was sitting with Dolly and took her seat.

A military band started to play "God save the King" as His Majesty George VI walked in, wearing his naval uniform. Everyone in the reception room stood up. With his bodyguard, a Yeoman of the guard, the King walked up onto the podium.

The investiture began, and each of the servicemen was called up by name. The King pinned their medals on the officer's service dress tunic or on the sailor's uniform.

When he mentioned those who would be awarded the Distinguished Service Medal, the Yeoman called, "Dominic King, for courage, enterprise and skill while serving aboard HMS *Tuna*."

Dominic stood up and walked up to the podium. The King took the medal out of the box as he approached. His Majesty reached forward, pinned the medal on Dominic's left breast of his dress uniform, and shook his hand.

Gertie could see her husband standing before the King, but she had trouble hearing what he said to Dominic. It sounded like he asked how he came to earn the medal. Gertie was not all that sure of what Dominic had done. He only advised her that he had earned the award after helping sink a German submarine.

After His Majesty the King finished speaking with Dominic, Dominic saluted him and started to walk back to his seat. The Yeoman handed the case to him as he walked by.

The medal felt heavy on his tunic, and the blue and white striped ribbon, attached to the bright silver medal, hung over his heart. He was so lost in thought that he missed what the King had said to Signalman William Huthwaite, who received his Distinguished Service Medal after Bommy.

The remaining naval officers and seaman were given their awards and the ceremony ended. His Majesty the King left the room with the Yeoman, by the same corridor they had entered.

Dominic walked over to where Gertie and Dolly were sitting.

"Congratulations Dominic. I am sure you earned the medal for bravery, I'm so proud of you little brother," Dolly said.

"I could sure use a fag right now," Dominic announced. "Shall we get out of here?"

He said his goodbyes to his former shipmates, wishing them well and hoping they would all meet again when the war ended. Then he walked back over to Gertie and Dolly, and they all left together.

Outside Buckingham Palace, Dominic took out his pack of cigarettes. He did not have a match so he asked a sailor—who was having his own—if he could get a light? Dominic took his investiture chit, ripped the bottom edge off, and twisted it. He lit his cigarette from the small piece of paper and then offered it to Dolly so she could light hers too.

His Majesty's Sailor *and the Girl in the* Blue Coat

They stood before Victoria Memorial, watching the people and vehicles going by. Dominic unpinned his medal, placed it into the case, and closed the lid, handing it to Dolly.

"Here, I'll ask you to look after this for me. If I should ever need it, I will know where it is."

Dolly placed the small case in her purse and said she would keep it safe for him.

It was early afternoon. Dominic's train back to Plymouth from Paddington Station was not due until four-fifteen. They decided it was best that he get there, so he should leave sooner rather than later. They walked to the St. James Park tube station together. There, the line would take them their separate ways; Dolly and Gertie going east, Dominic going west.

Gertie had tears in her eyes, when they embraced. "You take care of yourself," she cried. "And come home to me in one piece!" She added, as she gave him a big hug and a kiss.

"I will, I promise!" Dominic replied.

He turned and hugged his sister. "Say hello to Kate and Jack for me. We will meet again."

They travelled down their respective escalators to the platform. Dominic's train came into the station first.

Gertie strained to see if she could catch a glimpse of him through the carriage windows. He was heading to Plymouth, back to sea and the war.

London

When her mum and Aunt Gertie arrived back from Buckingham Palace, Eve was so excited to hear what it was like.

Her mum and aunt told her of the grand staircase, golden halls, and reception rooms with footmen everywhere. They showed her the bright, silver medal displayed in a black leather case and told how the King had presented it to her Uncle Bommy, pinning it on his chest. As Evelyn picked it up, it felt so heavy in the flat case. Her eyes lit up! The medal glinted in the light from the table lamps—it was so shiny.

Aunt Gertie's eyes welled up again thinking about Dominic. She worried about him going back onto the submarine.

Though Evelyn did not get to see her Uncle Bommy, she did enjoy the train ride down to London and visiting with her Aunt Florence and Uncle Denis. It was not pleasant sleeping in the shelter, but she knew it was for the best to sleep under the protection of the steel roof. She was thankful that there had been no air-raid sirens today, so far, and looking forward to getting home to her own bed. It had been an interesting adventure, riding the underground tube and experiencing the bustle of the city.

Paddington Station

Dominic exited the train at Paddington Station. He had over an hour to wait before his train left for Plymouth. He felt the familiar pang in his stomach, missing his daily tot. He looked around. Down on the right of London Street was the Sawyers Arms. There was a good place to have a quick one.

He walked down to the pub and into the front door. It was not too crowded, with primarily men having a pint of ale and chatting with each other. Dominic walked up to the bar as the barman came over and asked, "What can I get you?"

"I would love a double shot of Pussers Rum, if you please," Dominic requested.

"Righto," the Barman said. "Coming right up."

Dominic knew he could not be long; he had a train to catch. The barman walked back with a tumbler of dark amber liquid. A smile came to Dominic's face as he thanked him.

He picked up the glass and raised it to his lips. Inhaling the aroma of the rum deeply, he took a sip. It tasted weak. He did not get the burn down his throat and into his belly that he was expecting. He took another swig. He was sure now that the establishment was watering down the spirits, but he would not complain. What could he say? But he missed the warmth that it usually brought him.

He was unsure of the time. He looked around and there, over the bar, was a clock. He had more than enough time to get to the train station, but he decided it was time to go—just in case.

His Majesty's Sailor *and the Girl in the* Blue Coat

He asked the barman how much for the rum, took the coins from his pocket and left a small tip. Downing the last of his glass, he said his good-byes and walked back out onto Praed Street.

Turning left, Bommy made his way to Paddington Station. He looked up and noticed barrage balloons tethered over the train station. He walked into the concourse and looked up at the arrival and departure boards. On track three was the Plymouth train. He noted where the platform was and started walking towards it.

The rum may have been watered down, but it still had the desired effect. The pangs in his stomach had subsided, and his head was not hurting as much. He reached into his trouser pocket to check for the tickets that were issued to him last night for his return to Plymouth. They were still there, along with his travel pass in case he was asked to produce it.

On his arrival at the platform, the westbound train to Plymouth was already waiting. A clock suspended from the ceiling indicated the train would leave in fifteen minutes.

"Good timing," he muttered.

He walked to the nearest carriage and up the steps. A compartment on the right was empty,

"That will do," he said to himself as he walked in and sat beside the window.

"All aboard," the guard announced and a couple of moments later, the train lurched forward. Once it was underway, he came by asking for tickets. Dominic gave his to the guard, who clipped it and handed it back.

Putting the ticket into his pocket, Bommy settled back into his seat and closed his eyes. He was asleep before the train left the City of Westminster.

Epilog

I can only imagine the party and celebrations when the family reunited after the war ended.

There is no record of what Dominic's occupation might have been after the war or what a retired helmsman aboard a submarine might do once he was out of the service. It is hard to imagine him being a lorry driver.

One thing is certain: Dominic did not lose his fondness for the spirits. My grandmother would tell stories about how he walked to the local pub, accompanied by his dog. While he was inside, the dog stayed out—only to walk home alone after some time.

Family history had the Kings living at 40 Albany Road Liverpool before and during the war. So, it is somewhat ironic that a Google search now shows the location to be the Albany Road Pub.

My grandmother had been informed by Gertie that Dominic's health was failing, and she travelled from Scarborough, Ontario, Canada, to be with him before he died. He passed on 21 September 1972, and my grandmother arrived the following day. On that fateful journey, she took Dominic's Distinguished Service Medal back to England and gave it to Gertie.

Gertie and Dominic had no children, so the Distinguished Service Medal would have been passed along through the McArdle Family. It is hoped that whoever is the keeper of the award knows the history of the medal and the man who earned it.

Appendix A: Dominic King

This appendix follows the rest of Bommy's naval career. He continued to serve on the *Tuna* through to its final war patrol, and then into training duties, until 4 July, 1944. Bommy was transferred to the *Elfin*, the *Ambrose*, the *Cyclops*, and *Dolphin*, before ending up on brand-new T-Class submarine HMS *Totem*.

Bommy was part of the crew that tested this new style of submarine, putting *Totem* through its paces until its first war patrol on 8 April, 1945. Bommy remained on board the *Totem* until the end of the 2nd World War and the Japanese surrender.

On 16 September, 1945, he was transferred back to HMS *Dolphin*, where he served until the end of his 15-year naval career. Bommy was discharged on 7 February, 1946, and lived with his wife until his death on 21 September 1972.

On Board the *Tuna*
- *Wednesday, 25 August 1943.* HMS *Tuna* arrived at Holy Loch, ending her 21st and last war patrol. With the new submarines becoming available, Tuna was relegated to training duties. *Tuna* and other T-Class submarines had engine problems, which was also why she was based in home waters her whole service.
- *September 1943.* HMS *Tuna* conducted ASDIC/Sonar exercises in the Clyde area. The sub travelled north to Scapa Flow, where additional ASDIC/Sonar exercises were performed.
- *October 1943. Tuna* was back in Scapa Flow at the beginning of the month. She was chosen as the submarine to conduct the Commanding Officer Qualifying Course. The course tests prospective officers looking to take command of a submarine. It is considered one of the toughest command courses in the world, with a high failure rate. The course tests the participants in search detection, evasion, surveillance and simulated combat with up to

- *November 1943*: *Tuna* was ordered to Blyth, UK, on November 4th, with a refit scheduled at Swan Hunter at Wallsend on November 5th.
- *April 1944*: After the Wallsend retrofit, *Tuna* went on to conduct exercises off Blyth.
- *May 1944*: *Tuna* participated in training exercises in the Blyth area.
- *June 1944*: The *Tuna* was also used with the launching and recovering of Chariot Human Torpedoes at the shore establishment at Port HHZ on Loch Cairnbawn with the refit to launch X-Class midget submarines.
- *July 1944*: *Tuna* started off the month based out of Blyth, conducting training exercises for new submariners.

Transfer After Transfer
- 4 July, 1944: Dominic was transferred to submarine HMS *Elfin*.
- 16 July, 1944: Transfer to the submarine HMS *Dolphin*.
- 18 July, 1994: Transfer to the submarine depot ship HMS *Ambrose*.
- 20 July, 1944: Return to the HMS *Dolphin*.
- 11 August, 1944: Assigned to the HMS *Cyclops*.
- 26 September 1944: Assigned to the HMS *Totem*, a newly-built T-Class submarine.

HMS *Totem*
- The newest T-Class submarine; welded, whereas previous hulls had been riveted. Welding saved enough weight to thicken the pressure hull that would allow the submarine to dive in theory to deeper depths of up to 350'.
- Streamlined hull, eight bow torpedo tubes and three aft firing tubes, fitted with a snorkel that allowed the diesel engines to be run while the boat was submerged just below the surface.
- Skippered by Acting Lieutenant Commander Michael Beauchamp St. John, who had extensive experience in commanding submarines, including HMS *Tuna* from November 1941 to April 1942.

Testing the *Totem*

November 1944
- Dominic returned to Plymouth on the evening of 28 November 1944, after receiving the DSM in London.

January 1945
- Tuesday 2 January 1945 Plymouth: HMS Totem departed Plymouth for Holy Loch with an escort from HMS Cape Mariato, an Anti-Submarine Warfare Trawler.
- Thursday, 4 January 1945: Arrived in Holy Loch to conduct trials off the Isle of Arran in the Firth of Clyde.
- Monday, 15 January 1945–Saturday 27 January 1945: Totem was conducting torpedo discharge trials at Arrochar on Loch Long.
- Tuesday 30 January 1945: Totem conducted noise trials in Loch Goil, off Long Loch. The submarine was being analysed by ships with hydrophones measuring the sub's acoustic noise.
- Wednesday 31 January 1945–Friday 2 February 1945: The sub conducted attack exercises in the Clyde area with HMS Hastings, a Folkstone Class Sloop.

February 1945
- Sunday 4 February 1945: With the tests completed, HMS Totem returned to Holy Loch from Arrochar on Loch Long
- Monday, 5 February 1945: HMS Totem conducted attack exercises in the Clyde with HMS Ravager, an Attacker Class Escort Carrier in the Clyde area.
- Wednesday, 7 February 1945: The submarine conducted attack exercises with the Destroyer Admiralty class HMS *Sardonyx* serving as a target
- Thursday 8 February 1945–Tuesday 13 February 1945: HMS Totem departed for Loch Alsh to conduct exercises in the inlet between the Isle of Sky and the mainland.

His Majesty's Sailor *and the Girl in the* Blue Coat

- Saturday, 17 February 1945: Totem conducted ASDIC Sonar exercises in the Clyde area with HMS Hart and HMS Amethyst, both modified Black Swan sloops.
- Monday, 19 February 1945–Tuesday 20 February 1945: Totem depart Loch Alsh for Holy Loch.
- Thursday, 22 February 1945: HMS Totem was conducting exercises in the Clyde with HMS Searcher, an Attacker Class Escort Carrier.
- Friday 23 February 1945: HMS Totem was conducting attack exercises in the Clyde with HMS Jan van Gelder, a decommissioned Royal Netherlands Jan van Amstel Class Minesweeper.
- Saturday, 24 February 1945–Monday, 26 February 1945: Upon returning to Holy Loch, the Totem conducted attack exercises in the Clyde area with HMS Sardonyx, an Admiralty Class Destroyer.
- Tuesday 27 February 1945: Upon completion of the exercises in the Clyde, the submarine proceeded to Loch Goil.
- Wednesday 28 February 1945: HMS Totem returned to the Clyde area where it conducted attack exercises where HMS Bridgewater, a Bridgewater Class Sloop and HMS Sardonyx both served as targets

March 1945

- Friday 2 March 1945: Totem conducted attack exercises in the Clyde area with HMS Bridgewater, HMS Sardonyx and HMS Jan van Gelder.
- Saturday, 3 March 1945: HMS Tapir, a T-Class submarine, joined HMS Totem in attack exercises in the Clyde with HMS Shikari, an Admiralty S-Class Destroyer.
- Sunday 4 March 1945: HMS Tapir joined HMS Totem in exercises with HMS Bridgewater and HMS Hastings, a Folkstone Class Sloop.
- Monday, 5 March 1945–Wednesday, 14 March 1945: HMS Totem arrived at Loch Alsh on 5 March 1945 to conduct exercises in the area. These included night exercises too.
- Thursday, 15 March 1945: HMS Tapir joined HMS Totem and was escorted to Holy Loch by HMS Shikari. The group anchored the night in Rothesay Bay.

- Friday, 16 March 1945: HMS Totem and HMS Tapir were escorted back to Holy Loch by HMS Shikari.
- Sunday, 18 March 1945: HMS Totem conducted exercises in the Clyde area with HMS Bridgewater, HMS Sardonyx and HMS Shikari serving as targets.
- Tuesday, 20 March 1945–Wednesday, 21 March 1945: HMS Totem conducted exercises in the Clyde area.
- Thursday, 22 March 1945–Sunday, 25 March 1945: HMS Totem was in Holy Loch docked to an Auxiliary Floating Drydock #7.

The *Totem* at War

April 1945
- Sunday, 1 April 1945: HMS Totem departed Holy Loch for Lerwick with submarines HMS Tapir and HMS Varne escorted by HMS Bridgewater. HMS Scotsman, an S-Class submarine, travelled part of the way with the group.
- Wednesday, 4 April 1945: The group arrived in Lerwick.
- Sunday, 8 April 1945: HMS Totem departs Lerwick on its 1st war patrol. She was ordered to patrol the Norwegian coast of the Kors Fjord near Bergen.
- Thursday, 19 April 1945: HMS Totem completed her 1st war patrol and returned to Lerwick.
- Sunday, 22 April 1945–Tuesday, 24 April 1945: HMS Totem departed Lerwick for Holy Loch.
- Saturday, 28 April 1945: HMS Totem is docked at Holy Loch in Auxiliary Floating Dock #7.
- Monday, 30 April 1945–Tuesday, 1 May 1945: HMS Totem leaves the Auxiliary Floating Dock at Holy Loch to conduct noise trials in Loch Goil.

May 1945
- Sunday, 6 May 1945: HMS Totem departed Holy Loch for Gibraltar, the first part of the journey to the Far East and their 2nd war patrol.

His Majesty's Sailor *and the Girl in the* Blue Coat

- Tuesday, 15 May 1945: HMS Totem arrived at Gibraltar for a quick call before departing for Malta.
- Saturday, 19 May 1945: HMS Totem arrived in Malta.
- Monday, 28 May 1945: HMS Totem docked in Malta in Dock #2.

June 1945
- Friday, 1 June 1945: HMS Totem left the dock.
- Friday, 8 June 1945: HMS Totem was docked again, this time in dock #4.
- Wednesday, 13 June 1945: HMS Totem leaves the dock.
- Friday, 15 June 1945: HMS Totem departed Malta for Port Said.
- Tuesday, 19 June 1945: HMS Totem arrived in Port Said, Egypt.
- Thursday, 21 June 1945: HMS Totem departed Port Said for transit through the Suez Canal and the Red Sea to Aden, Yemen.
- Tuesday, 26 June 1945: HMS Totem arrived in Aden for a couple of hours before departing for Trincomalee, Sri Lanka.

July 1945
- Thursday, 5 July 1945: HMS *Totem* arrived in Trincomalee.
- Friday, 13 July 1945: HMS *Totem* departed Trincomalee for Freemantle, Australia.
- Thursday, 26 July 1945: After almost three months of travel, HMS *Totem* arrived in Freemantle, Australia.

August 1945
- Wednesday, 1 August 1945: HMS *Totem* was docked on a slip in Freemantle.
- Friday, 3 August 1945: HMS *Totem* was put back into the water.
- Monday, 13 August 1945: HMS *Totem* departs Freemantle for her 2nd war patrol, her first in the Far East, where she was destined to patrol in the Java Sea between Malaysia and Indonesia.
    - Two days after her departure, the Japanese accepted unconditional surrender on Tuesday, 14 August. *Totem* was ordered back to Fremantle.

The 2nd World War ended on 2 September 1945. Dominic served on HMS *Totem* until 16 September 1945, when he was transferred back to HMS *Dolphin*, Gosport, Portsmouth. Dominic served at HMS *Dolphin* from 17 September 1945 to 7 February 1946, when he was discharged from the Royal Navy after fifteen years.

His Majesty's Sailor *and the Girl in the* Blue Coat

Appendix B: London Gazette

Numb. 36229   4811

SECOND SUPPLEMENT
TO
The London Gazette
Of FRIDAY, *the* 29th *of* OCTOBER, 1943
Published by Authority

Registered as a newspaper

TUESDAY, 2 NOVEMBER, 1943

CENTRAL CHANCERY OF THE ORDERS OF KNIGHTHOOD.
St. James's Palace, S.W.1,
2nd November, 1943.

The KING has been graciously pleased to approve the award of the George Medal to:—
Acting Temporary Lieutenant-Commander Neil MacSween Waldman, R.N.R.
for great bravery and undaunted devotion to duty.

CENTRAL CHANCERY OF THE ORDERS OF KNIGHTHOOD.
St. James's Palace, S.W.1,
2nd November, 1943.

The KING has been graciously pleased to approve the following awards of the British Empire Medal (Military Division) to:—
Petty Officer Leonard Clinton, LT/KX.109662.
Petty Officer Samuel Dearness.
Petty Officer Leonard Herbert Henry Nicholls, C/JX.583654.
Shipwright Third Class Thomas Devonshire, 71088, S.A.N.F.
Acting Leading Seaman Wilfrid Henry Kyte, P/SSX.26945.
Stoker First Class Martin Greaves, 72551, S.A.N.F.
for outstanding courage in dangerous operations which led to the reopening of North African ports.
Regulating Petty Officer John Thomas Hunter, C/MX.583088.
for enterprise and fine seamanship by which he saved many lives when in charge of a lifeboat after a vessel in which he was taking passage was lost.
Able Seaman Ronald James Webster, C/JX.351165.
Ordinary Signalman Vincent Thomas Hurley, C/JX.202517.
for great bravery in diving into waters where there were known to be sharks to the rescue of survivors from a torpedoed merchant ship.

ADMIRALTY.
Whitehall,
2nd November, 1943.

The KING has been graciously pleased to give orders for the following appointment to the Distinguished Service Order and to approve the following Reward and Awards:—

For outstanding courage, enterprise and skill in a successful patrol in H.M. Submarine Tuna:

Second Bar to the Distinguished Service Order.
Lieutenant Desmond Samuel Royst Martin, D.S.O., Royal Navy (Vancouver Island, B.C.).

The Distinguished Service Cross.
Lieutenant (E) Nicholas Travers, Royal Navy (Plymouth).

The Distinguished Service Medal.
Acting Temporary Leading Seaman Dominic King, D/JX.135013 (Liverpool).
Acting Temporary Leading Stoker Thomas Alexander Abraham, D/KX.82152 (Renfrew).
Electrical Artificer Fourth Class Victor Frank Thomas Lammin, P/MX.79980 (Bath).
Signalman William Richard Huthwaite, P/CDX.2318 (Nottingham).

Mention in Despatches.
Lieutenant David Sivewright Brown, R.N.V.R. (Durham).
Acting Chief Petty Officer Alfred James Mallett, D.S.M., D/JX.130986 (St. Austell).
Stoker Petty Officer Charles Spencer Watkins, P/KX.84395 (Ballindaggin, Co. Wexford).
Acting Temporary Leading Seaman John Francis Wilband, D/JX.96550 (Llangryney).
Acting Temporary Leading Stoker John Arthur Wilkinson, C/KX.94292 (Leicester).
Engine Room Artificer Fourth Class Wilfred Jarvis, D/MX.74878 (Cutsyke, Castleford).

For gallantry and determination when heavily attacked from the air while serving in Light Craft:

The Distinguished Service Cross.
Temporary Lieutenant Robert MacKenzie Young, R.C.N.V.R.

The Conspicuous Gallantry Medal.
Able Seaman Michael Stanley Cooney, C/JX.236141 (Worthing, Sussex).

Able Seaman Cooney was serving a gun and was severely wounded when aircraft attacked, and the sights of his gun

Appendix C: Operation Frankton Team Members

Of the ten commandos launched from HMS *Tuna*, only two men—Major Herbert "Blondie" Hasler and Marine Bill Sparks—survived the assault. Six were captured and executed without trial by the Germans, and two died from hypothermia.

A Division
- Major Herbert "Blondie" Hasler and Marine Bill Sparks in canoe *Catfish*
- Corporal Albert F. Laver and Marine William. H. Mills in canoe *Crayfish*
- Corporal George. J. Sheard and Marine David Moffatt in canoe *Conger*

B Division
- Lieutenant John. W. Mackinnon and Marine James Conway in canoe *Cuttlefish*
- Sergeant Samual. Wallace and Marine Robert Ewart in canoe *Coalfish*

Left Behind on the Tuna:
- Marine W. A. Ellery and Marine Eric Fisher in canoe *Cachalot*:
    - Damage to the *Catchalot* meant they were unable to launch with the others.
- Marine Norman Colley.
    - He had been brought along as a reserve, in case the unit lost a man along the way, and was not intended to participate in the mission.

His Majesty's Sailor *and the Girl in the* Blue Coat

Dominic King

Michael D Gilston

An early photo of Dominic and Gertie

His Majesty's Sailor *and the Girl in the* Blue Coat

Dominic and Gerty's Wedding Day

Evelyn is the girl on the steps to the left and Sonny is at the top.

Michael D Gilston

	Gerty's Brother	Gerty's Sister	Dorothy Jackson nee King	
Gerty's Sister	Dominic King	Gerty King nee McArdle	Ellen King (Nana)	Charles Fitsimmons

His Majesty's Sailor *and the Girl in the* Blue Coat

Eleven-Year-old Evelyn and family friend Nancy Skelton

Evelyn Jackson Ration Book

His Majesty's Sailor *and the Girl in the* Blue Coat

> 2469
> **BUCKINGHAM PALACE.**
>
> Admit one to witness the
>
> Investiture
>
> (at 10.15 o'clock a.m.)
>
> 28 NOV 1944
>
> Lord Chamberlain.

Dorothy Jackson's Investiture Chit

TOOK PART IN ATTACK ON U-BOAT

LEADING SEAMAN KING AWARDED D.S.M.

Leading Seaman Dominic King, R.N., aged 30 whose wife lives at 1, Clydesdale Avenue, Crewe, has been awarded the Distinguished Service Medal, and was decorated by the King last week. The citation states that the medal was awarded "for courage, skill and coolness as helmsman in a most daring and successful attack by H.M. Submarine Tuna on a closely escorted U-boat in the course of a Mediterranean patrol."

Leading Seaman King is the eldest of the four sons of Mrs King, a widow, of 40 Albany-road, Kensington, Liverpool. All four are in the Forces one. Pte John King, R.A.O.C. having been a prisoner of war in Germany for three years Sergt David King R.A., is serving in East Africa. The youngest is Leading Seaman Thomas King. R.N. Dominic King had a course of training on the Indefatigable as a cadet after leaving St Nicholas' Church School, Liverpool, and before joining the R.N. 13 years ago. At the outbreak of war he was in China.

The investiture was attended by Dominic's wife and sister. The King talked with Dominic, who briefly told him the circumstances which gained him the award.

LIVERPOOL D.S.M.

Congratulated On His Gallantry By The King

Leading Seaman Dominic King, R.N., has been awarded the D.S.M. for courage, skill and coolness as helmsman in a most daring and successful attack by a submarine in the Mediterranean.

Aged 30, he is the eldest son of Mrs. Ellen King, widow, 40, Albany-road, Kensington, Liverpool.

Leading Seaman Dominic King was in the Indefatigable as a cadet after leaving St. Nicholas' Church School, Liverpool, prior to joining the R.N. 13 years ago. At the outbreak of war he was in China.

At a recent investiture at Buckingham Palace, the King, after pinning the medal on his breast, warmly shook hands with him and congratulated him upon his gallantry.

King has four brothers in the Forces. One is in the Navy, two in the Army, and one a prisoner of war in Germany.

Leading Seaman D. KING

LIVERPOOL MAN'S D.S.M.

Leading Seaman Dominic King, R.N., has been awarded the D.S.M. for courage, skill, and coolness as helmsman in a daring and successful attack by a submarine in the Mediterranean. Aged 30, he is the oldest of the four sons of Mrs. Ellen King, a widow, of 40 Albany Road, Kensington, Liverpool. All the sons are in the Forces, and one, Private John King, R.A.O.C., has been a prisoner of war for three years. Sergeant David King, R.A., is in East Africa, and the youngest of the four is Leading Seaman Thomas King, R.N.

Leading Seaman Dominic King was trained on the Indefatigable as a cadet after leaving St. Nicholls Church School, Liverpool, prior to joining the R.N. 13 years ago. At the outbreak of war he was in China.

Newspaper article mentions the Mediterranean in error.

Noting living at 40 Albany Road

GALLANTRY AWARDS

The following awards were gazetted last night:—

For outstanding courage, enterprise and skill in a successful patrol in H.M. submarine Tuna: D.S.M.—Acting Temporary Leading Seaman Dominic King (Liverpool).

For gallant and distinguished services in Sicily: Military Medal.—Marine (acting temporary sergeant) James Crooks (Royal Marines), Warrington.

KING — September 21, 1972, suddenly DOMINIC KING D.S.M., dearly beloved husband of Gertie. (So sadly missed, R.I.P.). Requiem Mass at St. Sebastian's Church on Tuesday next at 9 a.m., followed by interment at Yew Tree Cemetery at 10 a.m. — 4 Botanic Place, Liverpool 7.

Obituary

Michael D Gilston

| DOMONICK | DAVID | JOHN | THOMAS |

SERVING THEIR COUNTRY—Mrs. Ellen King, a widow, of 40, Albany-road, Kensington, Liverpool, and 114, Beversbrook-road, Norris Green, has four serving sons. They are: Domonick, aged 27, R.N. (married); David, aged 24, R.A.; John, aged 21, R.A.O.C (missing in the Middle East); Thomas, aged 18, R.N. A son-in-law, Charles Fitzsimmons, aged 26, is in the Royal Navy.

Ellen King's Four Sons

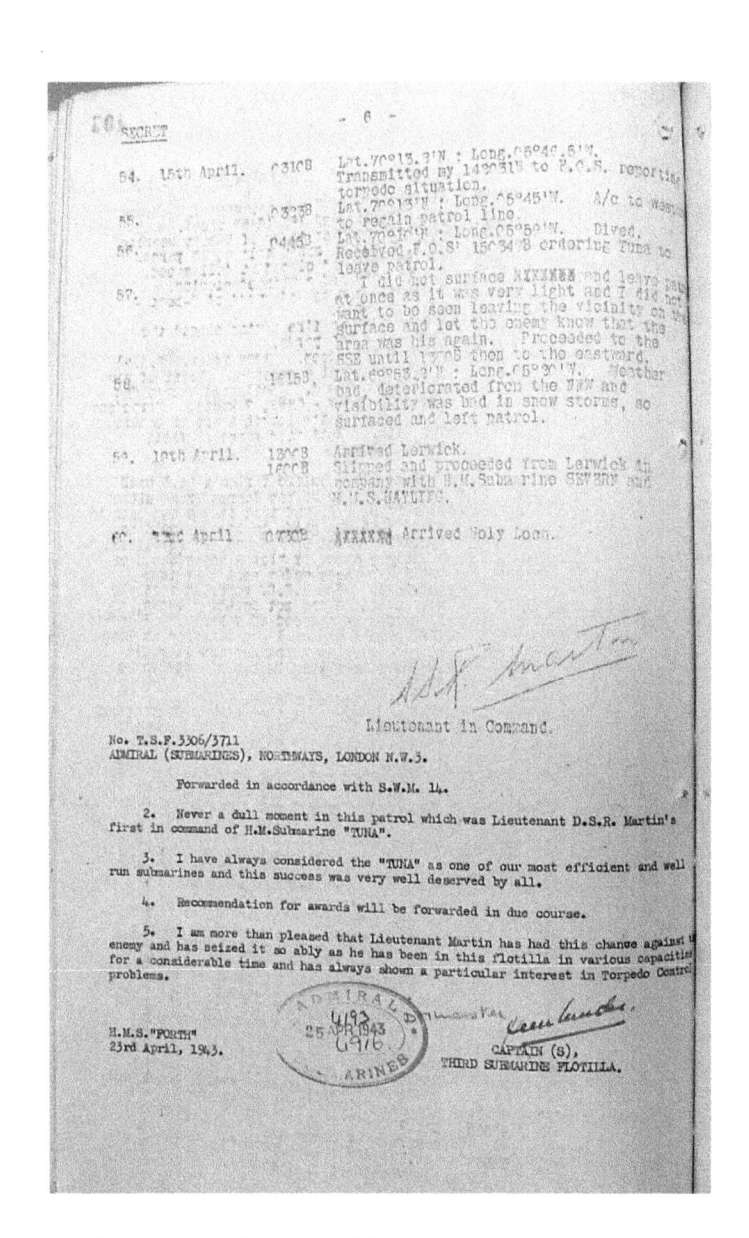

Tuna's Log 19-Apr-43 end of 18th War Patrol signed by Lt. D.S. Martin

SECRET   To retain for historical
                Purposes.   427

From: The Commanding Officer, H.M.S. Tuna.
Date: 6th June, 1943.   No: 286/11.
To: The Captain (S) Third Submarine Flotilla, H.M.S. Forth.
      Copies to: Captain (S) Fifth Submarine Flotilla.
                 Captain (S) Sixth Submarine Flotilla.
                 Captain (S) Seventh Submarine Flotilla.
                 Captain (S) Ninth Submarine Flotilla.
                 Comsubron 50.
                 Senior Officer Submarines, Lerwick.

H.M.Submarine TUNA's Patrol Report fro period
14th May, 1943 to 6thJune, 1943.

To patrol on line EE between positions 64°12'N 00°13'E
and 64°28.5'N 01°36'E. Object - U-boats.

All times Zone B

1. 14th May.   1430   Slipped and proceeded from H.M.S.WOLF in
                       company with H.M.S.BRYONY and H.M.Submarine
                       STUBBORN.

2.   2000   H.M.Submarine SEADOG joined company.

3. 16th May.   0001   Met H.M.T.STELLA PEGASI with H.M.Submarine
                       ULTIMATUM. ULTIMATUM joined company.
                       SEADOG detached to enter Scapa escorted by
                       STELLA PEGASI.

4. 16th May   1200   Arrived Lerwick.

5. 17th May.   0600   Weighed and proceeded from Lerwick for
                       patrol line EE.

6. 18th May.   1100   Lat: 64°07'N :Long.00°12'E. Arrived on
                       patrol line. Dived to periscope depth.

7. 18th May, to 24th May. Patrolled in the vicinity of patrol
                       line at periscope depth for 18 hours per
                       day and the remainder on the surface
                       charging. Visibility and A/S conditions
                       were excellent throughout.

8. 24th May to 29th May. Patrolled in the vicinity of patrol
                       line at 70 feet in heavy ENE and later
                       Easterly swell. (Periscope depth was
                       maintained during the afternoon of 26th
                       May, visibility being good.) A/S conditions
                       good whilst submerged. Visibility very
                       good and sometimes excellent whilst on
                       the surface except during the night of
                       27th and 28th when low cloud and mist
                       reduced visibility to 3 miles.

9. 29th May, to 30th May. Patrolled in the vicinity of the patrol
                       line at periscope depth. Visibility and
                       A/S conditions very good.

10. 29th May.   2358   Port Engine stopped for repairs (See

Tuna's Log 19th War Patrol

```
                                          442
         NAVAL MESSAGE.              S. 1320d.

To:                            From:

   TUNA (R) F.O.S.                      ADMIRALTY
          S.3.

                    CONFIDENTIAL.


         We congratulate TUNA on the destruction of a

   U-boat on MAY 30th 1943.

   VIA ADM                            19.17CCP.



   T/P   P/L   TOR. 1832 T.V. 19.6.43.   FULL MSG W.R.N.S.
                                         CYPHER OFFICER
```

> SECRET   Rear Admiral
>
> Commander-in-Chief, Home Fleet.
>
> 24th June, 1943.   N.H.F.1330/2/531.
>
> FLAG OFFICER (SUBMARINES).   437
>
> ---
>
> Patrol Report - H.M.S. TUNA.
>
> I am much impressed by the way in which TUNA conducted her two latest patrols. The destruction of two German U-boats is an example of her general efficiency and of the skill and initiative of her Commanding Officer.
>
> 2. I am very pleased to send my congratulations.
>
> ADMIRAL

20.	30th May.	1700	5 torpedoes loaded. One torpedo which had been removed from the first salvo during P Routines, still had water in its head. This was considered sufficiently drained down by 2130 and was loaded also.
21.		2200	Lat.64°,6.,5'N ; Long.00°28'E. Surfaced to charge.
22.	31st May	0555	Lat. 64°32,5' N ; Long.01° 29' E. Dived and patrolled at periscope depth.
23.		1040	Received S 9's 310231B ordering Tuna to leave patrol as necessary to pass XXr through position 00°° Muckle Flugga 8 at 1300 on the 3rd June. Considered I would have to leave patrol at 0001 1st June at the latest, as I was very doubtful about the port engine. Tremendous trouble was being experienced in making and fitting new connections to walking pipes for No.2 unit and I did not think we should have it running before arrival in Lerwick.
24.		2249	Transmitted my 3119?1B giving my intentions re leaving patrol port engine situation and requesting bombing restrictions.
25.	1st June	0001	Lat.64° 17'N; Long. 00°36'E. Left patrol.
26.		0352	Lat.64°10,5'N ; Long.00° 30' E. Dived to periscope depth.
27.		2153	Lat.63° 32.5' N; Long.00° 30'E Surfaced.
28.	2nd June	0342	Lat.63°19' N ; Long.00° 21' E. Dived to periscope depth.
29.		2206	Lat.62° 52' N; Long.00° 04' E. Surfaced and proceeded on the surface.
30.		2330	Port Engine running on reduced load.
31.	3rd June	1040	Arrived Lerwick.
32.	4th June	2300	Slipped and proceeded in company with H.M.S.CUTTY SARK,H.M.S.ULTIMATUM and H.M.S STUBBORN.
33.	5th June	0010	H.M. Submarine SYRTIS joined company.
34.	6th June.	2015	Arrived Holy Loch.

[signature]

Lieutenant in Command.

Tuna's Log end of 19th War Patrol 6-Jun-43 signed Lt. D.S. Martin

Admiralty Staff Minutes – Lt. Martin recorded with the destruction of two "U"boats

ENCLOSURE No. 1

Noon and Midnight Positions on passage

Date	Noon Lat. Long.	Midnight Lat. Long.
14th May	Holy Loch	55 31.6N 06 35 W
15th May	57 57 N 00 42.5 W	58 48.5N 03 16.7 W
16th May	Lerwick	
4th June	Lerwick	59 51 N 01 06 W
5th June	58 42 N 03 48.4 W	57 33.2N 05 50 E
6th June	55 43.2N 05 01 W	

ENCLOSURE No. 2

Daily Weather

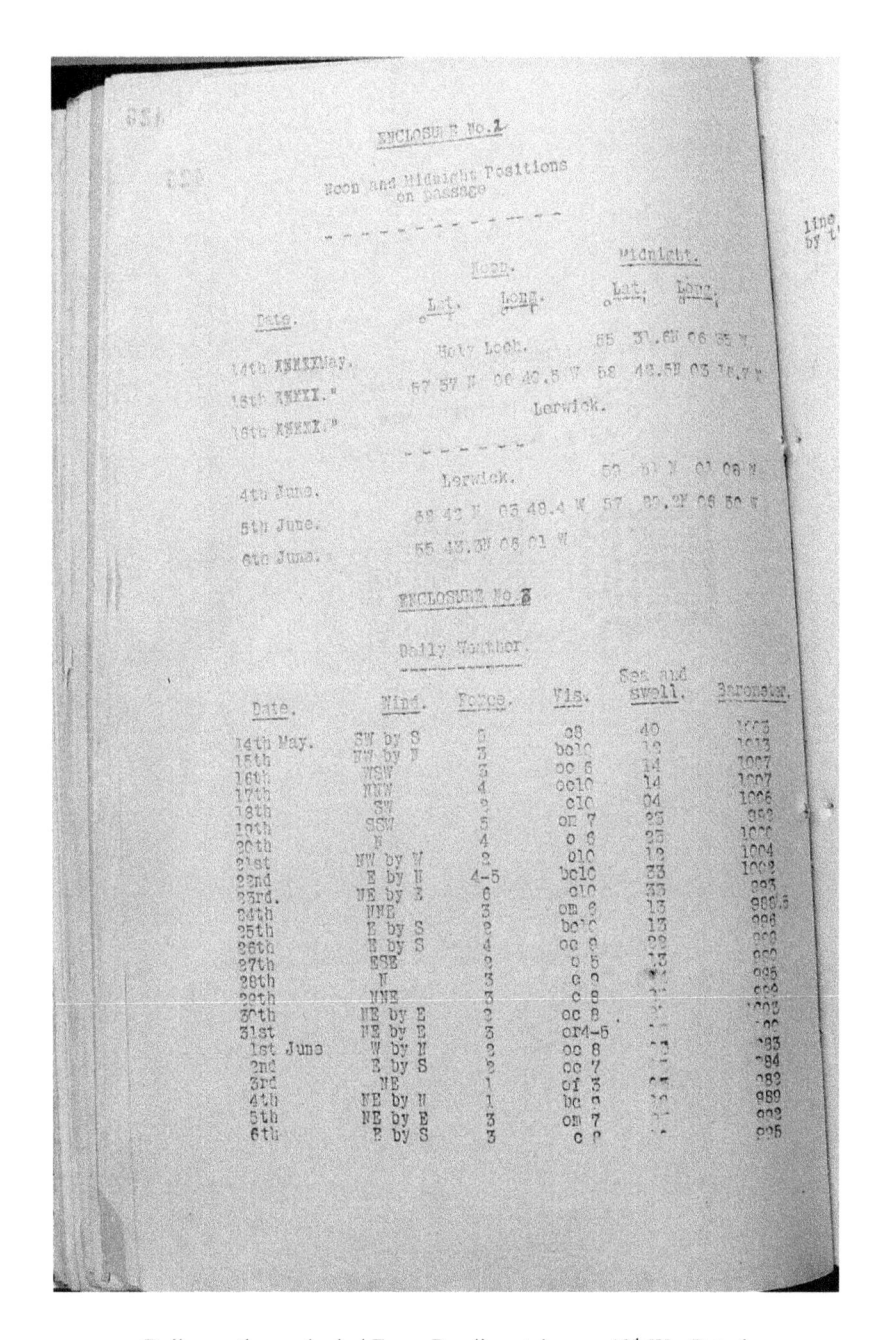

Date	Wind	Force	Vis.	Sea and swell	Barometer
14th May	SW by S	2	c8	40	1023
15th	NW by N	3	bc10	10	1013
16th	WSW	3	oc 6	14	1007
17th	NNW	4	oc10	14	1007
18th	SW	2	c10	04	1006
19th	SSW	5	om 7	23	992
20th	E	4	o 8	23	1000
21st	NW by W	2	o10	12	1004
22nd	E by N	4-5	bc10	33	1002
23rd	NE by E	6	o10	33	995
24th	NNE	3	om 8	13	995.5
25th	E by S	8	bc10	13	996
26th	N by S	4	oc 8	23	993
27th	ESE	2	o 5	13	990
28th	N	3	c 0		995
29th	NNE	3	c 8		998
30th	NE by E	2	oc 8		1003
31st	NE by E	3	cr4-5		990
1st June	W by N	2	oc 8		983
2nd	E by S	2	oc 7		984
3rd	NE	1	of 3		982
4th	NE by N	1	bc 0		989
5th	NE by E	3	om 7		992
6th	E by S	3	c 8		995

Daily weather and wind Force Readings taken on 19th War Patrol

Michael D Gilston

8AM Position M.S.T. HX 241. 68

Date	Lat.	Long.	Noon to Noon Dist.	Averages
26.	40.07	71.49	172.	9.15.
27.	40.33.	67.19	216	9.00.
28.	42.17	62.57	230.	9.58.
29.	43.20	58.09	196	8.17
30.	44.20.	52.19		
31.	46.34	51.41	148	6.17
1.	47.38	47.34	204	8.50.
2	50.43	45.06	216	9.39
3	54.01	43.32	200	8.33.
4.	56.19	40.24.	169	7.04.
5	57.09	35.17	191	8.30.
6	57.16	28.57	236	9.83.
7*	57.18	19.24	329	14.95.
8*	56.25	8.11		
9				

* Last Position Convoy.

J Kenneth Brook
Commodore
HX 241.

0800 Sun Position readings 19th War Patrol

APPENDIX II

Noon and Midnight Positions.

	Noon		Midnight	
	Lat.	Long.	Lat.	Long.
Date	° N ′	° ′	° N ′	° ′
April 1st.	— —	— —	58 36.8	34.6W
2nd.	59 43.2	7 23.5W	58 25	6 34 W
3rd.	59 03.7	2 21 W	60 20	0 40.5W
4th.	62 04.2	1 21.5W	63 57.5	0 46.2W
5th.	65 30	0 27.5W	66 03.1	0 46 E
6th.	67 17	2 00 E	68 11.5	3 00 W
7th.	68 59.5	5 50 W	69 36.1	5 56 W
8th.	69 54	6 00 W	69 49	6 33 W
9th.	70 02	6 36 W	69 44	5 29 W
10th.	69 29	5 02 W	69 08.2	5 11 W
11th.	69 19	5 04 W	69 48	5 34 W
12th.	69 58.2	6 06 W	69 48	5 52.5 W
13th.	69 52	6 06 W	70 13	6 24 W
14th.	70 21.9	6 44 W	70 13.2	6 05.3 W
15th.	69 56.9	5 35.5W	69 18.2	1 38 W
16th.	68 19	3 21.2E	67 13.3	5 04.7 E
17th.	65 29.3	7 47 E	64 10.5	1 33 W
18th.	65 29.3	7 47 W	61 42	1 13 W
19th	58 53	4 35 W		

Noon and Midnight positions 18th War Parol

229

Apendix D: N94 HM Submarine Tuna War Patrols

War Patrol 1	30-Aug-40	North Sea		1 U-boat sinking (Smell of diesel)		
War Patrol 2	15-Sep-40	Bay of Biscay		1 U-Boat sinking, German Merchant ship		
War Patrol 3	23-Oct-40	Bay of Biscay				
War Patrol 4	12-Dec-40	Gironde estuary		German French Tug sinking		
War Patrol 5	29-Jan-41	Patrol Azores				
War Patrol 6	22-Mar-41	Bay of Biscay				
War Patrol 7	01-Jun-41	Bay of Biscay				
War Patrol 8	07-Jul-41	Bay of Biscay				
War Patrol 9	20-Aug-41	Bay of Biscay				
War Patrol 10	13-Dec-41	Norwegian Coast				
War Patrol 11	23-Dec-41	Vågsøy, Norway		Navigational Beacon	Operation Archery	
War Patrol 12	14-Jan-42	Bay of Biscay				
War Patrol 13	19-Feb-42	Norwegian Coast				Operation EO
War Patrol 14	16-Mar-42	Norwegian Coast	No Logs			
War Patrol 15	23-Oct-42	Norwegian Coast				
War Patrol 16	30-Nov-42	Gironde estuary		Commando Raid	Frankton Operation	

His Majesty's Sailor *and the Girl in the* Blue Coat

War Patrol 17	25-Feb-43	Norwegian Coast				
War Patrol 18	1-Apr-43	Norwegian Sea		U-Boat sinking		
War Patrol 19	14-May-43	Norwegian Sea		U-boat sinking		
War Patrol 20	10-Jul-43	Patrol north of Azores				
War Patrol 21	15-Aug-43	Bay of Biscay		U-boat sinking		